STICK MAGIC

BOSTON BUCKS
BOOK 5

CATHRYN FOX

COPYRIGHT

Stick Magic
Copyright 2025 by Cathryn Fox
Published by Cathryn Fox

ISBN Ebook: 978-1-998943-87-6

ISBN Print: 978-1-998943-88-3

KALEN

S ummer Before College:

"I really don't want to be here." Despite my girlfriend Juliette tugging on my hand, my feet come to a resounding halt the second I enter the elite country club. I never did like the exclusive vibe here, or that I'm only accepted because I'm dating the mayor's daughter and was drafted by the Boston Bucks earlier this year. They think that makes me worthy.

As my gaze cuts across the room, taking in all the extravagant costumes, I shake my head. It's the end of August, not October, so why the board members decided on a masquerade party to celebrate the end of the summer season is beyond me. The ultra-rich are a strange bunch.

"It's going to be fun," Juliette assures me as she places her hand on my chest. Her blue eyes sparkle behind her mask as she gives me a wink. "I think the punch is spiked."

"You know what I think?" She arches her brow at my question. "That I'm allergic to this damn thing." I scratch my cheek, the hard plastic on the mask and the ridiculous feather irritating my skin. "It's giving me a rash." I'm about to tear the damn thing from my face when Juliette pouts and swats my hand away.

"Stop it, Kalen. You're supposed to be incognito."

I snort out a laugh as a few guests turn my way and nod. "I'm pretty sure I'm not fooling anyone here." While I'm not a member, I am a foot taller than most of the members here. Not only is that a dead giveaway, I've been playing for the Darien team since I was fourteen, and plenty of the guests here have cheered for me over the years.

Juliette shimmies closer. "Maybe, but I don't think anyone knows it's me," she tells me in a happy sing-song voice.

The fact that she's my girlfriend, and currently has her hands all over me, is also a dead giveaway, but I don't say that. Tomorrow, I leave for Boston College, and, well, I don't want to do or say anything to burst her bubble tonight—especially when a part of me knows this will be our last time together. Honestly, I only came because it was important to her—the country club is so not my thing—and a part of me wanted to give her one last great memory of us together.

A measure of unease grips my stomach at the thought of leaving Connecticut. Not because I know it will be the end of Juliette and me—long distance relationships just don't work—but I hate the idea of leaving my sister Taylor behind. While I'd like to take her with me, it's impossible. She has high school to finish, and I won't be able to watch out for her in Boston, not with my crazy college study and hockey schedule. She's better off here in Darien with our grandmother for now.

Juliette runs her hands over the lapels on the formal midnight black tuxedo and red tie that she insisted I rent for this event. "Did I tell you how great you look?"

Pushing those dark thoughts to the back of my mind and trying to be present for Juliette, I grin. "Yeah. Did I tell you how great you look?" I ask, even though I know I did. Numerous times.

"Yes." She grins and spins before me. My gaze drops to admire her curves in her red floor-length gown. I guess it's my red tie that binds us together, so to speak, and makes it a couple's costume. "But a girl never tires of hearing it."

"You look beautiful, babe."

She giggles and goes up on her toes to kiss me. I slide my hands around her back and hold her as I kiss her back. Someone clears their throat behind us. I inch back and turn to see a woman eyeing us behind her black mask.

"Juliette, Kalen, it's so nice to see you both." She puts her hand on my arm and gives it a little squeeze. "Oh my, you do fill that jacket out nicely."

Alrighty then.

"We were just about to get some punch," I tell her and slide my hand around Juliette's back to guide her away.

"Oh, Kalen. I wanted to congratulate you on your draft. Boston Bucks." Her eyes twinkle as she gives a low whistle. "That's very impressive," she adds, her French accent a little thicker than it was moments ago.

"Thanks." It's funny, really. I busted my ass off to get a full academic ride to Boston college, but not even my teacher seems impressed by that.

"I can't wait to watch you play. Maybe I'll make it to Boston for a game, and you can show me around."

What the hell...

"Yeah, okay. See you later." I back up, needing to get away fast.

"Oh." She pulls her mask down. "It's me. Connie DuBois."

"Right." Cougar DuBois...err...I mean, Connie DuBois. My high school French teacher. I guide Juliette away and she eyes me. "What?" I ask.

"That's going to happen a lot, isn't it?"

"If you mean women hitting on me because I'm going to be an NHL player one day, I think the answer is yes." I shrug. "Hockey culture, I guess."

She exhales, understanding dancing in her eyes as she nods her head. "Well, tonight you're mine, Kalen Coolidge."

I take her hands in mine and smile, because it's good to know we're on the same page, and both know that after tonight, we'll be going our separate ways, no hard feelings. And let's be honest, while I enjoy her friendship, nothing about us was ever love. Juliette is the most popular girl in school, and I'm the captain of the hockey team. We're together because she likes the way she looks on my arm.

"Tonight, I'm yours," I agree.

"Now let's get that punch." She takes a step and stops abruptly, a dramatic gasp catching in her throat.

"What?" Even though I'm used to her theatrics—why she's taking business instead of theater is beyond me—I glance around, trying to figure out who or what she's glaring at.

She points. "Ohmigod, what is she doing in my dress?" Juliette runs her hands down her jeweled red dress, smoothing it over her breasts and stomach. "I was told this was a one of a kind."

I follow her finger and spot a girl, who doesn't look like she wants to be here anymore than I do, pressed against the back wall, as she reads something on her phone. Her head lifts for a brief second and her long blonde hair falls over creamy shoulders.

Something about her holds my attention, and it has nothing to do with her uncanny resemblance to my girlfriend, right down to the blonde hair. "Wow, if it weren't for the glasses, I'd never be able to tell you two apart."

Juliette fumes beside me. "How dare she? She needs to go home and change right now." She grips her dress, lifting it slightly as she pulls away from me, like she's about to storm the castle, or rather the ball room. The second she starts toward the back wall, I grip her hand to stop her. I don't know why I suddenly feel protective of the other girl; maybe it's simply that I don't want a scene. Maybe not.

Making light of the situation, I begin, "Don't worry about it, babe." I touch her hair, brush it behind her ear. "You look better in it anyway." It's a small fib. Whoever that girl is hugging the wall, well, she looks good in her costume too. "Tomorrow they'll be discussing who wore it better?"

"And I'll win."

"Yeah, baby, you'll win."

A big smile spreads across Juliette's painted red lips. "I think you're right."

"Of course, I'm right. Now come on. I'm thirsty." I lead her in the other direction, and we run into our friends Jared and Mia at the punch bowl. Juliette and Mia instantly begin to gossip about Juliette's doppelganger, and I turn to our team's right winger.

"Kalen, dude what's up?" Jared asks me.

"How'd you know it was me?" I joke and once again resist the urge to tear my mask off.

He grabs the ladle and gestures with a nod toward Connie the cougar. "You getting with that later?"

"Jesus. You saw that, did you?" I laugh as I take in the interest in his eyes. "She's all yours."

He wags his brows. "You know what they say about French women?"

I rub my eye, which is watering from the feather threatening to blind me. "Actually, no and I really don't want to know."

He kisses the jointed tips of his fingers and joyfully spreads them out. "Passion, baby. Passion."

"What part of *I didn't want to know* did you not understand?"

"I also heard they don't shave." He winks at me. "I'll let you know tomorrow."

"Lucky me." I just shake my head and laugh as he grins and glances around.

He gestures toward the girl in red. "Who's the Juliette wannabe?"

I once again turn and take in the girl holding up the wall. She taps her thumb against her phone, repeatedly, almost uncon-sciously. A nervous gesture? As her gaze darts around the room, I study the way she's shifting from one foot to the other, and pushing her glasses up on her nose. Is she getting ready to bolt? She drops her phone into her bag and there's something familiar about her movements, but I can't quite put my finger on it. Her gaze lands on mine as I stare, and the next thing I know, she's pushing off the wall and disappearing into the big library off the main room.

"No idea," I finally answer and take a big drink of the punch, letting the liquid burn down my throat. "What's in this?" I sputter and wipe my mouth with the back of my hand.

Jared opens his coat to show me a flask. "A little something extra for you, dude."

I take another swallow to finish the contents in my cup and Jared fills me up again. I'm not much of a drinker, but I'm sure alcohol will help me get through tonight. Juliette slides her hand into mine, pulling my attention back to her.

"Mia and I are going to freshen up." She moves in closer, and goes up on her tippytoes. "Back there, in the library," she whispers. "There's a secret room behind the bookshelf, to the right of the window on the fourth shelf from the bottom look for the book on ancient Egypt. Pull on it, and a secret door will open. I'll meet you there in ten minutes." She slides her hand down and cups my crotch. "Let's make this a night to remember."

"Come on," Mia says, grabbing Juliette's hand after she too whispered something into Jared's ear.

"Don't get caught," Juliette warns as Mia drags her away.

Jared has a big grin on his face as the girls disappear down the hall. "I mean, it's not Connie DuBois, but it's not so bad," he jokes before taking a big swig from his cup. "Later." He steps away and I turn to take in the crowd. I recognize a few people from school, and while many of them go way back to kindergarten, I was fourteen when I moved to Connecticut from New York. Living with my grandmother isn't so bad. I snort out a humorless laugh. Truthfully, it's a million times better than living with my asshole father. Yeah, after Mom died, I was happy to get the fuck out of there, and I'm grateful my maternal grandmother took Taylor and me in.

A few people nod to me as they pass, and I check my watch. Has it been ten minutes? Setting my cup on the table, I walk toward the library, half expecting to find Juliette's twin lurking about, but she's nowhere to be found. She probably went out the back way, happy to get out of here and these ridiculous outfits.

I walk up to the wall and find the book. Feeling like a kid about to get caught with his hand in the cookie jar, I glance over my shoulder before I tug on it. Sure enough a latch releases, opening a secret door. I hurry inside, and my gaze rakes over the back of Juliette's red dress as light from the library chandelier shines in. Her dress flares as she spins, and I quickly close the secret door, plunging us into darkness.

"Hey," I murmur as I step into her. "I don't think anyone saw me." Her throat works as she swallows and the second I put my hands on her hips a low mewling sound crawls out of her throat. The strange, unfamiliar, almost silent sound coming from my girlfriend gives me pause. Juliette is usually way more demonstrative, loud even. She does like to put on a show. "Are you okay?"

A beat and then, "Uh huh."

Her voice sounds a bit scratchy. Maybe she's allergic to the feathers on the mask too.

"Let's get rid of these shall we." I pull off her mask, not that I can see her in the dark and then tear off my own. "That's better." Wasting no time, I cup her chin, and lift it, my mouth going straight to hers. Her lips are stiff at first, and I'm about to pull back—does she not want this—only to stop when her arms slide around my body. "Nice," I murmur into her mouth, and deepen the kiss as her lips become pliable beneath my ministrations.

I slide my tongue in, and taste spearmint and warmth and excitement. I moan and deepen the kiss as I back her up and push her against the wall. Fisting her dress, I tug on it, lifting it so I can get my hands on her bare flesh. I touch her panties, and my dick thickens as my fingers graze the soft lace.

I dip my hand inside, and her gasp wraps around my cock and hugs tight. Her nether lips are buttery soft, and she grows wetter as I part them with my fingers. "So wet, baby." I toy with her clit, circle it to tease her and the second I add pressure, her breathing changes, becomes a little erratic.

Her hands move to my chest, and she touches me, explores, like she's acquainting herself with my body. I slide a finger into her, and her warm spearmint breath washes over my face in a rush. What is going on with her tonight? I don't remember her ever being so reactive, like she's craving my touch and this is the first time I've given it to her.

"Yes," she murmurs, moving her hips, forcing my finger in deep. She untucks my shirt and I suck in a breath as her warm hands race over me. Jesus, I love the way she's touching me. I don't know what's going on with her tonight, but she's all over me. Sex was always about her and her pleasure. Tonight, she's touching me like I'm something to be worshiped, like I'm truly important to her.

I add a second finger and a deep cry full of pleasure fills the small space. I fuck her with my fingers, slowly, wanting to take her higher and higher, wanting to draw this out, before I take her over the edge.

Her hands continue to race over my body, her fingers splayed like she's trying to touch every inch of me. There's something incredible in the way she's moving, moaning, and exploring as she completely gives herself over to me like it's the first time she's ever been touched. This is different. She's different. Perhaps because she knows it's our last time. I really don't know what's going on, but if she can give herself to me like this—openly, honestly—maybe there's more between us than I thought. Maybe we could try the distance relationship thing.

Maybe I'm not ready to walk away from this.

I change the pace and rhythm of my fingers, brushing her G-spot and rubbing the butt of my palm over her clit. A loud cry erupts from her throat, and she grips my shoulders to hang on as her body bursts around me. Her liquid heat coats my hand and I'm seconds from dropping to my knees to press my mouth to her sweetness, when a noise grabs my attention.

"What the hell," Juliette yells and I turn back to the girl I just brought to orgasm. She lowers her head, her long blonde hair veiling her face as she scoops up her mask, brushes past Juliette and runs from the secret room. My gaze flies to Juliette's. "I thought..."

"You couldn't tell?" she accuses, anger flaring in her eyes.

Actually, now that I think of it, there were signs...I just ignored them. "Who..." I shake my head, and hurry from the library, running in to where the party is in full swing. I catch a glimpse of the girl in red as she runs from the country club and that's when I realize exactly who she is.

Darien Lewis.

Quiet.

Shy.

Socially awkward.

Book nerd.

Who I just finger banged and brought to orgasm in the library.

And I want more...

Fuck me.

"I think you should leave." I turn around and find Juliette standing there with her arms crossed. Angry blue eyes boring into mine.

"Yeah, okay," is all I mutter. I take a deep breath and try to get my spinning brain under control.

"Goodbye, Kalen."

"Bye, Juliette." With that, I walk out into the warm night and search the parking lot as I make my way to my car. I slide in and drive straight home. Taylor is at a friend's place for the night and Grandma is already in bed when I arrive, and I'm grateful I don't have to explain why I'm home early.

I drop into my bed, and stare at the ceiling, my mind going over tonight's events. Honestly, I don't know why Darien's touch, kisses and sweet moans messed with me the way they did, but I damn well want to find out. I close my eyes and eventually drift off. After a restless night, I push from my bed, make a fast trip to the bathroom and hurry back to my car.

I drive through town, stopping when I come to Darien Lewis' mansion overlooking Long Island Sound. She lives in the biggest house in Darien, and why on earth would her parents name her after the town she lives in?

A guy steps from the house. He makes his way to his car and slows when he spots me. "Can I help you?"

"I...uh." I scratch the back of my neck. "I'm looking for Darien."

He glances down the street. "You just missed her."

"Yeah?" I follow his gaze, but the street is empty.

"She left for college about an hour ago."

Well fuck...

2

SAHARA

P resent Day:

As the audience stands, and the other actors join me on stage for a bow, my heart jumps into my throat. I grin, as both pride and shock race through my blood. Honestly, when I moved to Boston over the summer, when the opportunity to work at Boston Library presented itself, I had no idea I'd be performing at a local theater—or that the audience would be on their feet, applauding the entire cast of Love Unbound.

Taylor Turner wraps her arms around my waist and gives me a big hug. We met during tryouts, and she's currently my only friend in town. Not that I have a lot of friends back home in Darien, but I've been so busy here, getting my apartment set up, settling into a new routine at the library, and practicing for opening night, that I've barely had time to sort my thoughts, let alone make friends.

Taylor beams at me. "You did great, Monroe."

"You did too, Turner," I tell her, loving that she chose the surname Turner for her stage name. I chose Monroe. Go big or go home, right? Taylor is a theater major at Boston college. We met during our auditions, and it's crazy that I got the lead when I know so little about acting. I mean, I did act at Columbia. I wanted to step out of my comfort zone and took a course. I really enjoyed it, but never intended to continue with it. Maybe I auditioned for this one because the story about a girl trying to get out from under her parents' control and find her way in life resonated with me so strongly.

Nevertheless, I felt bad that I got the role and she didn't. Not that she ever made me feel that way. She's a real sweetheart. But it's crazy to think that I, nerdy bookworm introvert extraordinaire, could even walk on stage, let alone toss out a performance that warranted applause.

But are you just *a nerdy bookworm introvert extraordinaire, Sahara?*

Honestly, I don't know. The sad truth of the matter is, that as the baby of the family, I've been under my parents' thumb for years, and have no idea who I am or what I like. Okay, that's not entirely true. I know what I am to my parents. A disappointment. And I probably gravitated toward this play and excelled at it because it represented what I was going through.

I can't even imagine what my folks would say if they saw me performing for a local community theater. I can hear my mother now. *If you want to perform, it had better be on Broadway.* This is so beneath them. Her kids had to be the best at everything they did, and this small stage in downtown Boston would be an embarrassment to her.

Much like my library science degree.

There was no way I was going to be a surgeon like my mom and dad, or my oldest brother and sister, Austin and London. Or a professor at Yale, like my middle brother Charlie. Oh, and let's not forget my other sister, Aspen, the fourth youngest—two years older than me—who is working in the aerospace industry.

Yeah, I'm a disappointment and it's hard to fathom that they caved and let me go into library science at all. Then again, I'm a book nerd and they probably figured I'd fail at everything else. At least this way they could spin it to their friends and make it sound like I was a historian, or something a little more special. I'm not any of those things. Deep down, they know it too, which is why they've been trying to marry me off to any successful guy in their social group. That would up my status, I guess.

The last straw, however, was when they set me up with their friend's son. On paper he looked good—a well-respected lawyer. But he was rude to our young waitress. I might come from a well-to-do family, but the one thing I won't tolerate is entitlement, especially from a man-baby who practically threw a tantrum because it took too long to get his drink.

So, I guess you can see why I took off to Boston when a library position opened up. If I had stayed in Darien, I saw only one path forward—unhappily married, and never knowing who I really was or what I liked.

Beside me, Taylor shades her eyes. "Where are you?" Her words pull me back as she peers out into the crowd, and my stomach tightens. She told me earlier that her brother and his friend were coming to watch tonight's performance—it's friends and family night, a performance for us to work out the kinks—and while I'm happy for her, I'm a little sad that there is no one out there supporting me.

I shade my eyes to block the spotlights. I try to help her look, which is a bit ridiculous. I have no idea who her brother is or what he looks like. She grabs my arm. "There he is. There he is," she chirps loudly, clearly happy to see her brother. While I love her dramatics and enthusiasm, my heart pinches a bit, a little envious that she has a brother who cares enough to come watch her. She gasps a little, and stands perfectly still and it pulls my attention.

"What?" I ask.

"He's with Elias. Oh God, Sahara, he's with Elias. I didn't know he was coming. I mean I left tickets for friends and family night. I just never thought. God, he came..."

Okay, I might not know her well, but I've never seen her thrown off her game before. "You don't like Elias?"

Her eyes widen as she turns from the crowd, offering them her back so they can't see her expression—or perhaps it's one man she's hiding from. That's when I see it's nervous excitement in her big blue eyes. "Oh, I get it. You *like* Elias."

"Yeah, but he's my brother's best friend." She wrings her hands and crinkles up her nose. "They're roommates."

"Uh, didn't you say you lived with your brother?"

She lets loose a tortured groan and twists and turns, like she's about to melt at my feet like the wicked witch. Maybe she should audition for the Wizard of Oz. "Yes, and you have no idea how torturous it is when Elias showers and walks around in nothing but a towel. Thank God it's a big house and I don't have to see that often."

I angle my head and arch a brow. "You mean you're not trying?"

She hangs her head in shame. "I'm trying. We share a Jack and Jill bathroom, so trying isn't really that hard. Ugh."

I laugh out loud at her antics. "Why don't you go for it?" Suggests the girl who's never gone for it. Ever. Okay, that's not entirely true. I went for it once—stepping completely out of character—and it was a spectacular disaster.

What were you thinking, girl?

"Bro code," she concedes with a frown. "I'd never do anything to come between my brother and his best friend. Besides, he's a lot older and thinks of me as a kid, I'm sure."

"Nothing wrong with an older man."

She flips her long dark hair from her shoulder. "Except when he thinks of you as a kid. Trust me, I've seen the women he used to go out with. All smoke shows."

"You're a smoke show too, Taylor." I frown. "Wait, did you just say the girls he *used* to go out with?"

"Yeah." Her brows bunch together, and I sense her worry for Elias. "I haven't seen him out in a while. Maybe one of the girls wanted something more and he's laying low. I think something happened but my brother would never tell me, and I think he has family problems."

Who doesn't...

"Family problems?"

She crinkles her nose. "He comes from a big political family, but like I said, no one tells me anything. I'm just the kid sister around the house, and I think Elias feels the same."

"He's not interested in anything more?"

"Nope, not with me and he is—or rather was—just like my brother. One and done usually." She gives me a cute, lopsided grin that any man would find attractive, I'm sure. "The girls that flock to them after a game." She snorts out a humorless laugh. "I can't compete, and they have their pick of women."

I'm about to ask what game her brother and Elias play, but stop when the lights dim and the curtain closes. The director comes out and gives us all high fives. While my body is tired, pouring my heart out on stage is exhausting, I'm not sure I'm ready to go home to sleep, despite my early morning at the library. At least it's Thursday, one more day to trudge through, and I'll have the weekend to sleep in. Our regular shows don't start for two weeks, and then we'll be non-stop. It's community theater, but we've worked hard.

The lights flicker on and behind the curtain, conversation buzzes around us. We all head off stage, and back in the change room, I pull my stuff from my cubby. Hurrying into my street clothes, I carefully hang up my costume and tug on my shoes. I'm about to head out when Taylor snatches my hand.

"Where are you going?"

"Home," I tell her.

"Why don't you come for a drink with my brother and me, and Elias..." She gives me a nervous grin. I'm about to say no, but she has a pleading look in her eyes.

"I'm not much of a wing woman."

She laughs. "Sometimes I think I stare too hard at him, and just having you there to nudge me would help."

"Girl, you got it bad."

She groans. "So bad, and I can't do anything about it."

I check the time, and since I am still keyed up, I nod. "Okay, one drink."

"Great. My brother knows this fun Scottish pub, Kilting Around."

"I've heard of it." It's not too far from the theater and within walking distance of my apartment. I've peeked in the window but have yet to go inside. "The guys all wear kilts."

"Maybe that will help me get my mind off Elias." She pauses and glances down. "Wait, nope. Now I'm thinking about Elias in a kilt."

I laugh and hike my bag up higher as I throw an arm around her. "Come on."

She smiles. "You never know, you and my brother might hit it off."

"What you're really saying is, if your brother is distracted, you can stare at Elias, right?"

"Damn girl, I can't get anything by you. He's just so overprotective of me. I love him and I love that he watches out for me, but sometimes it feels like I'm being smothered."

I nod, understanding that completely. My parents watched my every move. "I'll do my best to help." I push open the door and guide her outside. The late October air is warm as we walk to the front of the theater and search for her brother.

"There he is!"

She grabs my hand and people greet me as she drags me through the crowd. The second we reach her brother and I lift my head to meet his gaze, my breath leaves my lungs in a whoosh. I stand there, immobilized, hardly able to believe I'm staring at Kalen Coolidge—the captain of my high school's hockey team, and the guy I've had a crush on for as long as I can remember.

Taylor is speaking, doing the introductions as Kalen dips his head and looks at me with zero recognition. Which is no surprise. Why would a guy like him remember a nerdy bookworm like me? But I remember him. Remember when he slipped into the secret room at the library where I was reading on my phone and hiding from the crowd.

I didn't want to be at the damn masquerade party in the first place. My parents forced me, hoping I'd meet a nice young man. I met a nice young man all right. He just thought I was someone else. In that secret closet, though, when his fingers bit into my hips and his tongue sank into my mouth, I thought maybe, just maybe he knew it was me. I must have been high on the scent of old books because Kalen Coolidge does not go for girls like me.

"Sahara," he greets, his gaze searching my face, but there's nothing in his eyes to suggest he recognizes me. He has no idea who I am now, or that it was me in that closet that night. When Juliette swung that door open, and reality hit like a four-hundred-page hardcover to the side of the head, I obscured my face and ran like I was being chased by wild wolves. The next morning, at the crack of dawn, I took off for Columbia University, never giving Kalen Coolidge another thought.

Much.

Now here I am, staring at the Boston Bucks' hottest left

winger, about to share a drink at the local pub. I need to get the hell out of here, and fast.

"Ah, nice to meet you Kalen." I jerk my thumb over my shoulder. "I should go. I'm pretty tired after tonight."

"One drink," Taylor bursts out, sliding her arm in mine, her eyes pleading. Taylor glances at Kalen. "Sahara is new in town, like me." My gaze moves to Kalen's again, and he's watching me carefully. Even if he figured out it was me—Darien Lewis —in the closet that night, I'm sure he'd never recognize this version of me.

Not only is my hair shorter and a different color, I'm using a stage name, and I'm doused in makeup.

I switched to my middle name Sahara after I became a librarian. Honest to God, what were my parents thinking naming me Darien? Sure, we lived in Washington when I was born, but after we relocated to the coast, I had the same name as the town I lived in—a town where my mom had grown up. I spent my high school years there, before I went to Columbia to become a librarian. With the degree tucked into my belt, I had no choice but to change my name. No way was I going to be called Darien the librarian. Jeez. Adults are as cruel as kids.

Wait, is that interest in Kalen's eyes?

Whoa...

Does he like what he sees? I take a moment to see myself through his eyes, and what I see is the theatrical version of myself, a woman who is confident, vivacious, sexually open, a risk taker—everything I'm not. But like I said before, I have no idea who I am, so maybe I do have those traits buried deep inside me.

"I'd love it if you joined us," Kalen says, the deep tenor of his voice taking me back to that night when I moaned...and he asked if I was okay.

I wasn't okay.

I'm not okay now.

I might never be okay again.

Get your ass home, Sahara.

Or...pretend to be the girl from the stage, have a little fun... for a little while anyway.

3

KALEN

Taylor drags Sahara down the sidewalk and Elias falls into step beside me. He's a quiet guy, but much quieter than usual lately. I cast him a glance as he pulls his ballcap lower on his head. Perhaps he's just worried about being recognized...and swarmed. Last time that happened, and his face was splashed all over the papers, his parents paid him a visit.

His dad is high up in the government and feels Elias' actions —which are very carefully scrutinized by the public—are a reflection on him. I guess that's why he keeps his head down and nose clean. But he's a grown-ass man, and it's been a long time since I've seen him with a woman. Not that I can blame him. The guy never knows who wants him because he's a pro hockey player, or to use him to get close to his family.

I don't have that problem...but that's not to say I don't have demons of my own.

As though feeling my eyes on him, he angles his head, grins, and nudges me. "Taylor did great tonight."

I nod and a smile I have no control over spreads across my face as my sister laughs at something her friend said. "Yeah," is all I reply as pride wells up inside me. After high school, Taylor floundered for a bit, not knowing what she wanted to do, or what career she wanted to pursue. With my aging grandmother's health on the decline, we thought it was best she go into nursing care. Unfortunately, our grandmother passed before we could make that happen, and with no family left in Darien—yeah, our old man is still in New York—I knew it was time for Taylor to join me in Boston. I'm so fucking happy to have her here where I can watch over her again.

Taylor and me, against the world.

I wasn't ready for the responsibility before, not with college and hockey. Hell, who am I kidding? I wasn't ready for the responsibility at thirteen either, when Mom got sick, and I found Dad in bed with another man. Who the fuck sleeps around when their spouse is dying? My old man, that's who.

I didn't want anything to do with him after that, and I took over taking care of Taylor. Even after I asked Grandma if we could live with her, and she agreed, I still watched out for my kid sister. She's everything to me, and I want what's best in life for her.

Which is living under my roof and going to college to make something of herself. I've been with the team two years now, and my feet are on solid ground, so I knew it was time. Plus, my house over on Beacon Hill is big enough for a family of ten. My stomach tightens at that thought. All I ever wanted was a big family, seated around the table during the holidays. I know from some of the guys that big families can be chaotic and messy and loud. Heck, Tanner Bang has five siblings and while he might grumble, there's always love and happiness in his eyes when he talks about them, and dammit I want that for me and Taylor. But now, since our grandmother passed, it's always just the two of us.

My gaze strays to Sahara as she glances back at me, and something niggles in the back of my brain. There's something familiar about her. I can't quite place it, though. Perhaps it's just that she's flamboyant and outgoing like my sister. While I was at the theater to watch Taylor, I can't deny that my gaze strayed to Sahara numerous times.

"She's cute, huh?"

I glance at Elias as he grins at me. "Who?"

He pushes me. "Fuck off."

Laughing, because I damn well know who he's talking about, I shove him back. "If you want her, go for it."

He shakes his head, a dark storm flashing in his eyes. It hits me with the force of a hurricane and nearly sucks the air from my lungs before he quickly blinks it away. What is going on with him? I'm about to ask, only to stop when he speaks.

"She's your type, Coolio."

I turn back to take in Sahara. Tall, with dark hair and a lithe body, she kind of is my type. Not that I'm looking for anything serious. Okay, I am looking for something serious. I want the house with the picket fence and the SUV. I'm just too much of a chicken shit to put myself out there. Trust is hard for me.

Life has taught me that people hide things, that they aren't who they say they are, that they'll show you the side of themselves they want you to see. Tonight on stage, Sahara proved she's a great actress. But fuck, that doesn't mean we can't have a great time, right? Although I wouldn't want to come between Taylor and her friend.

We reach the bar and Taylor pulls the door open. Her cheeks are a bit flushed as she waves her hand for us to enter. "Age before beauty," she jokes and I nudge her chin.

"Wait, are you even old enough to drink?" I ask and she purses her lips and glares at me, but then her gaze strays to Elias as he moves past me. "I'm old enough for a lot of things," she tells me and lifts her chin.

"Ugh." I put my hands over my ears. "I don't want to hear it." Yeah, okay, I know she's old enough to do whatever she wants, but in my eyes she's still that kid who danced around the house in pig tails. She lost a bit of that spark when Mom died, and I made it my mission to protect her and get her through the hard times.

Who got you through the hard times, dude?

I glance up as Gavan, the owner of the place, comes from the back room to greet us. I put my arm around Taylor and tug her to me. "Eyes up here, sis," I tell her as her gaze rakes over Gavan's kilt.

"Kalen, Elias. How's it going?"

"Great." I give Taylor's hair a playful tug. "Celebrating Tay's opening night over at Chester Theater."

He grins at Taylor. "I saw the posters. Congrats, Taylor. I bet you killed it."

I smile at my sister. "She did."

Taylor drags Sahara to her. "So did Sahara. Sahara, this is Gavan. He owns the place."

After the two say hello, Gavan guides us to my favorite booth in the corner. Elias slides in and Taylor moves in beside him, leaving Sahara and me on the other side.

"What would you like?" I ask Sahara as she reaches for the menu.

"When in Scotland..." She smiles at Gavan. It lights up her face, and brings out the warmth in her blue eyes. "I'll have a Scottish whiskey." I stare for a moment, mesmerized, and that's when I realize everyone is staring at me.

"Oh yeah, I'll have the same and can we get a plate of nachos for the table?" Gavan walks away and I turn to Elias and Taylor. "Did you order?"

Taylor laughs. "Yeah, bro." She waves her hand in front of my face. "Where'd you go?"

I shake my head. "Oh, was just thinking about tomorrow night's game."

"You play New Jersey tomorrow," Sahara comments quietly as she sets the drink menu down.

Before I can respond, Taylor's jaw gapes open. Jesus, she's so dramatic. Her hands lift. "You know my brother? You recognized him? I don't think I ever told you he was a professional hockey player." Taylor's gaze goes to me, and her head angles, like she just had an epiphany. I'm not sure I want to know.

Sahara toys with the edge of the menu before she begins to tap her thumb on it. Oddly enough, that gesture reminds me of the girl I made out with in the library all those years ago. Not that Sahara is anything like quiet, shy Darien Lewis.

I never did see her again after that night. When I visited my sister and grandmother back in Darien, I drove by her house a few times. I never stopped. What the hell was I going to say? *Oh hey, remember me? I'm the guy who brought you to orgasm in the secret room at the country club because I thought you were my girlfriend.*

For years, I wondered why she didn't say something to stop me, to let me know she wasn't Juliette. I always assumed she knew it was me. I did talk to her, and figured she recognized my voice. Plus, one look at Juliette standing there glaring at us, and she had to know who I was, right? I guess I didn't recognize her voice because she pretty much only moaned and screamed yes...

Dammit, I can't tell you how many times I've wanted to hear yes on her lips again.

"You didn't," Sahara explains, pulling my thoughts back to the present. "I recognized him."

"You follow hockey?" I ask.

She looks almost embarrassed when she answers, "Yes. The Shooters are my favorite team."

Elias laughs. "I guess there's no accounting for taste."

Sahara grins at him. "They're my dad's favorite team, so it's kind of a family thing."

"Time to pick a new favorite team," I propose and nudge her.

She casts a fast glance my way. "I guess I could be convinced. You know, since I live in Boston now."

"Where did you use to live?" I ask, suddenly wanting to know a lot more about this woman. From my peripheral vision, I catch my sister's grin. Shit, does she think I'm hitting on her friend?

Is she right?

Fuck yeah. But I'm not going to do anything to come between friends. Taylor is new here. So is Sahara, and they seem like they've bonded. My sister could use a friend in her life.

She blinks, and her brow crinkles. Uh, does she not remember?

"Washington."

Elias laughs. "That's why your dad is a Shooters fan."

"For a while, I was a New York fan," she points out, and when I narrow my gaze, she laughs. "I went to Columbia University."

"Come to tomorrow night's game with me," Taylor says, and a shocked look moves over Sahara's face. Jeez, you'd think Taylor just asked her to fly to Mars and back. She opens her mouth, and hesitates. "It'll be fun," Taylor continues. "We can sit in the box together and get all the special treatment. Sometimes it's fun to have a professional athlete in the family."

"Sometimes?" I joke and when Sahara laughs I turn to her. "If you already have plans," I begin, giving her an out because I'm not so sure going to a game is her thing. Although she does follow hockey.

Our server, Cassandra, comes with our drinks. "Heads up." She gestures with a nod. "Couple of girls over there are losing their minds. You want me to talk to them? Tell them you want your privacy." Elias looks around, and once again tugs his hat low.

Gavan brings our nachos and sets them in the center of the table. "Enjoy."

After he walks away, Taylor picks up her whiskey. Honestly, I've never seen her drink whiskey before, and I'm a little surprised she ordered it. She must be following Sahara's example. "Oh, give them your autograph, big brother. Make a girl's day."

"Maybe they saw your play tonight and want your autograph, little sister," I shoot back and Taylor grins.

"Someday, brother..." She lifts her chin. "I will be the star in the family and my face will be splashed all over the papers."

Sahara laughs. "I have no doubt, Taylor."

"I can send them over?" the server asks.

I nod. "Sure."

Taylor takes a sip of her whiskey. "Ohmigod, this is horrible." She sticks her tongue out and waves her hand in front of it. "How can you guys drink this?" She pushes it away. "Just no."

Elias grabs a monstrous cheesy nacho and holds it out to Taylor. "Eat this cheesy one, it will help."

Taylor opens her mouth and Elias sets the nacho on her tongue. He pulls his hand away fast and his glance jerks to mine. I smile at him, thankful that he cares about my little sister as much as I do.

Taylor chews and Elias asks for water for the table before Cassandra walks away to talk to our fans wanting to come say hello.

"Thank you," Taylor says. "That helped a lot. Here, brother, you drink this." She pushes the glass toward me and I shake my head no. "I'm driving." I glance at Sahara, but she shakes her head no as well.

"Fine, I'll take one for the team," Elias says, and Taylor watches him as he takes a swig from her glass.

"I'm sticking with my girlie drinks. I'll be right back. Little girls' room." She slides from the table, and Elias looks like he's about to follow her to the bathroom, but settles when three girls come rushing over.

We spend the next few minutes autographing napkins and taking selfies and I note that Sahara doesn't seem fazed by the commotion at all. Normally the girls I date hate it when we're bombarded by fans. Not that I'm dating Sahara.

Once they disappear, Taylor comes back with a strawberry daiquiri, and we eat and sip, talking about hockey, and theater, and Elias and I tell Taylor and Sahara about our favorite Boston restaurants.

Once the drinks are gone, and the nacho plate is empty, Sahara stifles a yawn. "I should get going. Tonight was exhausting."

"Yeah, I have classes tomorrow," Taylor announces, and stands. "We on for the game, Sahara?"

"Uh, yeah, I think so. I'm free tomorrow night."

"I'll be glad when my full-time job is theater or dance and I don't have to study," Taylor moans. As we step outside, Sahara looks like she's about to say something, when Taylor interrupts, "I have my car. I can give you a lift."

"No, I'm just a few blocks over."

"I'm not letting you walk home alone in the dark." Taylor pulls her keys from her pocket, and just when Sahara looks like she's about to protest, Taylor suggests, "Why don't you walk her home, Kalen?"

"Sure. Elias and I can walk you home."

She waves a hand. "I don't want to keep you from anything."

"You're not."

"Fine then. I'm not putting you both out. I don't need two bodyguards," she jokes. "Elias might as well get a lift from Taylor."

"Yeah, right. Okay," I agree. Taylor grins at Sahara and hugs herself as a breeze rushes down the street.

"You cold?" Elias asks Taylor, and shrugs out of his jacket.

As he puts it on her shoulders, Sahara touches my arm and pulls my attention. "Thanks. It's not far."

We start down the sidewalk, and when someone passes us, my body brushes hers, and little electrical impulses zip through my body. I cast her a fast glance. Did she feel that too? "Have you been acting long?" I ask, searching for normal conversation, which is weird, because I'm pretty good at making small talk.

She nods. "A few years now."

We turn a corner and pass the Nook, a team favorite café that my buddy Ash's wife Gina owns. I've noticed Tuck hanging out there more and more, now that Gina hired her friend Maria as manager.

"You acted at Columbia?" I ask.

She nods. "I did." She tucks a strand of hair behind her ear and glances at me. "How about you? Been playing professional hockey for long?"

"A couple of years now. I was drafted a few years ago, but went to Boston college for a business degree." I snort out a laugh. "A guy needs something to fall back on when retired, or you know...injured." I wince thinking about that. My buddy James has been down and out with a concussion. We all work so hard to get where we are, we hate for anything to take us out.

"I get it. What did you major in?"

"Accounting." I cringe, and rub my hand over my arm. "Just saying that word gives me a rash."

She laughs. "Why did you choose accounting if you hate it?"

I shrug. "My dad is an accountant. I just picked something that would pay the bills." I try to keep the disdain from my voice. She doesn't need to know about my father. Not that I wanted to follow in my father's footsteps, but there's a lot of work in the field, and I needed something to support Taylor and me if hockey didn't work out.

"I see."

We turn another corner. "How long have you been in Boston?"

"Just a couple of months. Still getting my bearings." I glance around the dark street. I can't say she's staying in the best part of town. "I'm right here." She stops at the end of a drive-way, and I take in the duplex. "Thanks for the drinks and nachos, and for walking me home."

"Anytime."

She nods, and stands facing me, like she's not ready for this night to be over either. Does she feel this pull as much as I do? Fuck. A part of me wants her to invite me in. The other part of me remembers she's my sister's only friend in Boston and since I'm not into relationships, a fast hookup can only make things awkward.

"I hope to see you tomorrow night." I wink at her. "I'll make a Bucks fan out of you yet."

She grins, and then something I can't identify, something real, honest, and vulnerable—something different from the outgoing, vivacious woman that intrigued me earlier—moves over her face and hits me like a flying puck. But not in a bad way.

"We'll see." She lowers her head, an air of shyness coming over her. "See you later, Kalen."

"Later, Sahara," I respond and really fucking hope I do see her later.

I stand there, watching her walk to her door. She climbs the three steps to her door. But then she hesitates, and the next thing I know, a gasp fills the silence of the night and she inches back her arms wrapping around herself.

What the fuck is going on?

"Sahara." I hurry to her, and the second I see the panic in her eyes, and her door, which has been kicked open, my protective instincts kick into full gear and I put her behind me. Fuck. This isn't good.

Not good at all.

4

SAHARA

My body is shaking by the time the police arrive, and even though I'm hugging myself, I can't seem to calm down. On my stoop, I speak to the officers for a moment, and after they take my statement, they walk inside to do a search of the place. Kalen is about to follow them in, but stops and turns to me.

"Sahara," he says, and before I realize it, I'm in his arms, and he's rubbing his hands up and down my back. "It's okay. They're gone."

"I know."

He inches back and the concern on his face as he looks me over does weird things to my insides. While I had a major crush on this guy in high school, I didn't really know much about him other than the fact that he lived with his grandmother and was close to his younger sister. "I've got you. I won't let anything happen, okay?"

I nod. "Okay."

He takes my hand. "Are you ready to go inside and see what's missing?" I give him a grateful smile, so glad he walked me home, because everything about his presence has given me a measure of comfort.

"Thanks, Kalen."

He squeezes my hand. "Hey, of course."

With my hand in his, I follow him in, as the officers walk through my space. In my living room, I notice my laptop is no longer on the coffee table. It's not like I had a lot to steal. Jewelry and 'things' aren't that important to me, and everything that I own of value, I left back at home in Darien.

"My laptop is gone," I murmur.

"Shit. Was it password protected and backed up?"

I nod.

"Okay, let's check the other rooms." Kalen stays with me as we go from room to room and other than my laptop, some costume jewelry, and some money I had in a bowl in my bedroom, everything is okay. But the sense of violation I feel, to know someone has been in my place, in my bedroom, fills me with a new kind of panic. A hard shiver goes through me and once again, Kalen pulls me to him, holding me against his hard, but comforting body. We meet with the officers in the front hallway, and I let them know what's been stolen. I glance at the doorframe and take in the broken shards. The thoughts of everyone leaving and being alone, with a busted door, terrifies me.

The officer puts his notepad away. "We have everything we need, but I have to say, chances of catching the guy or getting your things back are slim."

"I figured as much."

"You might want to think about getting a door camera," he suggests.

"Good idea."

"We can help you get this door in place and locked, but it's not safe. Do you have somewhere to stay tonight?"

I open my mouth. I don't know anyone other than Taylor, but Kalen speaks first. "She's staying with me." My jaw falls open, sure that shock is causing me to misinterpret his words. "Let's grab what you need. You're coming home with me."

"Kalen, no that's not necessary."

"You're not staying here, Sahara. Someone just broke into your house, and they could come back."

Kalen wants me to stay with him?

Oddly enough, a part of me thinks he's not ready for this night to be over. Heck, I'm not either. I loved talking to him. But the other part of me, that part that is shy and insecure, wants to believe there's something more here, but is too afraid to believe it. Then again, that girl could be wrong, because the woman Kalen met tonight is very different from who I really am. What am I even saying? I have no freaking clue who I am.

"I'm sure—"

"I think you should stay with a friend tonight," the officer advises.

"Taylor would want this," Kalen points out. "She'd kill me if I didn't bring you home."

Yeah okay. Of course, that's why he's offering. I'm his sister's friend, and he's a protector at heart.

It's not like he wants you in his bed, girl.

Heck, maybe he's not even interested in the outgoing version of me. Nevertheless, I don't want to stay here and while I could go to a hotel, I think I need the company tonight.

"You should take your friend up on his offer," the officer points out.

I nod. "I will. Thanks, Kalen." I take a step toward the door, and my chest tightens with anxiety. I swallow, and turn back to Kalen.

He must read the panic in my face, as he instantly takes my hand. Without making me feel like a feeble, frightened female, he tugs. "You'll probably need help carrying things."

He guides me toward the bedroom as the officers both work to right my door, which is kind of them because it's not in their duties.

In my bedroom, I grab a duffle bag from the closet and toss it on the bed. Kalen stays close as I open my drawer and toss some clothes into the bag, and Kalen tucks them in.

"I shouldn't need much," I begin. "Probably just one night." He nods, but he doesn't look convinced as he pulls his phone from his pocket and slides his finger across the screen. "I can try to find someone to come by tomorrow or the next day to fix the door." I probably can't get someone that quickly. But I don't want to overstay my welcome.

"Yeah," is all he mutters, distracted by whatever it is he's searching for. I make my way to the bathroom to grab a few things, and he follows me, standing guard in the hall, and his presence gives me comfort.

Once I gather my toiletries and face products, I exit the bathroom, and he doesn't move, which forces me to squeeze by his large frame. My body brushes his and I fight down the shivers racing through me.

He tucks his phone away. "My buddy Ash is going to fix your door and install a camera."

"What?"

"Yeah, he's a jack of all trades."

"Ash Wheeler, the defenseman for the Bucks is going to fix my door?"

"Yeah. Do you know him?"

I shake my head and drop my things into my duffle bag. Am I in the twilight zone or something. "Not personally. Just from the team, and I can't ask him to do that."

"You didn't, I did."

"Okay, but still. I can find someone, I'm sure."

"You don't have to. Gina would kill me if I didn't call and ask for help." I arch a brow. Who the heck is Gina? Reading my curiosity, he explains. "Gina is his wife. They have a daughter, Zoe." He chuckles about something.

"What?"

He glances over his shoulder, like he's making sure the coast is clear. "When Ash met Zoe, he was terrified of her. She's like seven years old."

"Big Ash Wheeler, afraid of a seven-year-old?"

"Yeah, but you should see him with her now." His eyes almost glaze over. "He loves her so much and vice versa. There was this whole lumpy pancake wish thing…"

"What?" What the heck is he talking about?

"Nothing. Anyway, she loves helping her daddy out, and she'll probably come with him to help fix this door. It's adorable." As he grins, that look of melancholy back on his face, he zips up my bag and tosses it over his shoulder. "You got everything you need?"

"I think so."

"Let's go." He takes my hand again, and guides me to the front door.

We walk through the open door, and the officer who took my information tugs the door shut behind him. "This will hold for now, but you should get it fixed right away."

"Already on it," Kalen tells him.

"I'll keep you updated," the officer informs us and joins his partner in the car.

"My car is parked at the pub," Kalen tells me. We head down the street, and he doesn't let go of my hand. We reach his car and he hits the fob to open the doors and pulls mine open for me.

I climb in and he tosses my bag onto the back seat. I watch him circle the vehicle and when he climbs in, he suggests, "Why don't you text Taylor and let her know what's going on."

I pull my phone from my purse and shoot a text to Taylor, and she returns a message full of shock and concern. I let her know I'm okay, and that we're on our way.

As Kalen maneuvers his car through the downtown streets, I take in the worry in his eyes in the dashboard light. He scrubs his chin, and casts me a fast glance. "Not a great welcome to Boston."

"It's been good so far," I tell him and hug myself. "I'm just glad I wasn't home, and nothing of real value was stolen."

He flicks on his signal and turns. "Me too and I'm so glad Taylor lives with me." His fingers tighten around the steering wheel. "I'm not ready for her to be out on her own."

My heart squeezes. I love how much he cares for her. I know my folks care for me too, and want to see me successful. I'm just not sure I can fit into the mold they want for me. "You're a good big brother. She's told me that."

He laughs. "Are you sure she didn't tell you that I'm overprotective?"

I laugh with him. "She might have dropped a hint about that," I tease. It does make me wonder what happened in their lives to make him so protective. Heck, my parents are completely overprotective too, or maybe the better word is controlling. Since high school, all I wanted was to get out from under their thumb. I almost tell Kalen that he needs to be careful, otherwise he could drive his sister away, but it's not really my business so I keep my mouth shut.

"Are you sure all of this is okay, and that Ash won't mind fixing my door? I mean I will pay him."

Kalen nods. "You can try. He probably won't take anything."

I nibble my lip and think about that. I've heard about hockey culture, of course. The guys are like a family, and the wives and girlfriends are pretty close too. I think that's really special. We drive in silence and I sit up a bit straighter when he pulls into his driveway, parking beside Taylor's car. On the other side of Taylor's car there's a vehicle and I assume it's Elias'. I grin as I think about her crush on him and I can see why she's not about to pursue it. Her brother really is protective.

Kalen hops from the car and grabs my bag from the back. The front door is flung open and Taylor comes rushing out. She pulls me into her arms. "Ohmigod, Sahara. That must have been terrifying. I'm so glad Kalen brought you here. You can stay as long as you like."

I laugh. "I'm sure one night will be enough."

"You can't go back there. What if it happens again? You at least have to move."

"I can't move." I'm here on my own, making it without my parents' help or finances. I think they want me to go crawling back to them, so they could say I told you so. They never thought I'd make enough as a new librarian, and things are tight here in Boston, but I refuse to ask them for help. If that is all I can afford at the moment, that is where I'll live.

"But you can, Taylor," Kalen says as he comes up behind me. Taylor arches a brow, confused. "Move," he orders playfully. "You're in the way and we'd like to get inside."

Taylor rolls her eyes at her big brother. "Come on. I got the spare room ready for you."

I reach for my bag, and Kalen keeps it over his shoulder. "I'll carry it up. I want to make sure you have everything you need."

Dressed only in a pair of sweats that hang low on his hips, Elias comes down the hall, a bottle of water in his hands. "Sorry to hear about the break in."

I swear to God Taylor is about to melt into the floor beside me as she tries, unsuccessfully, to tear her gaze away from Elias. He really is handsome. I can see why Taylor likes him. I can really see how torturous it is to be here.

"What about a roommate, Sahara?" Taylor croaks out. Poor girl is a mess living here with Elias and not being able to do anything but dream about him.

"I...uh."

Kalen glares at his sister. "You have school to finish before moving out."

Taylor folds her arms and glares at her brother, and just when she's about to protest, Elias puts his hand on her arm.

"T, you do need to think about school. Living here is where you need to be right now."

Whoa...while his words are full of love and worry, the want I spot in his eyes really grabs my attention.

Taylor opens her mouth and closes it again, the hand on her arm totally messing her up. Needing to help her out, I say, "If you could show me to my room." I slide my arm through hers, and guide her toward the stairs. "I think I might get lost looking for it on my own."

"Yes, of course." We hurry up the stairs, and I'm fully aware of Kalen's presence behind us as he follows. Along the stairs I notice numerous pictures. Some of a woman I assume is their mother, and some of him and Taylor as kids. I see no evidence of a father.

His home is warm, cozy, and I can feel the love through his pictures. I have no idea why I felt it would be monochromatic decorating, done by a decorator, with no warmth at all.

Maybe he did this all for his sister...or maybe there's just a lot more to the man than I ever realized.

We pass a few rooms and Taylor waves her hand to the right. "That's Kalen's room." A couple more steps she waves to the left again. "That's my room. Elias and I share a Jack and Jill bathrooms. It's meant for kids, but Kalen doesn't have any."

"Keep moving," Kalen grumbles.

We stop outside the open door across from Elias. "This is you. You're beside Kalen."

I step in and take in the big bed against the far wall to the left of the window, which I think might overlook the back yard. There's a closet, chair, night tables and a dresser. Everything I could need.

"This is perfect for tonight." I turn back as Kalen enters, his big, hard body, and protective nature doing crazy things to me as he sets the bag on the bed.

He glances around, like he's inspecting the room for the first time. He hovers at the end of the bed, running his fingers over the wooden footboard.

His gaze finds its way back to me. "Do you have everything you need, Sahara?"

Oh, God, everything in the way his fingers are still grazing the wood sends my mind spiraling in a direction I don't want it going. "Uh, yes. I'm pretty tired so I'll just wash up and get to sleep."

"Help yourself to anything you want."

Gulp...

"The kitchen is downstairs, just at the end of the hall from the front door," he continues. "If you get hungry or thirsty, help yourself. There might be some cookies left in the pantry. I can't be sure. Taylor eats them as fast as I get them in the house."

I catch the grin on Taylor's face and quickly avert my gaze because I'm sure my face is turning many shades of red. "I think I'd like to take a shower. Wash the night off. Is that okay?"

"Of course." He points to my door. "Just a few doors down. You can't get lost."

"Actually, I think I could get lost in this place," I joke as I unzip my bag. "I might have to leave myself a popcorn trail."

"Yeah, you wouldn't want to end up in the wrong bed," Taylor kindly points out, an all-knowing grin on her face as she steps up to my window to draw the curtains closed to give me privacy.

"No, we wouldn't want to do that, would we, Taylor?"

Kalen's glance goes back and forth between the two of us, like he's trying to figure out if we're sharing some kind of secret. He gives up and shakes his head. "I'm calling it a night. See you both in the morning." He's about to leave and then turns back. "Wait, do you need to be anywhere tomorrow? You can use my car. I can get a lift to the arena with Elias. Or maybe Taylor can drive you to where you need to go."

My heart leaps. Honestly, I never told Taylor acting was my full-time job. I'm not sure how she came to that conclusion and I feel bad for not correcting her. I just don't want Kalen seeing me as a boring librarian, especially when I've been pretending to be the outgoing girl from the play. After tomorrow night's game, I don't expect to run into him again, so in the meantime, I'm just going to pretend to be that other girl.

"I do have some things to do tomorrow, but I can grab an Uber."

"No, here." Kalen takes his keys from his pocket and hands them to me. "If you can avoid going to your place until Ash gets it fixed, I think that would be for the best. There's a house key on there too. Come and go as you please."

Taylor folds her arms. "Yeah, you're not going back to your place," she states, and from the determination in her eyes, I think she wants me to stay here forever. "Besides, there's too much testosterone in this house." She fakes a shiver. "It's nice to have another woman in the house. Someone to have a conversation with that doesn't involve hockey."

I laugh at them both and shake the keys. "Thanks, Kalen." I point to the door. "I'm going to go get cleaned up and hopefully the door is an easy fix for Ash, and I won't need to put you out."

"Oh, he doesn't mind being put out." She whacks Kalen's stomach before walking to the door. "Right, bro?"

I nearly choke on my tongue when Taylor gives me a cheeky grin.

"Right. G'night." They both leave my room, and I follow, turning in the other direction. I hear them talking in the hall as I search for the bathroom. I find it three doors down, or maybe it was four. I'm not sure. Nevertheless, that doesn't matter, not when there's a huge tub calling my name. I drop my pajamas on the counter and find a bottle of bubble bath on the shelf above the tub. I run the bath water and pour in a generous amount. As it fills, I brush my teeth and fight a yawn. I have no doubt I'm coming off a big adrenaline rush after finding my place broken into.

After the tub fills, I slide in and moan as the vanilla scent and warm water relax me. I stay in the bath for a long time, letting my eyes fall shut. Quiet reaches my ears, and I'm not sure I've ever heard such silence before. My place is just off a busy street and I hear cars racing at all hours of the night. Kalen's place must be sound proofed.

I remain in the tub until the water grows cold, and then climb out. There's a big fluffy towel on the shelf and I help myself to it. Breathing in the fresh laundry scents as I dry myself off. I lightly towel dry my hair, and pull on my pajamas. I open the door and I'm met with darkness and silence. I run my finger along the wall, searching for the light but don't find it. Dammit, I should have brought my phone in with me. At least then I'd have my flashlight app.

I start down the hall on tiptoes, not wanting to wake anyone and when I reach my door, I quietly open it. The curtains are drawn, and a sliver of light spreads across the edge of my bed against the far wall. As my body aches for sleep, I walk quietly, slide in and when I roll, my body connects with something hard, something that is rousing from sleep...something that is reaching for me.

Oh God...

● **5**

KALEN

"Hey," I murmur groggily as the enticing scent of vanilla falls over me. I reach out, and as I try to wake up my brain, my hand connects with soft curves and warm skin. I'm not sure what is going on, but as my hand explores the soft curves beside me, my dick thickens between my legs. I breathe deep. "Mmm," I moan and when a small little gasp of surprise reaches my ears, my brain comes to life, flashing back to the night in the closet—with Darien.

I shift, and roll over to turn on my lamp. The sight of sweet Sahara, the blankets pulled up to her chin greets me. I blink one, twice. What the hell is going on?

"Sahara," I murmur, as understanding dawns. Sahara is in my bed. Clearly, she felt the pull between us every bit as much as I did, and yeah, I considered slipping into her bed, but she stayed in the bathroom so long I ended up falling asleep, which was for the best right.

Or not.

Hell, even Taylor could see my interest in her friend. But when she called me on it in the hall, as Sahara made her way to the bathroom, I denied it. But I wasn't fooling anyone. She laughed right in my face and told me to go for it. I ended the conversation. No way was I going to talk about my sex life with my sister. But at least I know if I hooked up with her only friend in town, she wasn't going to let it come between them. I can't say the reverse would be true. Not that I have to worry about any of my teammates. They know the rules when it comes to Taylor.

Wait, why the fuck does Sahara look so frightened?

"Sahara," I say again, and tug on the blankets as I shift closer, to assure her everything is okay. Maybe this has nothing to do with sex and she needs comfort from her scare tonight. "Oh sorry," I burst out quickly when I realize I misjudged the distance and now my hard cock is pressing up against her soft thigh.

"Kalen." As a sliver of light cuts across her face, her eyes meet mine, and I don't miss the desire reflecting there.

Okay, so maybe she's not looking for comfort, and maybe she likes what she feels against her leg.

I touch her face, lightly brush a strand of her damp hair from her soft cheek. That's when another thought hits. "Did you get lost?"

She hesitates—a vulnerability about her—and for a second something about that look feels so damn familiar. My mind once again goes back to that library closet, but I can't hang on to a single thought when a mewling sound catches in her throat and an inviting smile spreads across her gorgeous face, reminding me I'm with the exciting woman from tonight's stage.

Her warm fingers lightly graze the side of my face, and I suck in a fast breath as her heat travels through my blood and strokes my cock.

"I'm not lost, but if you don't—"

"I do. Oh, I fucking do," I shoot back quickly and she tugs her bottom lips between her teeth, laughter lighting up her eyes.

Her fingers trail lower, touching my bare chest and my muscles tighten. Her lashes fall for a second veiling her eyes when she agrees, "I just...one night."

"One night," I agree. With that I roll over her, spreading her legs with mine as I settle on top of her lush body. I brush her damp hair back and gaze at her lips. She wets them in preparation, and while I want to draw this out, I need to taste her so fucking bad.

I cover her mouth with mine, and a rumble starts deep in my chest and rises up, only to get smothered by her kisses. She tastes like minty toothpaste and I slide my tongue inside to tangle with hers.

My dick thickens even more, and I move against her body, wanting my boxers off, and wanting her naked. I inch back and bury my mouth in her neck. Breathing in her scent, I moan, and run my hand down the side of her body, working to figure out what she's wearing and the best way to get her out of it. No one has ever accused me of being inefficient, on or off the ice.

Once I realize she's in shorts and a button-down pajama top, I slow myself down and slide off her. I push off the bed and stand over her.

She blinks up at me. "Kalen," she murmurs, a hint of worry in her voice.

I tug on my boxers, fixing them around my throbbing dick. "Don't worry, baby, I'm not going anywhere. I just want you to sit up for me."

"Oh."

She does as I ask, and I let my gaze go from her cute painted toenails, up her long silky legs, to the lush bumps in her pajama top. My mouth drools, aching to lick and taste those hard nubs that highlight her arousal.

Dropping to my knees before her, which, judging from the widening of her eyes, seems to surprise her, I reach for a button on her pajama top and pop it open to expose just a tiny hint of her creamy flesh.

She swallows and glances at the lamp. "Should we..."

I pause for a second, not really expecting her to be self-conscious. Tonight, on stage she was the female character in a racy love scene. I guess that's different, though. On the ice, I'm a beast. Off it, I don't go around checking guys if they're in my way. I'm once again reminded that we are what we need to be in certain situation.

"If you want it off, we can turn it off." I undo the second button, and my gaze takes in her small mounds. I spread her top and get the tiniest glimpse of her areolas. I've been with many different women, bodies of all shapes and sizes, but this woman's breasts, small, pert, ready for my mouth, are hands down my favorite. I'm not just saying that because she's currently in my bed, offering herself up to me. Sure, that doesn't hurt, but it's what I'm attracted to.

I undo the third button, and fully expose her gorgeous breasts. Her head rolls back, her eyes flitting shut. "Sahara," I murmur quietly. "I'd like to look at you, but if you want the light off, that's okay too."

Her eyes open, and race over my chest. "I...I like looking too."

I grin at that and it seems to wipe away her uncertainty. "How about touching?" I ask. She arches a brow. "Do you want to touch?"

She nods eagerly, and I take one of her hands and place it on my chest. A little whisper of air flutters from her mouth and falls over me. A quiver goes through my body and now it's my turn to shut my eyes. Her fingers splay, her touch light as she acquaints herself with my body and I moan, leaning into her.

"You like being touched?" she asks.

My eyes open at the quietness in her voice and I respond with, "I like you touching me. What about you, do you like being touched?"

She smiles and shoots back, "I like you touching me." It's strange and I have no idea why, but I get the sense that this woman hasn't been touched in a very long time. I could be wrong, but if that's the case and we only have one night together, then I damn well want to make it good for her.

I finish unbuttoning her top and love the way her chest is rising and falling erratically as I slide the cotton from her shoulders. I shake my head, strangely overwhelmed by the near naked sight of her and she must misread me, because her eyes go wide and she slightly stiffens.

"You're fucking beautiful, Sahara," I breathe out. Her body

relaxes as I cup her breasts, shaping the undersides as my mouth waters and my dick nearly tears through my boxers.

"You are too."

I grin. "I've been called a lot of things, but never beautiful." A pink little flush spreads across her cheeks and I lean in and kiss her. "I like it, but it needs to stay our little secret."

She chuckles. "Okay."

I lightly brush my thumb over her nipples and she mewls again. "Kalen, that is so nice."

"You like being touched here?" She nibbles her lips again, and nods. "Tell me," I insist.

"I do," she says.

I lean into her and lightly nip her nipple and her hands move to my shoulders. Her nails dig into my skin as I pull the entire bud into my mouth and suck hard. "Oh my God, Kalen."

"Mmm," I moan, as my chest fills with pride, loving that I can turn her on with one little suck. Jesus, how is she going to react when I have my mouth between her legs?

I don't know, but dammit, I can't wait to find out. I treat her other perfect breast to my tongue and my hands land on her thighs. I knead her flesh before spreading her legs even more, giving my body, hands and mouth ample room to move, because yeah, I want to devour her. With hurried, almost anxious hands she continues to touch me, like I'm a damn sculpture on the last night of its display. My blood burns, my cock restless inside my boxers.

I get it, buddy. I get it. I want inside her too.

She leans back on her hands, her body open to me, as I toy with the string holding her shorts to her hips. I hold her gaze, watch her breath come quicker as I tug on the string. "Lift."

Her ass leaves the bed, and I work the shorts free. The second I expose her beautiful bare pussy, all warm, wet and pretty pink, I move back, push her legs together and get her completely naked.

After tossing the shorts away, I spread her again, and her fingers race through my mess of hair. I lightly touch her with my finger, barely grazing her as I run the tip over her soft outer lips.

"Kalen…"

"You like being touched here?"

"Yes, please."

I apply more pressure, widening her pussy lips and exposing her swollen clit. Circling it, and gauging her reaction as my dick aches, her hips lift again. I focus in on her clit, rubbing it with my palm, and her cries of pleasure curl around me.

"I wonder if you'll like my tongue as much?" I grin as she whimpers again, loving all the sexy sounds she makes. "Do you think we should try?"

"God, yes."

I lean in, breathing in her freshly showered skin. Warm vanilla and something else that's uniquely Sahara fills my senses. I glide my tongue over her hot, wet pussy, lapping at her sweetness. Her entire body quivers beneath my ministrations, and her hands run down my back as she leans over me.

I savor her as my dick screams at me to hurry this along. I

reach down, pull him free and give him a hard stroke to sate him a bit longer.

As pre-cum coats my palm, I lick her with the soft blade of my tongue, and then sharpen it to apply pressure to her clit, and her whimpering sounds curl around me as I learn what her body needs from me.

"What's the consensus?" I ask from between her thighs. I glance up at her to find her eyes glazed, lost in a haze of pleasure. "You like my tongue as much?"

Her eyes practically roll in her head when she realizes what I'm asking. "Yes. I like."

"Should we try a finger or two?"

"Please." I nip at her inner thigh before I slide one thick finger into her core, and her quivering muscles tighten around me. Before I can ask if she likes that, she moans and murmurs, "Yes, finger…"

I slide it in and out of her, and run my tongue over her sopping wet clit. Her body begins to rock against my face, and I crook my finger inside her. The second I brush that tight bundle of nerves, she gasps, and her entire body lets go. Liquid heat floods her sex, and I lap at her as it drips over her thighs. Fuck yeah.

I steal a fast look at her and her mouth is open, her gaze locked on mine, like she can't figure out what just happened. When was the last time this woman had an orgasm? I know she's new in town, but lots of experiences happen in college, right?

"I love the way you come for me," I say, encouraging her to give in to everything her body is feeling. I stay inside her, letting her ride out the waves and when I come up for air, she looks almost flabbergasted.

"Sahara?"

"I don't...I usually..." She shakes her head. Whatever it was she was going to say, she changed her mind. As I go back on my heels, I want to press, to ask, but lose focus when a change comes over her and she places her hand over my throbbing dick.

"Do you think this big guy would like my mouth?"

I let out a loud groan. Shit, I need to keep it down, otherwise my sister might come running. Although she seemed to like the idea of us, but finding us together is something else entirely.

"I take that as a yes," Sahara jokes, and I go up on my knees as she leans into me, tugging my boxers lower to expose my entire dick and balls.

"You can take that as a fuck yeah."

She chuckles and her hot breath caresses my crown as she puts her small hand around my swollen cock and takes him into her mouth. I grip her hair, push it from her face and watch her suck me. In and out, in and out, almost curiously, tentatively.

As I watch her, something niggles in my brain. Once again, I hate to admit that I've been with a lot of women, and while most are into oral sex, they usually like to put on a show. But Sahara here, she's focused, like this is as much for her as it is for me. What she doesn't do is glance up at me, all seductive and demure, and maybe, after watching her act tonight, I thought she would, expected oral sex with her to be like it was with everyone else.

Honestly, she's a bit of a contradiction. Outgoing and seemingly up for anything one second, and the next, quiet, reflective almost...explorative. I don't hate anything about the contemplative side of her. In fact, I think I might like it. A lot.

She inches back, her gaze latched on my cock, everything about the look on her face thoughtful...curious. She seems to be all over the place tonight.

I touch her chin and bring her eyes to mine. "Sahara?"

The vulnerability about her hits like a stick to the gut, bringing out the protector in me, as she blinks once, twice, and then her lips curl into a smile.

"Do you think you'd like to be inside me?"

His eyes darken, lust overtaking him, and I'm grateful for that. For a moment there, I thought he could see right through me. See that I'm just an inexperienced girl who basically has zero idea of how to please a man. Although, he sure as hell seemed to like it when I took him into my mouth. Until I had to inch back to examine his length and hardness, like he was a damn bug under a microscope.

I mean sure, I've seen a man's penis before, touched it, and licked it, but I'd never brought a man to orgasm that way because it always ended in intercourse. I kind of wanted him to come in my mouth, wanted to watch his seed spurt from his slit...to know if I could actually bring a man to completion that way. That's when I started contemplating the best way to go about that. Maybe that's the analytical librarian in me. Or maybe it's the woman trying to come out.

I don't give it any more thought as he pulls me to my feet and kicks off his boxers. His arms circle me and he pulls me tight. His cock presses against my pelvis and I rub against it, more for my own benefit than his. Let's face it. I'm with an experienced guy here and I'm taking full advantage of that. Using this moment to learn what I like and don't like. That's why I'm here in Boston. To discover myself, and figure out who the heck I really am. Why not figure out who I am sexually too, and who better to do it with than an experienced guy who was the first man to put his fingers in me?

He touches my chin again, lifts my face to his. "I don't think. I know."

I blink up at him. What were we talking about again? With a tender touch, he tucks my hair behind my ears and his smile disarms me. Wow, who knew a rough and tough hockey player could touch such tenderness.

"You asked if I'd like to be inside you," he explains.

"Right..." I nod. "Right, I knew that."

He grins again, and my damn heart wobbles. *Don't fall for him, Sahara.*

Ha!

What a freaking joke. I can go right ahead kid myself all I want, saying I forgot about him when I went off to college but I think we all know the truth. I've always compared every man's touch to his. So maybe, just maybe after tonight, I'll be over that. Hopefully, he'll be terrible at sex, leaving me hot, achy and needy, and completely unfilled. Yeah, running for my toys to finish the job might be the perfect thing to help me get over him.

He backs me up toward the bed, his hand between my legs touching, reading me again, and as his deft fingers stroke me deep, I nearly orgasm again.

Okay, I don't think bad sex is going to happen. Dammit.

He puts his hands on my waist and tugs until I'm sitting on the edge of the bed. "You want me inside you?" With his cock inches from my face, I focus in on his crown, the precum dripping and I nod. "Good." He gestures with a tip of his chin. "Why don't you get on that bed, and spread your legs for me."

It's happening.

As I move to the center of the bed, putting a pillow that has his scent all over it under my head, he reaches into his nightstand and retrieves a condom. Before he puts it on, he takes his cock in his hand and strokes himself and I try not to stare in awe, like I just watched a shuttle land on Mars. He grins, and it's clear at times that I'm an easy read for him. I snap my mouth shut, trying to reel my emotions in and pretend I do this sort of thing all the time.

His gaze moves over my body as he bites into the foil wrapper and rolls the condom over his long thick length. He sheathes himself with an expertise I've never before experienced as he climbs on top, pressing me into the mattress with his big, hard body.

My hands instantly go around his back and it's crazy how much I like touching him, exploring his hard muscles and tight skin. He might think my touches are for him—yes, I paid attention, learning how he likes to be caressed. While that's half true, let's face it, I'm being a little selfish here. I'm a girl on a mission to discover who she really is.

His mouth finds mine for a deep kiss, and I shift, anxious for him to be inside me. He groans, reaches between our bodies and positions his cock at my entrance. His eyes meet mine, and he must see the need. In one thrust, he's deep inside me, and as he pushes in, it draws out a long moan of pleasure from my lungs.

"Fuck, Sahara. You feel good."

I run my hands over his body, wanting his mouth back on mine. He kisses me again, and then his lips move to my nose, my forehead and my cheeks. It's kind of adorable, really. He begins to move, sliding in and out of me and I wrap my legs around his back and tug him in.

Look at that. I was right after all. He really is bad at this.

Not.

Unfortunately.

He shifts his body for deeper thrusts, and his breathing changes. Moisture breaks out on my skin as each downward thrust stimulates my clit and my eyes roll back as I concentrate on all the points of pleasure.

Actually, everything about this feels so incredible, I can't believe this is what I've been missing out on. Yeah, I really should have slept my way through the phone book back in college, although something tells me, nothing would have ever felt this good.

"You good, babe?" he asks and that's when I realize I went quiet for a moment.

I lightly scratch at his back and he sucks in a breath. "I'm really good."

"Yeah, me too."

He fucks me in this position for a few minutes, and his face twists, like he's in total agony. He taps my legs. "Let's flip you over. Up on your hands and knees."

Oh my...

I stare at him in utter shock and he angles his head, his gaze searching my face. Because I don't want him to figure out I'm inexperienced, I say in my best seductive voice, that probably sounds like an octopus on red bull, "I was actually thinking something else."

"Oh?" He grins as his brows spike up, and it's clear I've got his interest.

In a move that actually takes me by surprise, I push him and he rolls, while I follow him along with his cock still inside me.

"Babe," he murmurs, his hands gripping my hips as I straddle him. "I like the way you think."

I've never been on top of a man before, and I kind of like this power pose. Doing what feels natural, I grind against him, and move my hips forward and back. Judging by the tortured sounds in his throat and the way his face is twisting up, he likes this too.

"Jesus, Sahara."

I press my knees into the mattress and lift myself up, only to drop down again and he hits so hard and so deep, a gasp catches in my throat and my whole body quivers.

"Fuck yeah," he grunts as I continue the movement until my legs grow tired. "Let me help."

He easily moves me up and down over his cock, lifting like I weigh nothing, and I let my body go, handing myself over to him. His hips lift as he pulls me back down, and I cup my breasts, sweeping my thumbs over my nipples. His eyes go wide with pleasure—he likes it when I touch myself—and a crazy thought hits. How would this man like to watch me use my toys?

Not that that is ever going to happen. I mean I'm pretending to be a wild, experienced woman but that would be over the top.

The muscles in his jaw ripple as he half lifts himself from the pillow. His shoulders tense, and he moves me up and down faster, pulling me forward a bit to hit my clit just right.

"Kalen," I burst out, shocked that another orgasm is pulling at me. One orgasm—with a man—is unheard of, yet here I am, about to have my second.

I toss my head back and my muscles squeeze around his cock, liquid heat flooding my channel and trickling down my thighs. I begin to chant his name like he's some divine spirit who deserves praise and admiration—and I'm the sacrificial offering. I guess I did offer my body up to him, and damn did he ever do all the right things with it.

He grips my hips, tugs me down, and holds me to him as he releases high inside me. His cock pulses and I bite back a gasp as each throb ripples through me. I've never felt anything quite like that before. What would it be like to have his seed spill inside me?

Another thing that is never going to happen.

I lean over his body, collapsing on top of him, my small breasts crushed against his hard chest. I revel in the feel of his moist skin next to my nakedness, and warmth rushes through my blood as he puts his arms around me, and kisses the top of my head. Jeez, when he does adorable things like that it really messes with me.

"You good?" he whispers, his voice low, sated, and so very sexy.

"As long as I don't have to walk anytime soon," I joke, needing to lighten the mood.

"Sorry, I should have taken over sooner." He lets out a laugh. "I was just so caught up in watching you fuck me, Sahara. I lost my ability to think clearly."

I, Darien Lewis, made Kalen Coolidge lose all ability to think...

What the what?

Trying to keep the giddiness from my voice I point out, "Plus, no blood in your brain."

"Truth. But seriously, Sahara." He touches my face with soft hands. "That was...you are fantastic."

"You're not so bad yourself," I shoot back because there's a seriousness in his eyes that might be messing with my brain.

I roll off him and he winces as I move to the side of the bed, debating my next move. Do I snuggle in, or bolt?

Which do you want, girlfriend?

He throws his legs over the bed and discards the condom. He wraps it in tissue and drops it in the garbage and it's weird how intimate this all feels. Good God, I need to get out more.

He turns back to me, and he must sense I'm ready to bolt. "Just one second." I watch him as he walks to the ensuite, completely naked, completely comfortable in his own skin. Water runs and a second later he comes back, running a damp cloth over his cock. Oh, okay, he's washing himself up. That's a new experience for me.

He sets the washcloth onto his nightstand and crawls back between my legs. What the heck is going on? He spreads me and that's when I realize he has another washcloth in his hand. Heat races through my blood as he gently presses the soft, warm cotton to my sex, ever so gently washing me clean.

Yeah, okay...this is different...and amazing.

I try not to react to his thoughtfulness, try to pretend I'm used to a man caring for me after sex, when really, it's me caring for myself with my battery-operated boyfriend.

"Feel good?" he asks, and that's when I realize I'm moaning.

"Yes, thank you."

He grins, and once I'm clean, he sets the cloth on the night-stand with his, and crawls in beside me. I glance at him, then stare at the closed door, my brain on overdrive as I figure out my next move. His hand lands on my arm, like a predator sensing its prey is about to bolt.

His head is angled, his eyes full of questions as he zeroes in on me. "What is it that you don't usually...

My sluggish brain takes a second to catch up and when it finally does unease floods my body. I said those words...right after I had an orgasm. What was I thinking? I almost laugh out loud. Thinking? I wasn't thinking, I was too lost in euphoria to know what I was doing.

I give a fast shake of my head and pluck at the bedding. "Oh...nothing."

He shakes his head, not believing me. "Not nothing."

I sit up, press my back to the headboard. "Fine, then, I can't tell you that."

He gives my arm a squeeze and adjusts a pillow behind his back, mimicking my position. "No worries, you don't have to. I just thought it might be something you wanted to talk about." He crinkles his cute nose. "You did start down a path..."

"It's embarrassing, Kalen."

"I've been inside you, Sahara, and we share a secret already, remember?"

How could I not remember?

I think about the fact that I called him beautiful and that we'd keep that a secret. Honestly, I had no idea what I was saying in the moment, and I can't tell him that I don't usually climax with a partner. Not that I've had many, but I did do some experimenting in college. If you call three minutes with Tristan Haney in the back seat of his car experimenting or three and a half minutes with Jeramiah Godfrey behind the bleachers after a hockey game. Oh, and there was that one messy time with Levi Jessome. Just...no.

I really wish I had done more. Maybe even had done it a time or two in an actual bed. Although I kind of like that Kalen was my first real between the sheets experience. Ugh. I need to stop thinking like that. I'm once again kicking myself for not sleeping my way through the phone book at college. Maybe that way I wouldn't always be thinking about what happened in that library closet. Cripes, the man only touched me with his fingers, yet it's stayed with me for all these years and now, whenever I have a man's hands on my body, I compare them to that night.

Oh, but now I'll be comparing everything to what just happened here...

So much for bad sex getting him out of my system.

What the hell was I thinking? I should have just told him I'd wandered into the wrong room.

Ah, but then your pussy wouldn't be sated and still smoking like a fired gun. Not that a smoking pussy is a real thing. I glance down. Ohmigod, I can't believe I just glanced down to check.

He's watching me carefully. Can he hear my brain racing? Jeez, probably. But I can't tell him what I mean. He thinks I'm that vivacious, outgoing woman from the play. What would he think if he knew I used toys to get off. Would he think there's something wrong with me? Or maybe he'd think that no man could do it for me because I'm a needy girl who demands more than a quick wham bam.

What he would think is that you're a woman who knows what she needs.

Hmmm?

I square my shoulders. Here goes nothing. "I just...don't usually come without..."

He cocks his head, his movements easy as he pulls the blankets up to cover me from the hips down. "Without what?"

I cover my face with my hands as heat rushes to my cheeks. As I begin to chicken out, I blurt out, "Maybe this is TMI."

"Nope." He pulls my hands from my face and I expect him to be laughing, or at least grinning as I try not to embarrass myself, but he's not. There's a deep sincerity about him and it curls around my heart, and does the strangest things to my brain.

I blink repeatedly, as he continues to watch me. "Fine. I don't usually reach climax without my toys." I throw my hands up and let them land on either side of my hips. "Are you happy now?"

He frowns. "Actually, no, I'm not. I'm sad about that for you."

What the...what the what?

He pauses, as though searching for the right words and something about him, about this conversation feels very real and personal. Intimate. Even after what we just did. "I'm happy that I was able to do that for you, Sahara." I stare at him, a little shocked by his sincerity, and openness. His brow lifts, real curiosity in his eyes. "Why do you think you were able to orgasm with me?"

I worked to swallow the lump punching into my throat. Oh, because you've been the man of my dreams and fantasies for far too long now. I bite back a snarky laugh, because I sure as hell can't tell him that. He has no idea who I am, and I want it to stay that way. Heck, no one paid any attention to that quiet, awkward girl in high school, and he'd probably tell her to go fly a kite in a lightning storm, not do delicious things to her in his bed.

Do you really think that, Sahara?

No, not after tonight, but he had nothing to do with me all those years ago, and I'll never, ever forget the tortured, almost mortified moan in his throat when I ran from the closet, right after he realized he wasn't in there with Juliette. Thank God, he never figured out who he was touching intimately that night.

"I don't know, Kalen," I begin, playing it off because this is getting far too serious. "I guess you have the magic touch."

He holds his hands up and examines his fingers. His gaze moves back to my face and he offers me a devastating grin that warms me from the inside out. "Who knew?"

I knew.

His rough palm lands on my stomach, and his thumb brushes the sensitive flesh near my belly button. He wags his brows playfully, lightening the mood in the room. "You know what I think?"

I'm not sure I want to know, but answer anyway. "No, what?"

"That you haven't been with the right guys. That they never took the time to figure out what you needed."

"True," I agree.

"With a toy, you're able to touch yourself the way you like." He goes thoughtful for a second. "It's important to know what you want."

Oh God, now we're talking about masturbation. What is happening to my life? I just met this man, sort of, and now after incredible sex, we're talking about me touching myself. Although I must say when he took his cock into his hands...holy!

He shifts on the bed, moving closer. "Why didn't you tell them what you liked?"

Because I'm not that girl. "I didn't think it would have mattered."

"Ah." He nods, like he knows exactly what I'm talking about. "Selfish assholes. Care only about getting themselves off." He snorts out a humorless laugh. "I know guys like that." His smile is full of warmth as he moves his hand higher and sweeps his thumb over the outer edge of my breast. "There's a few of them on the team."

As my body heats up again, I work to speak. "I'm done with assholes."

"Then maybe we can keep doing this." He touches the blanket just above my waist, and rubs it between the rough pad of his fingers. "Do you think that's something you might like," he asks, like we're still playing a sex game. "You telling me everything you might need, or letting me discover it on my own. You think it's a good idea?"

Yes and yes and yes. Oh wait, was there only two things he was asking?

I gulp, pretty sure nothing good can come from this. I mean, orgasms can come from this, and that's good, but I've been hooked on this guy for a long time, and I don't want to get in any deeper.

I take a deep breath and as I let it out, I blurt, "I don't want to have sex again."

Girl, what the hell are you doing?

Shut up, vagina!

Also, just to clarify this to myself, I *do* want to have sex again. We just shouldn't.

He arches a brow, his gaze not quite so steady on my face before he drops it. "Yeah, no. I get it. You're right." He nods a couple times. "We shouldn't do this again."

What the ever-loving hell is going on? I don't know, but I just had sex with the man I've been pining over for years, and he's asking for more, and I feel like I need to make a run for it.

"Taylor," I say quickly. "We're friends. She's my one and only friend in town, actually. I don't want to mess that up. I'm sure you can understand that."

"Right. Absolutely."

"Okay, so no more sex." I steal a fast glance at his closed door. "I should probably get back to my bed." I push the blankets off and before I can stand, he touches my hand. My gaze flashes back to him.

"For the record, you now have two friends in town, Sahara."

I smile as my heart squeezes tight. "Yes, I have two friends," I agree quietly, my stupid heart swelling at his sweetness.

"Actually, make it three." I arch a brow and he explains, "Elias." I grin and he lets my hand go. "Are you still coming to the game?"

"I told Taylor I would, so yes."

"A woman who keeps her word. I like that."

More like a woman who has been pretending to be something she's not. How would he feel about that? Not that I'm ever going to find that answer out because come tomorrow, I'm gone.

I gather up my pajamas and feel his eyes on me as I slip into them. I try to keep my legs steady as I walk to the door. Unable to help myself I glance at him over my shoulder and he grins, like it was a sign he'd been waiting for.

"Later, Sahara."

Oh God, why is he saying it like this isn't over—and we both know it.

KALEN

There's five minutes left in the third period against New Jersey, and we're up by one point. Not that I've been a whole lot of help this game. Fuck. I need to get my attention off the gorgeous woman beside my sister, and back on the game before it's tied and we go into overtime. I turn my focus to Jesse as he moves down the ice like lightning, and I cross the blue line setting myself up for the pass.

Unfortunately, Dmitri Sokolov, New Jersey's star defenseman, cuts in front of me, and the fucker is so big it makes getting around him hard. Instead of using brute force, I call upon the skating skills our new coach taught me, and the next thing I know, I'm around him. The crowd goes crazy, and I ignore it, keeping my focus on the puck.

Jesse shoots it to me, and I catch it on the tip of my stick, instantly taking the shot, but I miss. Jesse and Noah close in on it, and Noah picks it up, shooting it back to Jesse who slams it. The buzzer goes off and the guys all skate to him. As I make my way over, I glance up and spot Taylor and Sahara jumping up and down and hugging each other. Sahara glances at me, and I grin, giving a tip of my head before I'm swallowed up in the group hug.

After we celebrate, we head down the tunnel and into the locker room. Coach comes in to talk to us, and I try not to fidget. I'm really hoping to shower and get outside before Sahara leaves. Maybe she'd like to join us for our usual after winning game drinks at Kilting Around. Once the coach is done, we all head to the shower, and shoot the shit.

I notice Elias is very quiet beside me, and I can't help but wonder if his family is giving him shit again. Although he played a fantastic game, and has been keeping out of the spotlight, so they have nothing to complain about. He must have something else on his mind, and as his roommate and buddy, I feel obligated to ask, though he's a private guy so I don't want to push. I can only hope he'll come to me when he's ready.

"Who's up for a drink?" Tucker asks.

A bunch of guys cheer, but a few are anxious to be home with their wives and children, and while I'm happy for them, my loneliness and the craving for more sits like a lump in the pit of my stomach. Fuck, man, I want what they have, and while a part of me says get the fuck off your ass and go out and get it, there's that damaged boy inside me who fears people just aren't who they say they are.

Thanks, Dad...

A hard quiver goes through me as the image of him in bed with another man cuts deep. I don't give a shit that he's gay, or bi. Fuck, not one little bit. To each their own and love is love. What I fucking hate is that he decided to come out when Mom was sick. Not that he really came out, he was actually having a goddamn affair behind her back, instead of taking care of her and his two kids.

Jesus. Talk about fucked up. At least I was able to shield Taylor from it, and raised her the best I could. She still has a relationship with our old man, and I'm not going to take that away from her. I just don't want her influenced by the cheating bastard. She deserves better, and I have high fucking standards for any guy she decides to date. Although I'm not sure anyone will ever be good enough for her.

"You good, Coolio?"

Ash's voice pulls me back, and I nod and smile as I stick my head under the spray to clear my negative thoughts. Once done, I turn off the shower, and Ash catches up with me as we walk back to our lockers.

"I really appreciate you fixing Sahara's door."

"Not a problem. I was able to install the camera, but she needs to download the app."

"What do I owe you?"

"Hey, any friend of yours is a friend of mine." He grins, and reads far more into my relationship with Sahara than there really is.

"She's my sister's friend," I point out, a scowl on my face as I try to stick to my story.

"Right." His eye roll is a good indication he doesn't believe me.

"She is, that's how I met her. She's the lead in Love Unbound, the same production my sister is in. Elias and I went to see it last night. It was great." Do I sound like I'm rambling? Jesus, I think I do.

He waits until I finish, and continues, "Anyway, make sure she downloads the app to get it all set up. I gave her the box with the instructions inside."

"You talked to her?"

"Yeah, she came home late this morning when I was installing the camera. It was really nice of you to put her up for the night."

If he wasn't one of my best buddies, I'd smack that knowing grin off his face. "Yeah. Like I said, Taylor's friend."

He nods. "She was super grateful. Gina even sent some carrot cake for her."

"Really?" I don't know why I'm surprised. That's hockey culture. The wives are amazing and inclusive and are quick to bring in anyone we're serious about. I guess since I asked Ash for help, Gina too must think there is more going on. "That was really nice of her. Tell her thanks."

"You can tell her yourself. She wants to have a Halloween party before we head to Dallas the Monday after Halloween." He pulls his clothes from his locker. "The weather has been nice, and she wants one last gathering before winter hits."

I crinkle my nose. "Isn't she like twelve months pregnant?" A group Halloween party is a hell of a lot of work.

He laughs, and puts his hand on my shoulder. "No, she's six months. Besides, everyone helps."

Just then, Elias walks up to his locker on the other side of me, and he looks like he has something troubling on his mind. I put my hand on his shoulder. "You look like you could use a beer."

He gives me a smile as fake as the one I just gave Ash. "Yeah."

We finish dressing and I gesture toward the door. "Let's go."

Elias, Ash and I follow the guys outside and we're greeted with numerous familiar women who always meet us after the game. Every now and then I go home with one, but tonight, I'm searching for someone else. I scan the parking lot and the street, and find Taylor waving at me.

"Kalen, over here," she yells. I wave back, and disappointment lumps in my stomach when I don't see Sahara.

Beside me Elias stiffens. "You okay, man?"

"Yeah, I'm tired. Maybe I'll just head back and catch up on some sleep."

"You sure?"

He nods and hikes his bag higher over his shoulders. Before he walks away, he grins and nudges me. "Say hi to Sahara for me."

Shit, did he hear us last night? Not that it matters. It's my little sister who doesn't need to know what goes on in my bed. Yeah, okay sure, I might be overprotective when it comes to her dating, and who she dates, but hey, I'm the older brother and that's how things work.

I turn to Ash. "What can I bring to the party?"

He nudges me, but his gaze moves from my face to someone closing in beside me. "Your new girl."

"She's not—"

"Hi."

The low, familiar voice curls through my blood, and raises it from simmer to inferno. I turn and dip my head to take in the two blue eyes shining up at me.

"Sahara," I say, wishing I didn't sounds so fucking anxious to see her.

She smiles and turns her attention to Ash. "Thanks again for helping me. It was so nice of you and please tell Gina I loved the carrot cake. I hate to admit it, but it's almost gone."

Ash laughs easily and holds his hand up. "I confess. It wasn't that long ago I ate three quarters of a cake in one sitting. Gina is pregnant, and I think I'm sympathy eating or something."

"It's called couvade syndrome, and don't worry, it's normal." She laughs and glances at his body. "I don't expect you'll gain pregnancy weight, though. You're in great shape."

"I didn't know it had a name but I'm glad to know it's normal because there are a dozen cinnamon buns on my counter at home."

She casts me an almost shy glance as I angle my head. "I read a lot," she tells me like she's admitting a dirty secret.

"I read too," I announce, like I'm an idiot. Maybe I just want to be a part of the conversation, or to let her know I think knowledge is sexy.

"Anyway," she continues, turning back to Ash. "I really appreciate you helping me, and please thank Gina for me. I really need to get into the Nook one of these days. I pass by it a lot."

"Yeah, you're just around the corner."

As they talk easily, my head bobs back and forth and I feel a strange sense of jealousy at their comradery, which is insane. Not only was conversation between Sahara and me easy last night, it was intimate, and very informative. Too bad she said we could only have one night.

"Actually, why don't you thank Gina yourself, Sahara," Ash suggests. "She's having a big Halloween party at the end of the month."

She plays with the zipper on her coat. "Oh...I...I don't think..." Her gaze strays to me, like she's looking for help.

I shrug. "It'll be fun."

"Invite Taylor too," Ash says, and waves to someone in the distance. "I gotta run. See you later, and Sahara, don't forget to download the app for your new video doorbell."

He walks away, and I angle my body, leaning into Sahara, my words for her alone. Her eyes are narrowed, deep with concern. "It's just a Halloween party, a great way for you to meet more people. The players' wives are really nice. I think you'll like them."

"I'm not sure I belong."

"You're with me. You belong." Her mouth inches open, and she wraps her arms around herself.

"Kalen—"

"We're friends, Sahara," I remind her quickly. "Taylor will be there, too."

"It's really nice that you include Taylor."

There's a measure of sadness—does she not have siblings?—in her eyes and when she turns her gaze, I follow it and find my sister on the sidewalk talking to Elias. He's leaning into her, probably to be heard over the crowd. "Just think about it."

She nods. "Do I dress up?"

I take a trip back in time, my mind revisiting the last 'dress up' party I went to, and the girl I found myself with in the secret room. "Only if you want to."

"Are you?"

I wink at her. "I might go as a hockey player."

Chuckling, she jerks her thumb out. "I should head home."

"How did you get here?"

"My car. Over there."

I guess I didn't realize she had a car. I didn't see one in her driveway but that doesn't mean anything. "Why don't you come out for one drink? Taylor is coming."

"Yeah, she asked me to join her. I'm kind of tired, though."

Just then my phone pings, and I pull it from my pocket. "It's Taylor." I run my finger over the screen and read the message. "Taylor is going to give Elias a drive home. She said she has some homework she wants to get at." I tuck my phone away, lift my head and give her a wave. Both she and Elias wave back. "I guess I might as well head home too."

An almost stricken look crosses her face. "Actually, I think I will have that drink."

I almost ask why the change of heart but instead say, "Meet me there?"

"I think I'm going to drive my car home and then walk. I'd like to change into something that's not so big and bulky." She laughs and I glance at her oversized sweatshirt. I don't think she needs to change. I think everything about her is perfect, but if she's not comfortable, I have no problem with it. "Plus, I'm so close and I won't have to search for parking."

"Okay, I'll follow you and then give you a lift downtown." I put my hand on the small of her back. Did she just quiver? I'm not sure. Her sweater is so thick I'm not sure I could have felt it. "Let me walk you to your car."

"I can get to my own car, Kalen," she huffs out.

I shrug. "I know, but if you were Taylor, I'd want someone to walk her to her car. People are rowdy after games, and I don't know..." I take in her smirk. "Fine, I'm overprotective. Shoot me."

"I think it's adorable."

"Adorable and sweet. Wow, I might soon have to hand over my man card."

She laughs at that. "Come on, I'm this way." We move through the crowd and I tug my hat low.

"I'd really like to pay Ash back for the work he did," she tells me.

"He won't take money. He doesn't take it from any of us." I think about it for a second. "If you have tickets to give away to your play, I know Taylor said you guys have more shows coming up, I'm sure Gina would like that."

Her face lights up. "Kalen, that's a great idea."

I grin. "Sometimes I have great ideas." I tell her.

We walk away a lamppost and it's hard to tell in the dark, but I think her cheeks are turning pink. Is she thinking about last night, and how I suggested sleeping together again was a good idea, and that she probably shouldn't have vetoed it? Even though that was probably for the best. Doesn't mean I don't want her again, though.

Someone bumps into us and for a second I lose her in a big group. Shit. As the group moves past us, I reach out and capture her arm, bringing her to me. Her body presses against mine, and I hold her tight. I hate the panicked look on her face, one she's trying to hide. She's absolutely not over yesterday's break in and why should she be? That shit is scary.

I keep her close as we reach her car and once she's safely inside, I tap the roof. "You go on ahead." I jerk my head to the left. "I'm back there." I pause and, in a casual tone, I add, "Why don't you wait for me in your driveway."

Knowing exactly what I'm getting at she squares her shoulders. "I'm fine, Kalen."

"Okay." I don't want to press the issue. "See you in a few minutes." I practically run back to my car. Even if she doesn't want to admit being a little wary after yesterday, I know it's messed her up, fuck it would mess me up if someone broke into my house, so I want to get to her place as fast as possible.

I find my car, jump in and curse under my breath as I hit every fucking red light in the city. By the time I reach Sahara's, I park in the driveway behind her and find her at her door. I'm surprised she got here only a few minutes before me. I watch her, and note her odd stance. What the fuck is going on? How long has she been standing there with her key in the door? I'm about to get out of my car, stopping when she glances over her shoulder and holds her finger up.

"I'll just be a second," she yells out.

Okay, so no invite in. I can live with that, and it's probably for the best.

I relax into my seat as she opens her door. Tapping my steering wheel, I glance around the neighborhood. Like I said before, it's not the best neighborhood. But as an actress, who is probably still getting her footing and building her career, it might be all she can afford.

As I wait, and wait, I grow anxious. Dammit, I should go make sure she's okay. But I don't want her to feel incapable of taking care of herself. She's a grown ass woman who no doubt does everything for herself, but still.

I shift uncomfortably, debating on what to do as a breeze blows down the street, shaking the branches of the big oak tree in her front yard. My phone buzzes, and I pull it from my pocket, to see that it's a text from Sahara.

What the...

SAHARA

God, what the hell am I doing?

I hug myself, and stare at my phone, waiting for Kalen to message back. The next thing I hear is Kalen's door slamming and his boots pounding on my outside steps. Damn. I'm being foolish.

My front door opens with a bang, and his worried eyes narrow as they reach mine. "Sahara?"

I gulp and try to act casual. "I'm sorry." I laugh it off. "I heard a noise, and..." I glance at the stairs, and laugh again like this is all silly, but I don't think I'm fooling anyone, least of all myself. "I heard something upstairs. It was probably just the wind."

Going straight into action, he locks the door behind him, takes my stairs two at a time and I stare at his back until he's out of sight. I hug myself as his boots echo on my wood floors, and door hinges creak as he searches all the rooms. A few minutes later, he comes back down. "No one there." He glances over my head. "Stay here though. I'm going to check down here."

"I'm pretty sure it's okay."

He takes my shoulders and moves me until I'm sitting on the second last step on the stairs. "Wait right here."

I curl into myself, and sit tight as he continues the exploration of my main floor, and the door to the basement, which I don't use, opens. He heads down and my body relaxes when my ears meet with silence. Yeah, it was just the wind, and I'm an adult and really shouldn't have panicked. Maybe it was silly of me to text Kalen, but I have to say, having him here is beyond comforting.

He comes back, and I'm about to stand, only to stop when he crouches before me. "No one here. I'm sure it was the wind, but I'm going to check around outside. Maybe a garbage can blew over or something."

"You don't have to do that."

"It's okay." His gaze searches my face. "How about we skip the drink, and you come home with me tonight?"

I gulp. My door is fixed and I have a camera. Running away because I heard a noise is ridiculous. "I don't much feel like going out for a drink now, to be honest, and I think I should sleep here. I have to face my fears and sooner rather than later is probably for the best." This time I take in the worry on his face. "We could actually have a drink here, if you'd like?"

"Sure. Let me just do a quick check outside first."

He stands, and holds his hand out to me. I graciously accept it and he pulls me up. Instead of turning, he holds my hand for a second, and I give him a grateful smile. "Thanks for checking. I appreciate it."

"I was thinking," he begins, his voice an octave lower. "You should probably just ease yourself back into staying here alone. Someone breaking into your house is scary, and unnerving. It can be hard to simply go back to normal."

"That's what I'm finding," I admit. "Any ideas on how I can ease myself back into staying alone?"

"Your lock is fixed and you have a camera, but I can add to that comfort by staying the night."

I open my mouth about to tell him it's not necessary, even though I love the idea, and he must think I'm going to protest, because he quickly adds, "I'll sleep on the couch..." He straightens his body, putting his arms at his side like he's one of the Queen's guards at Buckingham Palace, and with a very bad British accent, proclaim, "...where I shall protect the queen and guard over her manor."

A grin plays with the corners of my mouth. "Ah, what the heck was that?"

He bursts out laughing and it lightens the mood in the house...err...I mean, manor. He shakes his head and cups the sides of my face as he leans into me. "I don't know. But what do you think? Would having company help?"

"I think so and there's no way I could say no to such a noble offer." He sweeps a thumb over my cheek and my entire body warms. "Thank you, Kalen."

"It's not a problem." He pulls his phone out. "I'll just let Taylor know that you're scared and I'm going to stay the night." He shoots off a text and after one comes back he puts his phone away,

"There is a problem, though." I curve my mouth, as he lifts an inquisitive brow. "If you're going to stay the night, there's something you need to know about me, first."

He cocks his head, his eyes narrowing. "Oh."

"I'm not who you think I am." His thumb still on my face, and his muscles tense. He almost looks horrified, and that's not what I was going for at all so I quickly blurt out, "I'm not a woman who keeps her word." He begins to inch back, like I slapped him so I add, "I want to have sex again. When I said I didn't...I wasn't being entirely honest."

A mischievous grin tugs at his kissable lips. "Well, I think I can forgive you this time." He steps back into me, lifting my chin an inch. He dips his head, his mouth close to mine, and I smell minty toothpaste on his breath. My lids fall, and I lift my chin, waiting for the kiss and when it finally comes, I sag against him, my earlier worries evaporating around me.

"Problem is..." he begins, his lips leaving mine. "I don't want to have sex again."

My heart jumps. Omigod, I read this all wrong. Dammit, how could I have just assumed. I know these guys have revolving doors, but I just thought...I mean, he was the one who asked if we could keep doing it. Maybe I was really bad at it? No wait, that's not right. He wanted me to tell him what I liked, or discover for himself.

I'm so damn confused.

I inch back, ready to bolt, but he takes a step into me, and cups my face.

"Babe." There's a new kind of urgency in his voice as he dips his head, his eyes searching mine. "I'm kidding. I meant it as a joke and thought you'd take it that way. Jesus, I'm so sorry.

I'm such a dick. Of course, I want to have sex with you again, and again, and again." A tortured sound rises up from his throat. "I am so fucking sorry, Sahara."

"You're not a dick. But you do have one and…"

I let my words fall off, teasing him.

"And?" he asks.

"And maybe you could do something with it, an apology of sorts for teasing me with such a straight face." I chuckle. "Maybe you should be the one on stage."

"Nope, I'm not an actor, and I'm not a great liar." Something dark, and tortured passes over his eyes, before he blinks it away. "Now teasing…I'm good at that."

"Exactly how do you like to tease?"

"Take me to your bedroom and I'll show you."

I tap my chin. "Ah, I thought you said you were sleeping on the couch. Protecting the queen of the house like a noble servant."

"I don't remember saying anything about a servant, but…" His grin is wicked as he lifts me clear off my feet, and starts up the stairs. "I wouldn't mind serving you."

"Ooh, I love the idea of that."

He takes the steps two at a time and carries me to my bedroom. He sets me on the bed, and since we're the only two here, doesn't bother to close my door. "We don't have to hide what we're doing at your house."

I lower myself and settle on my mattress. "Does that mean I can scream and moan as loud as I want?" I'm teasing, of course. I think.

A grin curves his kissable lips. "Yes please."

I laugh at that, and his gaze leaves mine and strays to my nightstand. My heart jumps, because I think I know exactly what he has on his mind. "Kalen," I murmur. Oh, God is this really happening. How did I go from wallflower nerd to having Kalen in my room, about to go through my private things?

"Can I?"

I gulp. No man has ever been in my nightstand before. It's where I keep my toys and that's exactly what he's after. "I don't need them when I'm with you," I explain and it sounds feeble, even to me.

He rolls one shoulder, a big grin on his face "I know, but it sure would be fun to check them out, see what they do for you."

I inch back a bit, my breath coming a little faster. "You want me to...use one?"

"Do you only have one?"

"No," I admit.

"Then no."

Okay, I'm losing track of this conversation. "What? No, what?"

"I want you to use them all." He arches a brow as his fingers hover near the handle. I whimper, my heart pounding so hard, I'm not sure I can even hear anymore, but I can read the question on his face, and since I've decided to discover who I am and what I like, I nod. He pulls the drawer open and smiles. "Impressive collection." He pulls out my pink wand and examines it. "Of course, you don't have to use them *all* tonight."

"Oh, God," is all I can manage to say as he runs his fingers along the length of my wand.

I nearly orgasm just from the mischief in his eyes as he gazes at me. "What's this one called?"

"It's a wand."

He cocks his head. "You don't name them."

"Well, I mean…"

"You do?" He adjusts his pants and my gaze drops to take in the bulge. He's loving this. "Tell me," he commands in a soft voice that sends thrills racing through me.

"Kalen," I whine, as my body warms, my pussy throbbing for a little action. He holds his hand out, and starts flickering his fingers toward himself, as if to say give it to me.

Grinning, he says, "Come on, out with it. It will be our little secret."

I snicker at his antics. "Fine, that one is called *Clit* Eastwood."

He stares at me for a second, and then he bursts out laughing. "That guy from the old spaghetti westerns? Are you kidding me?"

I nod and I'm not even really embarrassed, which is strange. "I'm not kidding you."

"Is he your favorite? Oh, wait, maybe your toy is a she."

"It's a he, and he's…magical." My eyes practically roll back in my head as I recall the last time I used that toy.

He frowns. "Hey," he shoots out, but there's humor in his eyes. "I thought I was the magical one."

"Oh, you are, and I'd prefer your touch over Eastwood's any day."

"Good." He turns back to my nightstand, then, like he just had an epiphany, his gaze flashes back to mine. His dark eyes are vibrant with curiosity. "Do you have any toys for two?"

"No," I admit. "Do you?"

He laughs. "No, babe." He wags his brows. "But I'm open to the idea. I heard toys aren't a great substitute for a partner, but can really enhance things in the bedroom."

I really love that this man has no hang-ups. I once read that men were intimidated by sex toys, thinking they could be replaced, but not this guy, and not that any toy could do the job better than him. The human touch—Kalen's touch—is far more pleasurable and intimate than any toy.

"Mr. Eastwood isn't much into pillow talk and he's awfully hard to cuddle up with after sex." The grin Kalen offers me strokes me deep between the legs and I honestly can't believe how much fun I'm having right now. "Do you have any toys at all?" I ask, surprising myself with the personal question, but hey...apparently, I ask these kinds of questions now.

He chuckles, tucks my vibrator under his arm and holds up his hands, wiggling his fingers. "Don't need any. Got these. Oh, and hey..." His gaze goes from one hand to the other. "Since I have two hands, I guess I do have toys for two."

A soft laugh escapes my lips. I wiggle my fingers. "I have these, but..." I pause and briefly close my eyes. "It's nice to let the toy do the hard work."

"I wouldn't call bringing you to orgasm hard work, sweetness. In fact, it's fucking awesome and damn enjoyable."

I moan, hardly able to believe this conversation, but liking it just the same. "Glad you think so."

Setting Clit Eastwood on the nightstand, he steps up to me. He puts his hand on my face. "But I'm open to whatever you want," he tells me as I reach for the button on his jeans.

"What if I want a lot?" I admit. Wow, who have I become and what happened to Darien?

"I hope you do."

I grin at him, my nipples so hard from this insane banter, I'm sure he can see them poking out of my big bulky sweatshirt. But really, why is sexy repartee, or even talking about my most intimate—private—activities so easy with him?

"Yeah?"

"Yeah, because I want to give you whatever you want." His eyes darken with heat and lust. "What do you think of that?"

"I think that's a great idea." I nibble my lips and add, "Not that I *need* any toys when I'm with you."

"But it could be fun, right?"

"Yes, fun," I agree. "We can have fun for a little while longer." This thing between us can't last too long, for many reasons.

"Yeah, a little while longer."

Warmth moves over his face, and he bends and presses his lips to mine as I pull his zipper down. He growls, and I shimmy his pants over his hips to free his beautiful cock. He stands to his full height, and once again, I look at the long length of him and try not to stare in fascination.

He tucks my hair behind my ear, and when I spot pre-cum on his slit, my entire body quakes. As much as I want him inside me, I really, really want him to come in my mouth. I just don't want to sound needy or desperate or for him to know that I've never made a man come that way, never swallowed cum. But with him, I'm ready to experiment and try anything.

"Tell you what?" I breathe over his cock and it jumps before my face.

He swallows. "Yeah?"

I can barely believe what I'm about to do, but here goes nothing. "Let's show each other."

He stares at me with glassy eyes, zero understanding reflecting in his gaze. I grin, loving that I can do this to him. But he's a guy and once the blood leaves his brain, he's probably like this with all women. Not that I want to think about other women right now.

"I'll show you how I use my toys, if you show me how you use yours."

"But I don't—" Before he can finish, I grab his hand, and run my fingers over his palm. "Ahh…" His chuckle curls around me and a hard quiver rocks through my body as I envision myself sprawled on my bed, using Clit Eastwood. Am I really going to do this?

Holy God, I am.

He takes his cock into his hand, and wets his bottom lip. "One condition…"

9

KALEN

She blinks up at me, looking so fucking sexy it's all I can do not to give over to the orgasm pulling at me, but the last thing I want to do is shoot cum all over her pretty face—before we even get started, but let's be real here, I *do* want to shoot cum all over her pretty face, if that's what she wants. With her fingers on my palm, I link our hands together and pull her to her feet.

"Condition?" she asks. Lust-filled eyes move over my face, and the pink flush on her cheeks is almost the same color as her vibrator.

Clit Eastwood.

Jesus, I can't wait to hear the names of her other toys.

"Yeah." I run my other hand down her body, slipping it under the big sweatshirt that hangs mid-thigh, no doubt to keep her warm at the rink. But we're not at the rink anymore, and I plan to keep her warm for the rest of the night. I lightly stroke the soft skin on her side. She whimpers as I caress her before going lower, sliding my hand between her legs. Heat radiates from her sex, and my cock jumps. "Before the night is over, I get to put my cock in here."

She gulps, and nods. "I think that's a great condition."

"Good. Now let's get you out of these clothes and on that bed so you can show me how Clit Eastwood works his magic." I tug on the hem of her sweatshirt and she lifts her arms, making it easy for me to peel it off. I toss it away, and she grabs my sweater and pulls on it. Since I'm a lot taller than her, she can only lift it so far, so I take over and remove it. I quickly shed the T-shirt I'm wearing underneath and my dick jumps at her smile of appreciation as I strip.

Before I can continue to remove her clothes, I need to get out of my fucking pants, which are hovering around my hips and annoying the fuck out of me. I toe off my boots, strip off my pants, as well as my boxers, and kick them out of the way.

She continues to stare at me, like it's the first time she's seen my body, and I grab her hand and tug her to me. Sure, it's great to be admired, but I'm not sure I ever liked being looked at so much before. "Seems unfair that I'm naked and you're not," I growl.

She breathes out a soft mewling sound as she says, "Maybe you should rectify that."

"I plan to, babe. Believe me, I plan to." I reach behind her and unhook her bra, then she leans forward, letting it slip from her shoulders. I pull her to me, burying my face in her neck and run my hands over the soft angles of her shoulder blades. I moan as her gorgeous nipples press against my body. Christ, they're so hard and needy for my touch, I'm sure they're going to score my skin, and I wouldn't be mad at all.

Before I get to work on her jeans, I cup her sweet, delicate breasts. They fit in my palms like they were made to be there. "These," I begin. "So fucking perfect."

Her brow tightens, a skeptical look in her eyes when they meet mine. Christ, has no man ever told her how absolutely perfect she is?

"I always thought I was small," she admits.

Deciding to show her just how much I like everything about her size, I dip my head and suck one nipple into my mouth as my thumb caresses the other one. She rakes her hands through my hair, her body curving against mine. I suck her all the way in, and she gasps. Inching back, I stare at her dark nipple, swollen and wet from my mouth. "Perfect mouthful."

This time her eyes are full of lust and belief when my gaze goes back to hers. She arches her back, wanting more, and I give it to her. But I'd be a fucking liar if I said it was just for her. Nope, I'm not that altruistic. I want her tits in my mouth, I want to lick and suck and just gorge on her body like a fucking selfish bastard. When have I ever been this greedy?

Her hand slides between my legs and she grips my cock, stroking the long hard length of me, and if I want this to last long enough for her to use Clit Eastwood, I need to put a stop to it. But fuck, I sure as hell don't want to.

"Naked and on the bed, babe." Her hand slips from my dick and I don't miss her small intake of breath. I put my hands on her hips and study her face. "Only if you want to."

She hesitates for the briefest of seconds, and then she removes the rest of her clothes and backs up, answering me without words. Snatching her toy off the nightstand, she turns it on, and the buzzing sound fills the room. She reaches into her drawer again, and grabs the lube.

"I'm not even sure you need that."

"You're probably right. I'm really wet."

Fuck me.

She grins, like she knows exactly what her sexy words are doing to me. "But I use lube when I'm alone."

"Use the lube," I growl.

She climbs onto her bed, and spreads her legs. Flipping the cap open on the tube, she pours a generous amount onto her pussy, and I fucking nearly lose it.

"Jesus, Sahara. That is hot."

She rubs her pussy with her palm and spreads her lips in preparation for the toy. I'm so damn mesmerized, my entire body goes stiff and I'm not even sure I'm breathing. Sliding the buzzing toy between her legs, she lets out a small moan, and her head sinks deeper into her pillow.

"You've never done this for anyone before, right?" Jesus, why am I asking that? So, what if she has or hasn't. It doesn't make special, either way.

Do you want to feel special, dude?

Fuck.

"No, Kalen." She pushes the vibrator inside her sweet, sweet pussy and her moan of pure bliss heats my blood.

Torture.

Pure fucking torture watching what she does when she's alone. Maybe I shouldn't have agreed to any of this. I will never, ever get this image out of my brain, and in fact I'm worried I'm going to compare every other hook up to this one.

Her eyes slowly open and she turns my way. Her gaze drops to my throbbing cock. "I want to watch too," she murmurs.

Right.

I fist my dick, and ever so slowly run my palm from base to crown. I dip into my pre-cum and use it for lube, as she unconsciously wets her lips. Damn, what I'd do to have my cock in that sweet mouth of hers, or better yet, my mouth between her legs.

Two steps take me closer to the bed, so I can get a better look at the pink toy sliding in and out of her body, and I breathe in her aroused scent. It goes straight to my head, and I wobble, a bit lightheaded, but I don't close my eyes. No way am I missing a second of this.

She pulls the toy out and it's so damn wet, my cock aches to be inside her. Her hand moves quicker and I focus in on the movement, the toy going from inside her to her swollen clit.

"Kalen," she murmurs, and my gaze goes to her face. Her breath is coming fast, her cheeks a deeper shade of pink and I can't help but tug on my cock a little harder. "I'm so close."

"Show me how you come, babe."

She wets her dry lips again, and her breasts jiggle as she uses the toy between her legs, moving it faster over her clit. Her breathing is labored now as she slides the toy inside her, her mouth opening and her upper body lifting from the bed. She curls into herself, the bed practically vibrating as she comes.

"Holy fuck," I murmur, unable to help myself. I go still, wanting nothing more than to enjoy the show. She keeps the toy inside her body and collapses back onto the bed. As she breathes deeply, she turns her head on the pillow. Sated eyes latch onto my dick, and that's when I remember I'm supposed to be showing her too.

She grins as I begin to rub again, and she removes the toy, setting it on the nightstand. Her thighs are slick from her juices, and she puts her hand on her belly, her breaths slowing as she comes back to me.

"Sahara," I whisper.

"You liked?"

"Yeah, babe. I liked."

She chuckles. Jesus, I love how open and free she is with me. I know at times I spot vulnerability, and a part of me wonders if it's just me she can only show that side of herself to.

I have no time to think about that, because she's pushing from the bed and dropping to her knees in front of me. Fuck yes, I want this, but I really want to be inside her too. Wait, she's not supposed to be touching me. She's supposed to be watching.

I need to put a stop to this.

"Hey." Her gaze lifts, and lust imbued eyes brim with something that looks like determination and curiosity. What the hell is going through her mind? "How is this fair? I didn't get to touch you?" Sure, I'm protesting, I think. But I also think it sounds pretty lame, even to my own ears.

"But you will. Later."

Her tongue snakes out and circles my crown, and all thoughts of stopping this die an abrupt death.

"Yeah, I will and I'm going to put my cock in you so deep and fuck you so hard, Sahara, you won't be able to walk tomorrow."

The hard quiver racing through her body pulls a moan from my throat. She fucking likes the idea of that. You know what I like. A fucking woman who knows what she wants and takes it. That's fucking honesty right there and honesty is the most important thing in the world to me.

She leans forward, taking me to the back of her throat. I rake one hand through her hair and grip the back of my neck with the other. I'm about ready to climax, but I can't yet, not when she's rolling her tongue around my cock and exploring it like it's her fucking job. Why is she so good at this, and why do I get the feeling that she likes it, that this is about her as much as it is for me? Most women I've been with don't explore me with such care, don't savor every inch of me with their tongue, dipping into my pre-cum and moaning like they're eating a goddamn chocolate fudge sundae.

If she keeps this up, I'm not going to be able to stop myself from coming, and neither of us want that, because we both want my cock inside her. One small hand slides between my legs and cups my balls. She gently massages me, and heat bursts through me, flooding my body like a broken pipe. As my body prepares for release, I clench down on my jaw, trying to postpone it. Sahara doesn't look like she's nearly done and I want her to have her fill.

I rock into her, being careful not to choke her, but I want to push so fucking badly. She moans and the sound vibrates through my body, bringing on a shudder. She must know I'm struggling, because she glances up at me, a new kind of determination in her eyes. Wait, does she want me to come in her mouth?

"Sahara," I grunt out, and touch her shoulder. Nudging her, I try to push her back, to remove my cock from her mouth but she's having none of that. For real? She wants me to come in her mouth? "Babe, I'm going to lose it."

It's only a murmur, but everything about the way she settles deeper between my legs in preparation, tells me she's happy about this. Fuck me sideways. I hold her head, my hand moving as she rocks back and forth. As she continues to caress my balls, her other hand joins her mouth on my cock.

I hiss, because that trifecta is more than any man can take. "Babe, I'm there." She continues to stroke with her hand as my cock slips from her mouth, and when she holds out her tongue, waiting for me to shoot my load into her mouth, I'm sure I must have fucking died and gone to heaven. The sight of her on her knees, her mouth open, waiting... Everything about it is so incredibly honest and truthful, like she's laying bare her soul, my heart can't help but get involved, and thump a little harder.

My body lets go and my cum spurts onto her tongue, and her chin. She moans and continues to stroke like she needs every last drop and I put my hand over hers, and squeeze along with her. Her eyes lift to meet mine and the pleasure I see dancing there fucks me over.

"Babe," I murmur, barely able to get that one word out as my heart races.

She stays poised between my legs, swallowing me as I continue to pulse. Once I'm depleted, she closes her mouth, her eyes drifting shut as a small smile pulls at the corners of her mouth. She moans, and licks her lips, savoring every last drop like it's the first time she's ever tasted a man. That can't be true though, right?

My throat squeezes tight as she opens her eyes and smiles up at me. As I let my gaze race over her face, I quickly remind myself this is Sahara. My sister's best friend. Someone I probably shouldn't be hooking up with. And while there was something very different about the openness and honesty in the sex, I've been wrong about people and situations before.

Do I not want to be wrong this time?

Jesus, I don't think I do.

"Sahara," I begin. "That was…"

She grins up at me and goes back on her heels. "…fun?"

My heart sinks, her words quick to remind me this is just sex, and I can't help but wonder why I needed the reminder.

Jesus this is just sex, dude.

Goddamn, what is going on with me?

10

SAHARA

For the briefest of seconds, something painful flashes in his eyes. Jeez, was it something I said? But how could it have been? He's the one who wanted to use toys because it would be fun, and it was fun. Not as much fun as bringing him to orgasm with my mouth, though. That was an insane ego boost. Honestly, I'd never been confident having sex before, but Kalen makes everything so easy and natural, even the sexy talk. Being Sahara Monroe is so much fun.

He reaches down and pulls me to my feet, and he lightly brushes damp strands of hair from my cheek. I pout playfully. "I guess it's time for you to go sleep on the couch?"

"Like fuck," he laughs, and I laugh with him. He glances down. "Little Kalen might be spent, but I'm sure he'll be up for more later, and I want to be in that bed when he's ready."

"Little Kalen." I make a tsking sound. "That's the best you can do?"

"I guess I'm not as creative as you and your Clit Eastwood." He leans in and lightly presses his lips to mine. "Can you think of a better name?"

I close one eye and glance up. "Hmm, I'm going to think on that. But one thing I do know is we can't call him little." Just then an idea hits and I laugh.

"What?"

"Well, your last name is Coolidge, like our thirtieth president."

He cocks his head. "Uh, I know Coolidge was president, but no idea which number. How do you even know that? Did you study history, too?"

I shake my head, not wanting him to know that I'm a book nerd. That I'm Darien Lewis from the closet. "Something like that." I poke my finger into his chest. "Hear me out. You're Coolidge. Like the president." I point at myself. "I'm Monroe, like Marilyn, and she sang Happy Birthday, Mr. President, so..." I pause and reach down and touch his cock. "What do you think about Mr. President?"

He tugs me to him, his hand sliding down my back to cup my ass. "Mr. President, it is." He glances at my open nightstand drawer. "I can't wait to meet all your other friends in there."

"Oh, I'm sure Bugs and Octopussy are just as excited to meet you."

He roars with laughter. "I can't wait to hear the story behind those names." He taps my ass. "Right now, how about we shower, and I'll order us in some food?"

"A shower yes, but let me make you something."

"I don't want you going through the trouble."

"It's no trouble. Besides, I need you eating nutritious food. I won't be responsible for you being sluggish on the ice." I tap his nose. "I need you in the zone."

"You mean the 'O' zone."

Unable to help myself, because I simply want to keep touching him, I lightly brush his damp hair back. "Look at you. Clever after all."

He brushes his shoulder. "I got game."

"Yeah, you do." I go up on my toes and kiss him, and it seems to take him by surprise. "What do you like to eat?" I ask, and when he gives me a cocky grin I shake my head. "Do you have a one-track mind?"

"Two. Hockey and sex."

"Good god." I laugh but I'd be a fool to think there wasn't more to this man. With the way he protects his sister—me—there is something deeper there. But if that's how he wants to play this, and not get to know each other, I'm game. Actually, it's for the best. Keeping things light and superficial is exactly how I want this too. No way am I going to get in deeper.

Hahahaha...

Shut up, Darien.

He takes my hand and walks me into the hall, and I watch the muscles along his back play as he moves. My God, how much does this man work out? "Ah, do you always walk around naked?" Honestly, what is happening in my life? I agreed to a drink, to give Taylor alone time with Elias, and now, after an incredible time in my bedroom, I'm walking around my place with a naked NHL player, who I've crushed on for years.

Who are you, girl? I don't know, but I think I like her.

"Whenever I can."

His gaze rakes over my nakedness. Dammit, I should feel self-conscious but I don't.

"You don't like it?" he asks, tugging me to him.

"Oh, I like it. It's just not something..." Not wanting to give too much of myself away, I redirect. "I mean, I was just wondering."

"No clothes until I leave tomorrow."

"But I'm going to cook," I protest. "What if I burn myself?"

He lightly brushes my shoulder, running his hands down my hips, like we touch intimately like this all the time, like it's the most natural thing in the world for us to be doing. "Then let me do takeout."

"Nope. I'm making nutritious food."

"As an actress, I guess you have to be careful, huh?"

He's so honest and sincere, I almost blurt out that I'm a librarian and can eat whatever I want. "Yeah," is all I say.

"That's tough, babe."

"I don't know. You have to stay in shape too."

"How about this," he begins. "Let's do takeout tonight, and tomorrow we'll go for a run." He rubs his completely flat, completely hard stomach. "Work off those calories."

I nearly swallow my tongue. "A run?"

I must look horrified, because he throws his head back and laughs. "You don't have to if you don't want to, and I mean there are other ways to work off the calories."

"I like that idea, and actually, a run does sound like it would be fun…" I twist up my face, like I'd just dropped a hard cover book on my baby toe. Been there, done that. "…in a masochistic, painful kind of way."

"You're in?"

"I'm in. One condition." I lift my chin an inch, loving the playful banter between us.

"Oh, you have a condition, do you?"

"We get something really, really delicious, and I'm going to leave that up to you, since I don't eat out much and don't know many places."

He nods, and since he'd searched through my entire place twice now, he leads me to the bathroom, knowing exactly where it is, and hauls me inside. "I think I'm up for the challenge. But what happens if it's not really, really delicious? No run tomorrow?" He starts toward the shower, only to turn back a horrified look spreading across his face. "Wait, you're not going to hold out on me. No sex?"

I grin, loving this playful Kalen. "Why would I want to torture myself like that?" I eye him. "Sex is not off the table."

He wipes his brow, his eyes teasing. "Whew, and after the shower, food will be on the table." He winks. "Unless of course you want to have sex on the table."

I roll my eyes at him, not hating that idea, and he turns again. He takes two steps to my rather small shower, built for one, and reaches in and turns it on. My heart beats a little faster as I watch his muscles flex and relax again.

I haven't known this man long—okay, that's not true. I've known him for a very long time—so I guess I should say, I haven't been intimate with this man long... Okay, again that's not entirely true. Technically, I have been intimate with him —he just doesn't know it was me.

So, what are you trying to say, girl?

Oh, just that in the last two days, I've experimented more than I have my whole life, and I might be addicted to sex.

"Tell me what you like?" I cock my head and grin. Okay, maybe he isn't the only one with a one-track mind. He shakes his head. "Food wise," he clarifies with a grin, and when he lightly runs his fingers down my arm, warmth sweeps through me. "When you were growing up in Washington, what was your favorite food?"

A measure of guilt grips me as I think back to my 'young' days in Washington. I spent my teenage years in Darien, like Kalen, and actually consider that where I grew up for some reason and I feel bad keeping that from him. Truthfully, we shouldn't be having a conversation that could lead him back to my true identity. He never looked twice at that girl—or even once.

Are you that girl, anymore, Darien?

Yes, that girl still exists inside of me, and while I liked her no one else did.

"Beecher's cheese," I finally tell him, and close my eyes as I recall the rich, delicious taste. "Their mac and cheese is to die for. What I'd do for a big bowl right now."

He tugs me into the tight shower, and our bodies are meshed together. The space is tight, but I'm not mad about it. "I think we can get Beecher's cheese here."

"Yeah, but no one can make the mac and cheese quite like they can. At the market you could see the cheese being made in big vats. I wanted to do a deep dive."

"I can almost visualize that." Chuckling, he reaches over me and bumps the side of my head with his elbow. "Oh, sorry. Did I hurt you?" He lightly touches my head, his lips thinning as worry floods his dark eyes. The man really is a protector at heart. Where does that come from?

Don't go there, girl.

"No, I'm okay." He studies me for a second and once he seems satisfied that I'm okay, he squirts some body wash into his palm. He brings his arm back between us. I duck to dodge another hit. Although this time his movements are slow, cautious, extra careful.

I'm about to get a squirt of my own, only to stop when he starts washing me. Ah, so this is what happens when people shower together. I can get behind that. I don't hold back a moan as his big palms begin at my neck and travel downward, sneaking into all the tiny, hidden spaces, a few that have only ever been touched by him.

He reaches between my legs, and I bite back a small wince as he washes my labia. I haven't had sex in so long, and after last night, and then again just now, I have to admit, I might be a little tender.

With the utmost gentleness, he slides his fingers between my folds, and reaches around my body to run a finger along the crevice of my virgin backside. Hello! If he noticed me stiffening, he doesn't mention it, and again, I can't believe how he just touches me like it's natural, and easy, like he's not running a finger along my most private parts. Once he's done washing me, he shifts so I'm completely under the spray.

"Hair?" he asks.

I reach up, grip a handful and squeeze out the water. "No, it doesn't need washing. What about you?"

"I showered at the rink."

Desperate to put my hands all over him, I groan, "You need a bit of soap, though." I squirt body wash into my palms and go straight for his half-swollen cock. Does that thing ever go down? Honestly, I don't know how they walk around with them, let alone play hockey. "Mr. President seems to like this."

"Fuck," he murmurs. "Keep that up and Mr. President will be hard again in no time."

"Is that a bad thing?" I ask.

"Not if you want me to turn you around and take you up against this shower."

My stomach flutters. "Of course, I want that."

"I don't have a condom," he explains. All humor drains from his face as he lightly strokes my cheek with the back of his fingers. "I don't have sex without a condom, babe, and you were a little sore."

He noticed that?

Cares about that?

Jeez Louise. As my grandmother's 'curse' words ring around in my brain, I blurt out, "Right. Me neither." I'm on the pill, and probably could have sex without a condom. If he always uses one, I'm guessing he's clean. I'm not putting voice to any of those thoughts, though. With no barriers, it might be a little too intimate. That almost makes me laugh.

Everything we've been doing, from touching, to talking, to teasing has been completely intimate. Still, I guess I don't want him to think I'm too eager, too needy. Which, of course, I am.

He slicks his wet hair from his face. "Plus, I want to feed you and there's always tomorrow. After run shower sex."

"We're doing this again tomorrow?" Honestly, I can't wait. I keep that to myself, and remove the nozzle from the hook so I can wash away the soap.

"If you want to."

"Of course, I want to," I blurt out quickly, too quickly, and decide to add, "It's fun."

"Right, fun. I was thinking maybe we could do it until after the Halloween party. We're on the road to Dallas right after that."

I shrug. More time with Kalen? Have I died and gone to heaven? "Sure," I agree in my most casual voice which is ridiculous, because I just practically screamed, *of course I want to.*

Once I'm done rinsing him, he takes the nozzle from me. "I didn't realize this came off." He puts it between my legs, to better rinse me. Or maybe he's just playing with me, to see how I react to the spray. The man obviously knows I need enhancements to get off when I'm not with him.

He puts the nozzle back into the handle and reaches behind me to turn off the spray. Keeping our bodies close, he opens the glass door, and grabs my towel off the hook. I'm about to take it from him, but he practically lifts me from the shower and sets me on the mat. The next thing I know, I'm wrapped in the cotton while he stands there dripping wet.

"In the cabinet." I gesture with a nod and he turns and pulls a towel from the cabinet. He scrubs it over his hair and body and while I expect him to knot it around his waist he doesn't. Instead, he hangs it on the hook. Right, for the rest of the night we stay naked.

"When our food comes, are you going to answer the door like that?"

"I'll have them leave it on the deck."

"Kalen," I burst out. "You can't open my door naked. What will the neighbors think?"

He makes two fists and bumps them. "They'll think you've been knocking boots, babe."

I cover my face. "Ohmigod, you can't do that."

"Fine," he grouches. "I'll pull on my jeans, but that's it."

I roll my eyes. "I had no idea you were a nudist."

"I prefer the term naturalist, thank you very much."

I laugh. "What am I going to do with you?"

He leans in and lightly brushes his lips over mine. He inches back and that's when I realize the sigh in my throat, the way I'm still leaning into him. I open my eyes and find him smiling, as he reminds me, "I'm open to anything, remember?"

11

KALEN

I can't help but smile as I take in Sahara's scrunched up nose as she sits on the bench near her front door and ties her sneakers. "You don't have to go if you don't want to."

Her head lifts. "I want to run...said no sane person ever."

I laugh at that, and squat down in front of her. Pushing her hands away, I finish tying her sneakers and she leans back against the wall. "It'll be fun."

She snorts out a laugh. "Fun or not, I need to run. I ate far too many tacos last night. I'm mad that you introduced me to Antojo's."

"No, you're not."

"Yes, I am. Now I'm going to be craving tacos. I think I actually dreamt about them last night."

"Babe." I kiss her softly. "Go ahead and eat as many tacos as you want." I stand and pull her to her feet, and when her body collides with mine, I wrap my hands around her and grind against her. Jesus, why can't I get enough of this sweet girl? "I promise to always help you burn the calories."

She narrows her eyes. "By running."

"Nope, by taking you to bed and putting my cock inside you." A fine shiver goes through her, and my body reacts. Last night after tacos, we found ourselves back in her bed, and we had sex a couple more times. I would have gone for round three, but I only had two condoms. I make a mental note to store a box in her nightstand, next to Clit Eastwood. Yeah, we plan to do this more, at least until after Halloween.

She lifts her face to mine, her eyes half closed. "Mmm, I like the sound of that."

"Good." I pick up her wool hat and put it on her head. It's chilly this morning and fortunately I always keep a change of clothes in my car, which means I don't have to run in my jeans. I fix my own hat and open her door. A cool gust of wind whips around me. I glance up and see the sun trying to break through the clouds. "It should warm up."

"Yeah, I checked the forecast. It's supposed to get nice later. We really have been having a great October." She hugs herself. "I'm not looking forward to winter."

After living in New York and Connecticut. I'm used to the cold. "Much different from a Washington state winter."

She glances at her feet, her hair shielding her face. "Yeah."

"Ready?"

She waves her hands. "Lead the way."

I step out onto her porch and she follows me, locking up behind herself. On the road, I start off slow, and check in with her to make sure the pace is okay. The air feels good against my face as we run, and when I notice she's easily able to keep up, I round the corner and go a tiny bit faster.

Our feet hit the pavement, and we run in place when we come to a red light. It turns green and we're off again. As I keep a close eye on her, we manage to put some distance behind us. I turn the corner and we do a big loop, circling another block.

As her steps become a bit slower, I stop jogging, and instead do a brisk walk. She does the same and smiles up at me.

"This is actually kind of nice," she states, looking a bit surprised.

I nod in agreement as the downtown streets grow busier, everyone out shopping on this Saturday morning. "Endorphins."

"How did you get into hockey?" she asks, completely changing the subject.

"My father was a fan." I try not to sound bitter as I say that, but whenever I think about what he did to our family, it leaves a bitter taste in my mouth.

"Did he play?"

"No." My voice comes out much harsher than I meant.

She winces. "I'm sorry. I was just curious." She nudges me with her elbow. "We can talk about something else."

"No, I'm sorry, Sahara. It's just." I scrub my face and the image of my dad fucking around flashes in my brain. "I don't really talk to my dad. We don't get along."

"Sorry to hear that. My parents and I don't get along all that well either," she admits quietly me, and glances at the sidewalk. "I mean, we get along. They just want to run my life, you know." She gives me a smile that doesn't reach her eyes. "No matter what, they'll never be proud of me." Her face pales as she turns away, shaking her head, and I get the sense that she didn't mean to tell me any of that.

"Do you have siblings?" I ask, curious.

A tortured sound jumps from her throat. "Sorry," I begin. Nudging her, I take a line from her playbook. "We can talk about something else."

She goes quiet for a moment, and then begins, "I do have siblings. Four. Two older brothers. Two older sisters."

As she opens up to me my head rears back, surprised by her answer. "That's amazing." A hard wave of longing grips my gut.

She must recognize it because she responds with, "You can have them."

"Why, you don't like them?"

She shrugs but there's pain in her eyes. "I like them, I just don't think they like me." She moves closer to me as a group of people come our way. "I'll take your sister. Maybe we'd be close."

"Why do you think they don't like you?"

Jesus, that's gut wrenching. I can't imagine not being close to Taylor. She's everything to me.

"My two older brothers are best friends, and my two older sisters are best friends. Each pair do everything together. I was never much involved. I'm different from them all."

"I'm sorry."

"It is what it is," she responds, working with the cards life dealt her, but she's hurt. It's obvious in the way she's curling into herself. "Do you want a big family, Kalen?"

"I...I don't think that's going to happen for me." She angles her head and stares at me, because yeah, I didn't really answer her question.

"You should have a big family. Find the right woman and start popping out babies."

"I don't think that's going to happen," I respond under my breath. She doesn't say anything, so I'm not sure she heard me and that's good. She doesn't need to know anything about my demons. Quickly changing the subject, I begin, "I actually didn't think you had any siblings."

Her head jerks back a bit. "Why?"

I shrug. "I guess...after the game when you said it was nice that I involved Taylor. You seemed a bit sad. I assumed you wanted, but never had, brothers or sisters." She stares straight ahead, her body stiff. "I'm sorry you're not close, and as far as being different goes, nothing wrong with that. If we were all the same, how boring would that be?" I try to put a smile on her face but it doesn't work.

Instead, she briefly closes her eyes like what she's about to say next pains her. "They're all *very* successful. Mom and Dad are so proud of them."

"Ah, I see." I shouldn't probe but I can't help but state, "Your parents aren't happy with your acting choices."

"You could say that." She eyes me, and something flickers there, something that looks like hesitation. It's like she wants to ask questions, but isn't quite sure she should. Sure, she just opened up to me, but I can only assume she doesn't really want to forge any kind of relationship outside of the bedroom. Last night she didn't want to go for a drink and then something came over her and she quickly changed her mind. My sister always tells me it's a woman's right to change her mind, so I didn't ask, but it doesn't mean I'm not still curious. "Taylor said you grew up in Darien with your grandmother," she finally says.

Darien...

My mind instantly flashes back to the night I kissed and touched Darien Lewis in the closet.

"Yeah. Moved there in high school." I fall quiet for a long time, missing my mom and happy that she never knew what Dad was up to behind her back when she was so sick. I have no problem with Dad's sexuality or partner, it's the way it all went down that guts me and I wished he'd been honest with Mom. Honest with who he really was.

She looks a little hesitant when she asks, "Are your folks still there?"

Her hesitation once again reminds me this is just sex. She's just making conversation. Which is fine. I'm fine. I don't want more either, and we do have to talk about something on this run. We've already discussed the weather.

"No, my grandmother took care of us. Mom died when I was fourteen, and I didn't want to stay with my father. He's still in New York."

Her hand lands on my arm, and she gives it a squeeze. "I'm so sorry, Kalen. I didn't know."

"Thanks. It was a long time ago."

"Still tough."

As my heart aches with longing, I glance at Sahara. "She would have loved to see Taylor on the stage. She was supportive of everything we did. I'm really sorry that it's not the same for you. You're amazing on stage."

She pulls her hand back, and her lips thin to a fine line as sadness washes over her face. After a long moment, she responds with, "She would have been so proud of you, Kalen. Making it to the NHL."

"Yeah." We both fall quiet lost in our own thoughts, as we approach the Nook, Gina's café. I'm not sure if Gina is working today. She usually takes weekends off. Which is too bad. I'm sure Sahara would like to meet her. "Want to grab a coffee and breakfast?"

She glances behind us. "We really didn't make it very far."

"Is that a no?"

"That's a yes."

I laugh. "We did enough for today. I don't want you to hate running with me." Fuck, what am I saying? Why did I even ask her to come today, and am I really suggesting we do it again?

Yes, because you like hanging out with her.

"I actually enjoyed it."

I laugh. "Liar."

She flinches a bit at that one word, but then quickly counters, "No, it's true. Endorphins. I've got all the good feels."

I pull open the door, and we're instantly greeted with the delicious smells of pastry and coffee. "I'm working out with a few of the guys this afternoon, and I can hop on the treadmill. Unless of course you want to finish our run after we eat."

I hold the door open and Sahara enters. The place is packed, not a free table to be found. She glances back at me. "This place is so cute." Just then I spot Tuck and Roman. This is one of Elias' favorite places too. Where is he this morning? Last night, he seemed distracted by something. I consider texting him, but decide to wait until I'm home.

"Hey Coolio, what's up, dude?"

Catching me by surprise, Sahara goes up on her tiptoes and whispers, "Coolio is cute, but I like Mr. President better."

"Jesus," I curse. "You can't say that to me in public." I resist the urge to adjust my tightening sweats, which do little to hide a boner.

"I can, but I'm guessing I shouldn't?" The adorable twitch in her lips thickens my cock even more.

"No, you shouldn't. I'm going to say hi to the guys. Do you want to wait here?" She hesitates. "Unless you want to say hi."

"No, I'm good." Shit, did I insult her? "I didn't think you'd want to be bombarded with questions, and Roman, while I love the guy, can be an ass sometimes, in the nicest possible way." Not that he's rude to any of our girlfriends or wives, but we've been at bars and as soon as he flashes his grin at a girl—even if she came with another guy—she always left with Roman. I don't think he'd do that to any of his teammates, though.

Are you worried about that, dude?

Fuck me sideways.

She laughs at that. "A nice ass." She goes onto her toes again, and whispers, "Like yours."

"No more running for you. Too many endorphins."

She laughs and breathes in the scent of cinnamon, as a server comes from the kitchen with a new tray. "Cinnamon rolls also give me endorphins, but probably won't do much for my ass." She gives me a nudge. "Go say hi. I'll grab that table there." She points to a table that's clearing out.

"Be right back."

As she waits for the table to be cleared, I walk over to the guys. "Why aren't you sitting with us?" Tuck asks.

"Afraid your girl will dump you and fall for this?" Roman teases and points to the dimples on either side of his cheeks.

"She's not my girl," I correct. "She's a friend of Taylor's, and she had a problem last night, so I was helping her out."

Roman snorts. "Yeah, I bet you were."

"Roman," I warn and glance over my shoulder to make sure Sahara can't hear him.

"That's why you didn't come for drinks?" Tuck asks, not an asshole at all. I nod and can't seem to tear my gaze away as Sahara tugs off her hat, takes a seat and picks up the menu. As if feeling my eyes on her, she lifts her head and gives me a small smile. I smile back and she lifts her arm and waves. I'm about to wave back, when I realize she's greeting Tuck and Roman. I turn back to see them wave.

"She's cute," Tuck says, his brow furrowed, as his gaze briefly searches the café. Is he looking for someone? Maybe Elias is here.

Before I can ask, Roman opens his mouth. "How's Taylor?" he asks as he takes a big bite of his cinnamon roll.

"Stay away from her."

"Dude, these." He points to his dimples again. "I can't control what they do to the women. You know this."

I roll my eyes at him, but yeah, I do know this. "Fuck off."

Tuck laughs and gestures with a nod. "Go sit with your friend. Tell Taylor I said hi."

I pause. "Is Elias here?" I ask. Maybe he went to the bathroom or something.

"Nah, couldn't make it today," Roman answers around a big bite of cinnamon roll.

"Maybe he's having family troubles, again." I don't miss the concern in Tuck's eyes. We're a team and all care about each other. Maria steps up to the table, and Tuck sits up a little straighter as she says hi to me.

"Hey, Maria." I tap the table, unease taking up residency in my gut. I hope Elias' family aren't being too hard on him. Poor guy doesn't even go out anymore. He spends most of his time off sitting at home. "I'll talk to you guys later." As I head back to the table, my heart beating a little faster as Sahara smiles up at me, I think about asking her if she knows any single actresses she works with. Elias could use a nice girl in his life, and hey, maybe we could all double date.

Double date?

What the fuck am I even saying?

12

SAHARA

"Everything good?" I ask when Kalen comes back, a new kind of snarl tugging at the corners of his lips. Wow, who said what to annoy him?

"Yeah." He gives a dismissive wave of his hand, like he's playing something off. "Roman was asking about Taylor."

Sensing his worry for his sister, I lean back and takes another peek at Roman. "He's cute." As Kalen's gaze zeroes in on me like he's worried his sister might think so too, I add, "In an ass kind of way."

He laughs at that, his shoulders relaxing. "Yeah?"

I tap the menu with my thumb, something I do when I'm thinking and I note the sudden distant look in Kalen's eyes as he notes the movement. "So basically, what I think you're saying about Roman is that he's a player, but he's also a good guy?"

"Something like that. I just...don't want him with my sister."

I reach across the table and put my hand on his, but he maneuvers his fingers so he's lightly brushing his thumb over the back of my hand. Alrighty then. "Don't worry. Taylor is a smart girl. She's not going to get caught up in a guy who has no intentions of settling down for a while."

"You think she's looking to settle down."

Honestly, all I know is that she's got it bad for Elias. "I don't know, Kalen. Not all women want the white picket fence."

He opens his mouth and closes it a few times and then he finally says. "I just worry about her."

"I love that you do, and you know what…" My words fall off as the server brings us coffee. She smiles at me, and Kalen quickly introduces us. After we exchange pleasantries, Kalen asks, "Is Gina in today? I wanted to introduce her to Sahara. Ash fixed her door for her the other day."

Maria's eyes go wide. "That was you?" I nod and she continues, "I'm so sorry to hear that. Thank God Kalen was there."

I smile at Kalen. "Yes, thank God." God, isn't that what I screamed when he brought me to orgasm. I take a fast drink of my coffee, hoping to hide the blush I feel crawling into my cheeks.

"Well, you two have a look over the menu and I'll be back as fast as I can. We're a bit short-staffed this morning."

With that, she leaves and Kalen turns his attention back to me. "Do I know what?" he asks as soon as Maria is out of ear shot.

I blink, my mind backtracking to our conversation. "Oh, I was just saying, it's okay to not want deeper things in a relationship. I believe it's okay as long as Roman makes it perfectly clear who he is and what he wants. I think women can respect that. They know what they're getting into, know what they're getting out of it. I actually appreciate that quality in a man."

One and done...

I recall Taylor's words as I glance into his eyes to see if he fully understands what I'm saying. He needs to know I'm not asking for anything more than a few hook-ups. The man doesn't even know who I really am. If he ever found out...

"Yeah. Okay." He takes a sip of his coffee, and the table begins to vibrate. I glance down to see the way he's bouncing one leg.

"What?" I ask.

"I just...I was thinking. We know where we stand. I just...I'd like it to just be us, exclusive until...you know."

I try to still my suddenly racing heart. He just clearly likes the sex. "Until after the Halloween party?"

He laughs, but there's an uneasy edge to it. "Yeah."

"I'm good with that, Kalen." Maybe he thinks I'm the kind of girl who has more than one man at once. Not that there is anything wrong with that, there isn't, as long as everyone involved knows the score and are on the same page. But I'm not entirely sure that's the vibe I want to be giving off. Sure, I'm trying new things, even a new personality, or maybe not new, maybe it's a personality that's been inside me all this time, just repressed. "Are you sure that's what you want to do?"

He nods, and just then his head lifts and he glances at the door as the bell above it jingles. A gorgeous pregnant woman with dark hair and eyes steps inside, and a big smile full of fondness comes over Kalen's face.

"Hey," he calls and stands as the woman walks straight to him. Kalen gives her a hug and her gaze drops to me.

"You must be Sahara."

Her bright smile is welcoming and contagious. I return it. "You must be Gina."

She puts her hands on her belly and there's a glow about her. "That is me and I'm so happy to finally meet you, Sahara."

It's so weird because hearing her say Sahara, and not Darien, makes me feel like such a fraud, even though it is my middle name. I stand and hold my hand out to her. Catching me by surprise, she brings me in for a hug. "Any friend of Kalen and Taylor's is a friend of mine."

"Hey, where's my hug," Roman yells out and she rolls her eyes at him. "Eat your cinnamon roll, and hush," she teases and Roman and Tuck both laugh. Everything about the comradery between all of them is like a fist to the chest. My God, it's all I ever wanted. My sisters and brothers excluded me, whether they realized it or not, and I was a nerdy misfit in school. Sure, I've changed everything about myself, but for some reason, I don't think these people would care which woman I am.

"Thank you so much for the carrot cake. It was delicious. That was so nice of you."

"No problem. I just felt so awful that your place was broken into and I'm glad Ash could help. Besides." She pats her belly. "I've been craving carrot cake with this pregnancy and you were saving me from myself."

I chuckle. "You look great. I didn't know you were pregnant. Kalen only told me about Zoe." That day I met Ash fixing my door, Zoe wasn't with him, and that's too bad because I was looking forward to meeting the girl a grown-ass man was afraid of. "When are you due?"

"Not soon enough," she jokes and adds. "January, actually." Without missing a beat, she continues, "You're coming to the Halloween party, right?" I don't say anything, because I'm still not sure and she turns to Kalen. "You told her, right?"

I bite back a grin, because while Gina might be small, she's damn mighty.

"Yes, I told her. She might have had plans, though. She's busy with her play."

"Do you have plans?" Gina asks directly, and the honesty in her eyes, the real hope that I don't, has me shaking my head.

"I have performances Friday and Saturday night."

"Good thing the party is on a Sunday, to accommodate everyone's schedule."

I laugh. "Looks like I'm coming, then. I just have to figure out a costume."

She waves her hand. "Don't put too much work into it. I'm going as a beluga whale and don't even have to dress up." I laugh with her and she adds, "Most of the guys think they're so clever..." she pauses to roll her eyes again. "...dressing as hockey players. "

I laugh at that. "I'm sure Kalen can do better." I toss out that challenge to him and he folds his arms, a playful disgruntled sound rumbling in his throat.

"Ash was telling me that you are in a local production of Love Unbound with Taylor. That sounds amazing. I need to get out and catch a show soon. I've been dying to see Taylor on stage."

I glance at Kalen. I guess he must have been talking about me. An almost sheepish look comes over him. "We had our friends and family opening night on Thursday, but our regular show starts next weekend. They run until just before Christmas. We have Thanksgiving off, thankfully. It's going to be busy." I don't tell them that I'm actually super busy, because I also hold down a full-time job. "I actually have some tickets for you."

Her jaw drops open. "Are you kidding me?"

I crinkle my nose as I look at her belly. "If you're able to go?"

"I can go, and I'm so touched that you thought of me."

"I wanted to thank you for all you and Ash have done for me. I don't think I could have gotten anyone to fix my door so quickly."

She laughs and waves her hand. "No thanks needed, but I'll take those tickets."

"I'll bring them to you. We were jogging and I didn't know we'd be stopping in. They're good for any night."

"That is perfect. I'll gather up the girls and we'll make a night of it. Wait, do you read romance?"

I blink at her fast change of subject again. "Yes, I love to read."

"She's wicked smaht..." Kalen jokes doing his best Boston accent.

A little embarrassed, I lean forward to shield my face. "I don't know about that." Honestly, I'm not used to compliments, so I never know how to take them.

"I have no doubt you're wicked smaht," Gina adds. "Are you free Thursday night?"

I do a quick mental check of my work schedule. "I am."

"Come to book club. We're reading a steamy firefighter book this week. We've been trying to get Taylor to join, but she's so busy with school, and her play."

"I do not want to hear this." Kalen puts his fingers in his ears and starts humming, which makes us both laugh.

"We're having it at Brighton's place." She whacks Kalen's hands from his ears. "She lives in Sparrow Springs. Kalen can give you the directions. Actually, when the guys have a night off, they usually drive us, then get together for a game of pool and drinks while we have book club, so Kalen can drive you."

I'm about to protest when Kalen salutes her. "Yes, ma'am." He laughs and adds, "You know I don't remember you being so bossy."

"When you're fourteen months pregnant, you're allowed to be bossy. Kalen, text me Sahara's number and I'll send you the name of the book. There's not much time to read, but we mostly chat and drink wine..." She touches her stomach. "I miss wine." We both laugh and she points to the chairs. "Now sit, and let me get you some food." We both drop down into our chairs.

Kalen glances at her belly. "Are you sure you should be working?"

"My God, you sound just like my husband. He'd have me on bed rest if he had it his way, but we're short-staffed and a girl needs to get out of the house every now and then."

"Agreed," I say.

"Besides, Zoe and Ash were having daddy daughter time. They need to soak it up before this little one comes." I note the soft, melancholy look on her face, much like the one I just saw on Kalen's.

"What do you recommend?" I ask.

Gina points to the specials on the menu, and I squint. I had eye surgery a couple years ago, but sometimes I still need glasses when reading, or putting books back on the shelves at work. "A little birdy told me the waffles were extra fluffy today, and the cinnamon rolls are to die for."

"I want both," Kalen announces, and drops his menu.

I wince. "I think I do too, but it sounds like a lot of food."

Gina laughs. "I won't tell if you don't, and besides, you can take home what you don't eat." She gazes at our clothes. "And weren't you both just jogging?"

"Yeah," Kalen confirms.

Gina winks at me. "One of many great ways to burn off those extra calories."

She walks away and I almost have to pick my jaw up from the table. "She knows."

Kalen holds his hands up. "I didn't tell her." He leans in. "Maybe we just have sex written all over us."

"Ugh, do you think Tucker and Roman know too."

He shrugs. "Does it really matter?"

I consider that. "I mean, I guess not. I just...I don't want anyone to get the wrong idea."

His brow knits together as he wags his brows. "You mean the right idea?"

"No," I correct quickly. "The wrong idea, that we're a couple or anything. I don't want anyone thinking you're off the market."

"I am," he says quickly, his eyes piercing mine. My breath catches as I hold his gaze, and I consider the seriousness of his words. What exactly is he saying? "Until after Halloween, remember?"

"Right." Of course, that's what he meant. Jeez, did I really think Kalen Coolidge wanted a relationship with me. He's in it for the sex and so am I. Besides, Taylor doesn't want to break bro code and upset her brother by starting anything with Elias. Likewise, I don't want to do anything to come between my friendship with her, either.

So basically no one else can know, because I do not want anything more than a few hook-ups with this man.

Liar.

KALEN

In the locker room, I slick my damp hair from my forehead and pull my bag from the locker. Here it is Tuesday, and this morning, after waking up early in Sahara's bed, I hightailed it home to get ready for today's skate and team meeting. I'm pretty sure my sister is on to me, judging by the knowing grins she keeps giving me I'm guessing she's happy that I'm preoccupied, and not constantly asking about her every move. My phone pings, and I pull it from my bag and read a message from my sister.

Taylor: hey bro, are you going to the costume store on Newbury?

Me: Wasn't planning on it.

Taylor: (Sad face emoji)

Me: What do you need?

Taylor: I called them and they have one Wednesday costume left.

Me: What the hell is Wednesday.

Taylor: Brother get with it. It's that character from the Addam's family series. Anyway, they said they'd hold it for me for the next hour because it's so popular, but I'm in class and can't get there in time. Can you get it for me? Pretty please big awesome brother.

Yeah, she thinks I'm awesome when she needs something. Most other times she's annoyed with my constant overprotectiveness.

"Everything okay?" Ash asks as my fingers fly over the phone.

I nod. "It's Taylor. She wants me to go to the costume store for her."

"Which one"

"Newbury."

"I'll come."

My head rears back. "Why?"

He laughs. "Because I've been looking everywhere for a Beetlejuice costume for Zoe. Apparently, it's pretty popular this year. That's the one store I haven't tried yet."

I nod and send Taylor a text.

Me: Yeah, okay. I can get it.

Taylor: What are you going as, and don't say hockey player.

Me: A man with a jersey and a hockey stick.

. . .

Taylor: (Emoji eye roll) I was talking to Sahara and she doesn't have a costume yet. You guys should do a couple's costume. How about Marvel characters?

Me: No

Taylor: Chips and Salsa?

Me: No.

Taylor: Waldo and Wendy?

Me: No.

Taylor: Bro, you're no fun.

Instead of answering, I tuck my phone away and find Ash grinning at me. "What?"

"What's wrong with a couple's costume?"

"You were reading my texts?"

He shrugs. "No, well yeah." He gives me an almost apologetic look. Almost. "Gina was asking what everyone was wearing.

You said you were texting about costumes, and I couldn't help myself."

I shake my head. "Dude, back off."

He holds his hands up, palms out.

"What's this about costumes?" Brady asks. "I need to figure out something and Mel will kill me if I go as a hockey player."

"Me too," Noah pipes in.

"Are we all going somewhere?" Roman asks, coming around the corner.

Ash nods. "Looks that way."

"Road trip," Roman yells, and snatches his bag from his locker. "Wait, where are we going again?"

Tuck laughs and throws his arm around Roman. "Follow me, kid."

As everyone files out, I message Sahara to see if she needs anything from the store. She told me she had a bunch of errands to run today and things to prepare for the theater, so I have no idea where she is right now. I do know she hasn't got a costume yet.

Me: Hey, I'm heading to the costume store to pick something up for Taylor. Need anything.

I wait a second and I'm about to put my phone away when I see three dots.

. . .

Sahara: I really don't know. If you see something you think I'd like, maybe just grab it.

Me: Taylor said something about us getting couple's costumes.

Now why the fuck did I message that?

I wait a long time for her to message back and as the locker room clears, my stomach knots. Shit, did I scare her off with the couple's comment. Finally, I see three dots.

Sahara: Sorry, just really busy. Yeah, okay that sounds good.

I stand there for another second, waiting for more to come in and when it doesn't, I tuck my phone away and head outside. The guys are in their cars, and Roman and Elias are standing by mine. Roman and Elias both grew up in the same neighborhood—both their parents are in politics—and Elias pretty much looks out for him here in Boston. I expected Elias to be at my car considering we traveled together this morning, and clearly Roman needs a ride. He has a car but likes to walk most places, even when those places are far.

"Shot gun," Roman yells as I approach, and Elias pushes him out of the way.

"Rookies in the back."

Roman grumbles, but when I press the fob to unlock the doors, he hops in behind Elias. I back out of the lot, and Elias pulls his phone from his pocket. I catch the way he's scrubbing his chin, deep in thought.

"Everything okay?" I ask.

He nods. "Yeah, Mom was just asking me about Thanksgiving. Wants me to fly home."

For him, home is California and we do have the time off, and my only plans were having a big turkey with Taylor and eating leftovers for a week. "Are you going to go? If you want to stay back and celebrate with Taylor and me, the more the merrier." I know his Thanksgivings are much different from ours. Big elaborate gatherings, with numerous people—most of who are acquaintances. That's how it is in politics, I guess.

While I crave a big family sitting around the table, sharing a meal and laughter, I don't want to do it with acquaintances. Longing wells up inside me.

"I don't suppose you and Taylor would like to tag along? At least then I'd know who my real friends were."

"Hey, I'll be there," Roman pipes in, looking all indignant.

"Dude, really." Ignoring Roman, I cast Elias a fast glance. "If you need me, you know I'll come."

He laughs and pushes back in his seat. "No. I'd never torture you or Taylor like that."

Roman scoffs. "But you're okay to torture me?"

"You know it." Elias laughs. "I need someone there charming the women so my parents don't try to marry me off." His laugh is followed by a sigh as he turns to Roman. "Just promise me you'll run interference with whoever it is Mom is going to try to set me up with this year."

Roman leans forward and pats Elias's shoulder. "You can count on me, dude. But you could always bring a girl and pretend you're engaged or something."

Elias and I exchange a look and both grin before I say, "Dude, you watch too many romantic comedies. That shit never works out."

"Especially with my family," Elias responds. "They'd grill her from head to toe, and no woman should have to stand up to that."

"Taylor is tough enough for that," Roman says, and I laugh. He's not wrong, and I'm proud that Taylor could hold her own.

"Probably, but then she'd need to go with me to Easton's wedding in Vegas to keep up the charade." I arch a brow, and he continues. "Easton was my best friend growing up. His younger brother Rip was Roman's best friend. If I show up without a date, Mom will have some socialite ready to pounce."

Roman laughs. "I can't wait to check out the bride's maids." I shake my head at him and he continues with, "I'm sure Taylor would love a trip to Vegas."

Why the hell does he keep bringing up Taylor?

"Leave my sister out of this," I growl, and glance at him in the rearview mirror.

He holds his hands up palms out. "Just saying."

Elias glances out the side window, and Roman pulls his phone from his pocket. As I drive through the downtown core and pull into the costume store parking lot, I consider Roman's ludicrous idea, which oddly enough, doesn't quite seem so crazy anymore.

I glance at Elias. "Maybe Roman's idea isn't as outrageous as it sounds. Taylor has a break over Thanksgiving and depending on when the wedding is she might love to go to Vegas." I shrug. "I wouldn't let her go with any of the other guys." Jerking my thumb toward the back seat I add, "Especially that one, but with you, it's different."

Elias looks like he's about to swallow his tongue. "I don't know, Kalen."

As I warm to the idea, I park and say, "Maybe just ask her. Hell, if she can handle my overbearing ways, I'm sure she can handle your parents in the nicest possible way." I snort out a laugh. "I wouldn't be surprised if they loved her."

"She's pretty loveable," he mumbles, and then clears his throat quickly. He points. "We should go." I lift my head to see the guys are hanging out in the parking lot waiting for us.

"Think about it. She's been working hard, and this would be a nice break for her."

He nods and hurries from the car like it might be on fire, and we all head inside. I wince under the bright overhead lights and all the music that's supposed to be spooky, not annoying. I glance around. The place is huge, with many aisles.

Ash gestures with a nod. "I'm going to find the kid stuff."

Everyone goes their own way and before I head to the counter to get Taylor's Wednesday costume, I begin to browse the aisles, my sister's words and Sahara's agreement that we should do couples costumes is bouncing around inside my brain. The last time I dressed up as a couple...

What ever happened to Darien Lewis?

I glance at the costumes and pull a couple from the racks to look at them, but nothing feels right. Continuing my search, I make my way to the next aisle, and Roman comes running up to me.

"What do you think of this one?"

I arch a brow. "You want to go as a firefighter?"

"Girls dig firefighters." He puts the helmet on his head and gives me an award-winning smile.

I shake my head at his antics. "I think it's perfect, Roman."

"Yeah?"

"Yeah," I tell him and he looks pretty pleased with himself as he saunters off. I search a little more and I'm almost ready to give up when I come across Red Riding Hood and the Big Bad Wolf.

"You getting that?" Tuck asks, a knowing smile on his face. How many times do I have to tell him Sahara and I are just friends?

I let it go. "I don't know." Why am I suddenly embarrassed?

"Get it, dude." He pulls it from the rack. "This is perfect for you and your girl."

Okay, here we go. "She's not my girl. She's Taylor's friend."

"Right. You said that. Are you at least going to introduce us to her at the party?"

"Yeah, shit. It was—"

"Roman, I know. Dude says the first thing that comes to his

mind. I wouldn't introduce him to my girlfriend...I mean friend...either."

I eye him for a second, and he turns his attention to the costumes on the rack. "You don't think this is too...?"

"Suggestive...sexy," he responds, finishing my sentence. I nod and he laughs. "Dude, you're going to make any costume sexy."

I shove him. "Asshole."

"Kidding. What's wrong with sexy?"

"I don't know. I don't want her to think I'm trying to..." What am I even saying? "...you know. Show off her body or something. Fuck, I don't want the guys to be staring at her, or think they can get with her."

He gives me a sincere smile, and puts his hand on my shoulder. "You really like her, huh?"

Fuck.

"She's my—"

"Yeah, I know. She's your sister's friend." He turns his attention to the costumes and pulls out a different one. "How about this?"

I let my gaze fall over the chips and salsa outfits. I laugh because this was what Taylor suggested. I guess my sister knows her friend, and I should trust her judgement.

"I'm doubting you could make these chips sexy."

No, I can't, but I have no doubt Sahara is going to make the salsa costume sexy. Shit, she could wear a potato sack and I'd still want to rip it from her body.

"Son of a bitch," we hear Ash curse from the next aisle. I put the wolf and red riding hood costume back and take the chips and salsa from Tuck. We hurry to the next aisle where we find Ash standing there, a huge smile on his face as he holds out a child-size Beetlejuice costume my heart stalls.

Jesus, knowing he's going to make his daughter happy really looks good on him and I can't deny that I want what he has.

"I found it," he says. "It was hidden among these superhero costumes." Jesus Christ, I could practically fucking cry seeing the excitement on his face. Ash is a huge guy, and with his big hands, he gently holds the costume out, laying it over one arm for a closer inspection. "Zoe is going to love this."

As the guys pile into our aisle, all checking out the costume, I see the warmth, comradery and love between players. It's strange, really. I'm a part of this team, but sometimes, I feel like an outsider looking in, watching a big family at play. I don't know, maybe it's because a lot of them are settling down with their own families and I never really felt like a part of a family, outside of Taylor and me.

I stand there for a moment, just watching my teammates. Ash finally looks up and when he catches my eyes, I smile and nod. As if reading my emotions, he angles his head, and I simply hold up my costumes. "I think I found mine too."

"Now I'm hungry," Roman announces, lightening things up, and I'm grateful for that. "Who wants to get food?"

We all chime in, and since we're not too far from Kilting Around, we decide to head there for nachos. After we head to the cash register and pay, we make our way outside.

"I'm going to win best costume," Roman says.

"Don't think so," Tuck counters.

Roman frowns. "What are you going as?" he asks, considering Tuck is the only one not buying anything.

"You'll see."

Laughing, I pay for my purchase and head outside. As I make my way to my car, Roman and Elias in tow, Ash calls out. "Hey, I'm going to make a quick stop at the library."

I glance across the street, and take in the looming building. Boston Public Library. Sahara has been looking for that firefighter book for book club and ended up downloading it onto her reader, but I've noticed the way she complains it sometimes hurts her eyes and she'd much prefer the print version. Perhaps I should check.

"I'll come with you."

"Dude, I'm starving," Roman complains, and rubs his stomach.

Ash tosses his keys to Elias. "Take my car. I'll catch a lift with Kalen and meet you there."

Ash and I make our way to the streetlight and head across the street. "Zoe is going to kill me, coming here without her."

"You know, parenthood looks good on you."

He grins, and I expect him to come back with a smart-ass comment but instead he says, "You should try it sometime."

I laugh, like the idea of that is ludicrous, because that is my go to move, but then I stop, something strange coming over me. "Maybe I will."

He chuckles. "I see the way you are with Taylor." He shrugs and cocks his head. "I mean, you might be a little too overprotective of her, at her age, but you'd make a great dad."

Me, a dad.

I don't hate it.

Honestly, I never hated it. I just...well, I guess I just have been so closed off.

I fall quiet as we make our way up the steps of the library, and once inside, I glance around. "I'll meet you back here in ten?" Ash asks. He clearly knows where he's going and I clearly don't spend enough time reading anymore. But today, I'm not looking for a book for myself.

Walking quietly, I head toward the information desk, but there's a line. How hard can it be to find the romance section? I start meandering through the aisles. Whispered voices reach my ears when I walk to the end of a row, and spot a group of students seated around a circular table.

I head down another aisle and that's when I see a very familiar person pulling a book from a shelf. My heart picks up its pace. What the ever-loving hell? I walk closer, and she's so engrossed in the book in her hand she doesn't notice me.

I lean in, my mouth near her ear and whisper, "Are you stalking me?"

14

SAHARA

I spin quickly at the sound of Kalen's voice in my ear, and as my blood drains to my feet, I nearly fall to the floor. "Kalen," I murmur breathlessly, my hand on my chest. "You scared me."

"Sorry. I was surprised to see you here." He jerks his head to the left. "I was next door getting costumes."

"Oh, right. I didn't realize you were going to this particular one."

"Taylor asked me to. I got us costumes."

I try to relax as he grins at me. But how can I? I haven't been honest with him about who I am and what I really do for a living. The last thing I expected was for him to find me shelving books at my place of employment.

He inches back, his gaze moving over my face. "Look at you in glasses." His grin turns wicked as he looks me up and down, taking in my knee-length skirt, sensible shoes and buttoned up blouse. "You look different."

"Just ahh..." I smooth my hand over my skirt.

"I love this whole sexy librarian thing you've got going on."

Oh God.

"You could have worn this for a costume," he tells me, lust in his eyes.

I'm two seconds from confessing, even though I know it will be the end of us, and truthfully, I have been enjoying myself and was looking forward to the Halloween party, but before I can get the words out, he speaks. "Are you preparing for another role?" Something in his expression changes as he focuses in on my glasses. Ohmigod, are they triggering a memory? No that can't be right. He didn't know it was me that night in the closet.

"Yeah, something like that," I agree and he turns his attention to the book in my hand.

"Whoa?" As he takes it from me, and turns it over to read the back, I tear off my glasses and hook them in my blouse. "Kama Sutra." He arches a playful brow. "Part of your upcoming play, or part of our play?"

I gulp. I was only reshelving. I can't tell him that, though. He lifts his head and starts running his fingers along the spines of the erotic books. Why oh why did he have to catch me in this section? Then again, I do want to try new things, discover who I am, so maybe I can use this to my advantage.

"That's for me to know and you to find out," I tell him playfully as I snatch the book back. His grin widens and it does crazy things to the needy juncture between my legs.

"I'm looking forward to finding out."

"What are you doing here?" I ask, and the lust disappears from his eyes as he stands up straight, looking a little bit sheepish. What is going on?

"Oh, well, I was across the street, as you know and you were telling me that you were having a bit of a hard time with the e-reader so I thought I could find that book club book here for you."

My heart misses a beat, and it might be just a tiny bit harder to fill my lungs. He was going to do that for me? That is so incredibly sweet and means he's been thinking about me, outside the bedroom. "Kalen," I begin. "I—"

I'm not sure what he's reading on my face, but he quickly cuts me off. "No biggie. I was just across the street. It's what Taylor would have wanted me to do."

Okay that's a weird thing to say and I think he knows it too by the strange way he's now averting his gaze. But I guess he doesn't want me getting the wrong idea. That he's kind and adorable and might be thinking about me.

Got it, Kalen. You want me to know this is just about sex. Duly noted.

"I actually already checked and we don't have it." We? Shoot, why did I say we? I put my hand on his arm, hoping he didn't pick up on that. "That was really nice of you though."

"Like I said, I was in the area." He glances over his shoulder. "I'm here with Ash. He's looking for a book for Zoe." A big, warm smile touches his mouth. "He was so excited that he found her the Beetlejuice costume she wants. It was the cutest thing."

There it is, that longing. I have no doubt this man wants a family of his own, but there's something there, something keeping him back. It has to stem from his childhood, from losing his mother and moving in with his grandmother. Along with not having a relationship with his father. That all makes me sad and a part of me wants to fix it for him. Not that I know how, and I can't forget that he doesn't want to tell me anything about his father. I could ask Taylor, but that feels like an invasion of his privacy.

"The guys and I are headed to Kilting Around for some food. I'll catch up with you later. You're probably busy."

"Yeah, I'm busy."

He hesitates for a second. "I'll see you tonight?"

Before I can respond, he leans in and catching me by surprise, kisses me. He looks as shocked as I am when he inches back, and not wanting to make this more awkward than it already is, I blurt out, "What costumes did you get for us?"

"It's for me to know and you to find out."

I laugh as he shoots my words back at me. Really, do I even have to ask? I have no doubt that it's something low cut and sexy. Isn't Halloween a reason for girls to dress sexy and for guys to ogle them? Since I agreed to go in a couple's costume, I guess I'd better prepare myself for sexy cop, or a cheerleader or something along those lines. Although I'm not looking forward to having my boobs on display. Sure, I'm trying new things, but I'm not much into nudity outside the home.

Nevertheless, I'm in this role because I let him believe that was me. I handed that persona over to him and he's just going with that. Can't fault him for that.

"Does that mean I'll see you tonight?" he asks.

"Actually, I will be at your place." He cocks his head, confused. "Taylor has lines she has to run for her theater class and asked if I could come over and help her."

"Oh." He frowns and rubs an eyebrow, something about what I just said clearly bothering him. "It's nice that she has you to help."

"Are you sure?" I ask, and glance at his eyebrow. He seems a little uneasy about something.

"It's just that, I get the feeling that Taylor likes the idea of us hooking up. I just don't want anything messing up your relationship with her, when we're...you know..."

"...done," I respond finishing his sentence for him. I spot Teresa at the end of the aisle. She pauses when she sees me talking to Kalen, and her brow raises with curiosity. She must be wondering what a guy like Kalen is doing talking to a book nerd like me. We're in the erotic section, so maybe she just thinks he's looking for some sexy reads. She must know the reputation of the Bucks.

"Yeah," he agrees, and I turn my attention back to him, expecting an interrogation from Teresa later. "When I leave for my away game. You and me..."

"...are done," I finish again.

I try to ignore the lump dropping into my stomach, the reminder—once again—that this is sex and I shouldn't be upset. Why the hell am I? I don't want more. Ugh. Maybe I do. But I can't go there. Not with him. Maybe I'm upset because everything about this man screams of settling down, and having a big family...just not with a girl like me. I'm not the kind of girl he'd bring home to meet the family, if he had one. Heck, he doesn't even know the real me.

How can he, Darien...you don't know the real you.

"I'm a big girl, Kalen. Nothing is going to come between Taylor and me." He looks so unsure, I add, "Just like if she fell for one of your buddies, nothing would come between you two guys, right?"

"She's not dating a hockey player," he bursts out, his face reddening a bit.

I cringe, knowing how she feels about Elias, but I'm not sure Elias reciprocates those feelings and that must be so hard on Taylor. I need to make tonight fun for her, maybe even take her out for a drink so she can meet someone else. There's no way Kalen will like that, or ever approve of any guy with his sister, but maybe that will get her out of her funk.

"Why not?" I ask, pushing this a bit farther.

"I just..." He shakes his head and frowns. "The thought of one of the guys touching her..." He pauses, a hard quiver going through him. "Roman...Jesus."

"Not all the guys are like Roman, and you just watch, one of these days a woman is going to take him to his knees."

"It's possible," he responds and glances down, like he's considering that. Is he warming to the idea? "When Taylor is ready to settle down, I want her with a good guy. She's just too young, right now. She has school."

"Okay, Dad."

"Hey," he warns in a soft voice. "I'm not her dad, I'm..." he pauses for a second. "I mean, okay, maybe I act like it at times, and something tells me you don't think I'm good at it."

"Not at all, Kalen. I think you'd be an awesome dad. Taylor is lucky to have you."

"You just think I'm overprotective." I whistle innocently, and he shakes his head. "Maybe you're right. I want her to have a father figure. I want what's best for her."

I don't know the story of his father but my heart squeezes for the young boy who had to step in and take over that role. "You're the best, Kalen."

Tenderness moves over his face as I go up on my toes and kiss his cheek. From the corner of my eye, I spot Ash walking around looking for Kalen and I inch back. "You should get going. I think Ash is ready."

"Right, okay. So, I'll see you tonight, but I won't see you tonight."

"Something like that."

"What about sneaking into my room?"

"I'm not sure I'll be able to do that."

His gaze moves to the book in my hand. "You're checking that book out, right?"

I'm about to hand it over, have him check it out. But that would mean he'd have to come back and return it and next time he might find me behind the desk. I can't have that happen.

"I am." He quickly scans the shelf and pulls another one out.

"What about this one? Erotic bedtime stories for couples."

I chuckle. "You want me to read you a bedtime story, Kalen?"

He steps into me, his hands sliding around my back, pulling me to him. I feel the beginnings of a lovely bulge between his legs and the blood in my vein's boils. Ohmigod, now is not the time or the place for this kind of arousal.

He puts his mouth near my ear, his warm breath stirring the growing need inside me. I have no doubt my cheeks are turning pink. "Maybe I'll read you one, and maybe you can wear the glasses and we can play sexy librarian," he whispers.

I take a couple of fast breaths as his words ping around inside my lust-saturated brain. Jeez, maybe he would have liked the quiet librarian persona better. Maybe he would have thought of her as the serious type, someone he could have a future with. Clearly the vivacious woman on stage, the one I'm embracing, is fun to sleep with but not long-term worthy. But no, that can't be right. He ignored me all through high and I'm nothing like Juliette. Sexy librarian is a stereotype, a fantasy. A game people play. Then they go back to the real world.

Ash starts down the aisle and since I don't want him to see the books in my hands, I shove Kalen. "Go." I wave to Ash as Kalen turns and meets him and I let out a breath of relief. Did I really think my two worlds wouldn't cross? Boston is a big city, so yeah, I guess I did. I'll have to be extra careful from here on out.

I hold the books to my chest, air suddenly harder to come by as another thought hits. I haven't been honest with Kalen, or Taylor. If Taylor and I are to remain friends, eventually she'll want to know about my past, right? Friends share things.

Dammit.

Kalen might have been right to worry about my relationship with his sister. I might have told her all about my past if her brother hadn't been the man to intimately touch me in the secret closet all those years ago.

I continue to hang out in the erotic book section, my body still burning from his touch, not to mention the pictures on the covers, until I'm sure Kalen and Ash are gone. Once I'm sure the coast is clear, I head back to my desk, and before I sit, I do one last glance around. The second I sit, my phone pings, and I reach into my drawer and pull it out. I read the text from Kalen, and my heart jumps.

Kalen: When you come over tonight, keep the glasses and wear your hair up in a bun....

15

KALEN

"She's coming for dinner?" I ask Taylor for the third time. "Tonight? I know she said she was helping you with your lines, but she didn't say anything to me about dinner when I ran into her today."

"Kalen, yes, I told you she was. I invited her a little while ago, after you ran into her, and she said yes. I told her you were cooking." She plants one hand on her hips. "Can I set the table or are you not done interrogating me?"

"She likes this kind of wine?" I hold up the bottle of red to read the label.

Taylor laughs. "I told you she did. What's wrong with you, big brother? Did you take one too many hits to the head at practice today?"

"Yeah, probably."

"So, it's not that you're interested in my friend?"

Shit.

"No." I grab Taylor and put her in a headlock, running my knuckles over her head, lightly of course. She pinches my side, and I yelp and let her go.

She smooths her long hair back, and flicks it over her shoulders. "What if I said I didn't believe you weren't interested in her?"

"She's your friend and if she's coming to help you, the least I can do is make a nice meal."

"You know it's okay if you do like her, right?"

Ignoring that, because she doesn't know that bad tension between Sahara and me could come between their friendship, I pick up the wooden spoon, dip it into my homemade spaghetti sauce and hold it out to Taylor to taste.

She moans and closes her eyes. She glances upward. "Thank you, Grandma, for teaching this man how to cook."

"Good?"

"Excellent." She reaches for the plates, and pulls them from the cupboard. "I miss Grandma." Her voice is low, a deep longing lingering in her words.

"Me too." A moment of silence, which means she has something on her mind. "What?"

She begins to place the four plates onto the table. "Dad messaged me?"

I set the spoon down. I try to be mature and in control whenever she mentions Dad. It's not always easy and even though I don't want him having any influence over her, there's a part of me that knows a girl needs her father. I can only fill that role so much.

"What did he want?"

"He asked about the holidays. Asked if we might want to visit him for Thanksgiving this year."

My breath comes a little faster. "I thought you and I were going to have Thanksgiving here." Shit, I don't want to put pressure on her, or keep her from her father. "Taylor, if you want to go see Dad, you should."

"He and Miles bought a new house."

"He...he sold the family home?" I pinch my eyes shut, and squeeze the bridge of my nose as happy childhood memories flood my brain. "He didn't...why did he do that?" I know I don't go home, but the thoughts of never seeing my old bedroom, where Mom read to me as a child, is like a hard puck to the gut.

Her fingers are a bit shaky as she curls her hair around her finger. Dammit, I hate that she's nervous to talk about Dad with me. I don't want that for her. "Dad and Miles want to start making new memories. They bought Mrs. Williams' house after she passed, not too far from our old place. I've always liked that place, but I'm not sure I want to go without you." She moves the plate around on the placemat, centering it, but I suspect she just needs something to do with her hands.

Just hearing the name Miles brings back memories I wish I could vanquish from my brain. I'm just glad Taylor didn't walk in on them, and is oblivious to what really went down. All she knows is that there was tension between us.

"You should go."

"If I do, I'd want to go with you." She lifts her gaze, her big blue eyes, so full of vulnerability and loss, meeting mine. "I want to be with you for the holidays."

I step up to her and pull her in for a hug. "I want that too, T. Let me think about it, okay?"

"Kalen, I need to tell you something." She inches back and pushes the chairs out for us to sit. I'm not sure what's going on, but I suddenly feel like I'm going to be ill.

I drop into a chair, and she sits, facing me. Her eyes hold so much sorrow and pain, my stomach twists and I take her hand. "Taylor?"

She glances down, stares at our hands for a second, worry radiating from her body. "I know what happened."

I take a fast breath. Surely to fucking God she's not talking about Dad and Miles. No, she can't know that. I protected her from that.

"Taylor?" I say again, doing a shitty job of keeping my voice level. "What do you know?"

Her eyes lift to mine, and I see love and forgiveness mixed with the worry from earlier. "I know what Dad did. I know he was involved with Miles when Mom was sick."

I push back in my chair, my stomach churning harder now. "Jesus, Taylor. I'm so sorry. I thought...I didn't want...You were too young."

"Kalen," she says firmly, centering me back to our conversation. "You're right. I was too young. Too young to really understand what was going on when it happened, and I didn't talk to you because you were so angry. What Dad did was so incredibly wrong. As I grew up and started to live life, and I saw loss and grief and even love all around me, I realized that back then Dad was hurting, badly. He reached out to a man he loved for comfort during a difficult time and—"

"No," I burst out. "He cheated on Mom when she was sick." And I couldn't fucking protect my mother from it, and that guts me to this day.

"I know. I'm not saying what he did was right. I'm not. After we moved, I spent years trying to understand why he did what he did. He loved Mom, and he loved us, Kalen. You have to know that. Don't you remember him taking me to ballet and acting classes and you to the rink every day, even when Mom was sick? He made sure you got to practice and games, all while he worked full time. He was doing all the cooking, cleaning, laundry and he was exhausted, and alone, and...scared." She swallows a big sob as she puts her hand on my heart. "You can't keep this pain inside you. It's messing you up whether you realize it or not. It's keeping you from living the life you should be living."

I shake my head, the anger inside me still so strong, it's blocked out any good memories. "I...Taylor..." A sob wells up in my throat, and as I fight it off, pain radiates down my neck.

She leans into me and hugs me as she swallows a big sob and she puts her hand on my heart. "I'm not sure you're okay in here, Kalen."

"I'm okay," I lie. I'm not okay. I haven't been okay in a very long time. At least when I'm on the ice I can forget about all this crap. But when the game is over and the guys go off to their wives and families, that loneliness, wanting what they have, washes back over me like a tsunami.

Her lips turn down in a frown. "I'm sorry for bringing this up right now, just before dinner, and Sahara coming. We just don't have a lot of quiet time anymore." I'm about to apologize, assure her that I'll find more time for her, but she holds her hands up and makes light of it. "I have a very overbearing brother, so I'm not saying I don't appreciate my space, I do, and I know you're overbearing because you love me." I smile at that. "I just thought it was time to talk."

I nod. She's not wrong. "Okay."

"I'm not asking you to forgive him, I'm only asking for you to find a way past the hurt and anger, and maybe try to find understanding. For your own sake."

I shake my head. "My God, when did you get so smart?"

"I have an awesome big brother watching over me, and teaching me."

I snort out a laugh. There's warmth and hope in her eyes and I know she really wants me to go to our father's new house for Thanksgiving. I am not sure what will come of it, but if Taylor needs that, I have to give it more consideration. "I'll think about it, okay?"

"Think about what?" Elias asks, coming into the kitchen. Before I can answer, and not that I want to tell him what we'd been talking about, he sniffs and says, "Damn, that smells good."

"It's me." I tug on my shirt and push our conversation to the back of my mind to think about later. "New aftershave," I tell him and both Taylor and Elias moan. "Glad you like it. I was rather worried about that."

Elias shakes his head and glances at Taylor. "Thinks he's a comedian."

"Thinks he's something," Tylor groans, and smooths her hair

back as she steps up to the counter and pulls out the utensil drawer.

Elias goes completely serious, his gaze going from Taylor, to me, back to Taylor. He swallows, and I'm not sure he's ever looked so uncertain before. "Taylor, I need to ask you something."

Her body stiffens, and her hands still, holding four forks. She glances at Elias over her shoulder. Is it just me or does she seem nervous about something? "What's up?" Before he can answer, the doorbell rings. "That should be Sahara." She drops the forks onto the table, and Elias picks them up as she darts down the hall to the front door. Laughter reaches my ears as they share some story, and the next thing I know, both women are entering the kitchen and I try not to smile like an idiot.

My sister and Sahara are the actors. I'm not so good at it. "Hey," I say and nearly bite off my fucking tongue when I see that she has her hair up. Too bad she didn't wear her glasses. Or maybe that's a blessing because I'm not sure I'd get through a meal without wanting to ravish her. From the way her face is flushing, she must know what's going through my brain.

"I love your hair up like that," Taylor comments. She stands back and grins. "You have this whole sexy librarian thing going on."

Oh my, Jesus Christ.

Sahara just waves a hand. "I'm always trying new things for new roles."

All I can hope is that tonight's role takes place in my bed, between the sheets.

Sahara inhales. "What smells so good?"

"My grandma's famous spaghetti sauce."

"Looks like it's Kalen's famous spaghetti sauce."

I grin and try not to get a boner when she walks up to me. I dip the big wooden spoon in and hold it toward her for a taste. I try not to be jealous of the spoon when it slips between her lips. She runs her tongue over her bottom lip.

"Kalen, this is amazing. Is it a secret recipe or can you teach me?"

"I'll teach you."

"I had no idea you were such a good cook."

I shrug, but inside I'm just a dork who loves the compliment. Truthfully, I'm a hockey player, but I'm also a nerdy guy who likes video games, books, and cooking. I just haven't had much time for any of those things since joining the Bucks. I want to start reading more—haven't read anything other than books on hockey plays in ages, and with any luck, I'll be rectifying that tonight.

"You know what they say, a way to a man's heart," Taylor pipes in and laughs.

"Wait." Sahara frowns. "What's the way to a woman's heart?"

Catching us by surprise, Elias laughs and we all turn to him. "Oh, sorry. I clearly spent too much time with Roman today because I was thinking about what he'd say."

Taylor holds her palms up. "God, I do not want to hear it." She continues with, "I think a way to a woman's heart is a guy liking you just the way you are, and not wanting to change you into something else."

"Like his mother," Sahara laughs. "I've seen that happen before."

"Exactly."

"I'm not looking for a mother figure." Elias quivers. "Hell, one overbearing mother is enough, thank you."

"Does that mean you *are* out there looking for someone?" Sahara asks, as I reach for a spoon to stir the pasta. When the three of them fall silent behind me, I turn to see Elias tearing his gaze away from Taylor. Oh right, he wants to ask her about Vegas, but I take it he doesn't want to give her the wrong idea, especially after Sahara's question.

"No, I wouldn't say that, exactly," he answers.

"Wine?" Taylor asks, a small smile on her lips. I have no idea what's going through her head, but whatever it is, she's happy about it, and that makes me happy.

"Can you grab the pasta bowls?" I ask Sahara and point to the cupboard. Elias takes the bottle of wine from Taylor and opens it, pouring us each a glass, and Taylor sets them on the table.

As they both drop into their seats, Sahara goes up on her tiptoes to get the bowls but she can't quite reach.

"I told you, you keep them too high," Taylor huffs out. "We're not all giants like you and Elias."

"Here." I step behind her and reach over her head, my body pressing against her back and yes, as my cock enjoys the soft swell of her backside, it rises to the occasion, like he too is in search of the bowls. Mr. President is far too happy at the moment and that's just not good. I get the bowls and keep my back to everyone as she sets them on the counter.

"What did you want to ask me?" Taylor asks Elias, and I'm grateful that I don't have to talk. I'm sure my voice would come out a little high pitched at the moment.

I check the pasta, and set the colander in the sink as Sahara remains standing beside me, her back against the counter.

"Oh, uh...it was actually Roman's idea."

"What? This can't be good," Taylor bursts out.

"Believe it or not, the guy had a good idea."

"Okay, I'm all ears. Spill."

"I'm heading home for Thanksgiving, and Mom and Dad will be asking about my plus one for my buddy's elaborate New Year's Eve wedding. I'm sure there will be lots of women around the dinner table during Thanksgiving and they'll all be swarming me. I'm not saying that because of ego. It's just that Mom and Dad always invite women from the right families because they want what they call, the Ariti family's most eligible bachelor to 'choose wisely', you know." He does air quotes around the words choose wisely.

Taylor frowns. "I'm sorry, Elias. It must be hard to know if a woman wants you for you, or to be a part of your family, or even to get into politics."

He nods. "Anyway, Easton is my oldest childhood friend, and if I don't show up with a date to the wedding, my parents will ensure there's a woman, who they deem fit, on my arm. Whether I like it or not." I turn to see him briefly close his eyes, like he's in utter pain. "Anyway, Roman said something about bringing a date to prevent that from happening. I was thinking, I can tell them about you during Thanksgiving dinner, and then we could go to the wedding together."

Taylor's eyes go wide, as she points at herself. "Me? You want me to be your date?"

"Pretend date," I point out quickly, and Elias glances at me and nods.

"I understand if you don't want to do it. My parents are...a lot." He cringes and adds, "They probably won't like the idea of you, because...I don't know how to say this without it sounding awful."

"Because I don't have the right pedigree. Because I want to be an actress."

He glances down and nods. "Yeah, exactly."

"All the more reason I want to do it," she says with a big grin.

"Really?" Elias asks, his head lifting, surprise all over his face.

Taylor holds her glass out for a salute and Elias taps his against it. "To a Vegas wedding, and me being a pretend date to keep the sharks at bay." The smile falls from Taylor's face as she glances at me. "We didn't have plans, did we?"

I shake my head. Look at her worried about me when it should be the other way around. "Go to Vegas and have fun." I narrow my eyes. "Just not too much fun." I glance at Elias. "You'll see to that, won't you?"

He scrubs his face, and nods. "Yeah. Of course." He seems a bit twitchy as he toys with the corner of the placemat. Heading home for Thanksgiving next month, and this whole fake dating scheme must be worrying him.

The timer I set for the pasta goes off and I turn back to the stove. Sahara helps me plate and serve the food and after we all sit, I lift my glass in salute.

"What are we drinking to?" Sahara asks.

"To friends," I respond, loving that all four chairs are filled at the table, just like when we were kids, before Mom got sick and Dad well...I don't want to think about that right now.

Everyone nods in agreement and we all dig in. "Do you do all the cooking?" Sahara asks as she twirls pasta around her fork.

"We all take turns."

"I like it when it's Kalen's turn," Taylor says. "Not so much when it's Elias."

"Hey," he shoots back. "I'm a good cook."

I exchange a look with Taylor and we both laugh.

He squares his shoulder. "Okay, fine. I wouldn't say great, but I get by."

Sahara takes a sip of her wine. "It's nice that you all share." She looks a little lost, maybe a bit sad. "I grew up with four siblings so my place gets quiet sometimes."

"If you're ever looking for a roommate?" Taylor pipes in.

I sigh. "Are we doing this again?"

She purses her lips. "I can't live with my brother forever. I need my own space. Besides, someday you're going to get married and need the extra rooms for kids." She holds her hands up. "I don't want to be the one keeping you from that."

I shake my head. I think sometimes she just likes to poke at me. "At least finish school before you consider moving, T, and I'm not getting married anytime soon, or ever." I realize she'll have to move someday. This is a big city, and I like her close to me. Yes, I'm overprotective, I know.

"Speaking of moving," Elias pipes in and I turn to him. "The house at the end of the street is going up for sale."

"I drove by it on the way here. They were just putting the For Sale sign up," Sahara mentions. "It's huge."

He nods in agreement. "It is huge. Maybe I'll get a roommate."

I set my fork down for a second, this all taking me by surprise. "I didn't realize you were looking."

"Brady mentioned it to me the other day. He knows the family selling and I guess it got me thinking."

Elias focuses on his food, twirling the noodles around his fork. He seems uneasy, and I can't help but think he's worried he's upsetting me by moving. But I'm not upset. Sure, I like his company in this big place, and I consider him my brother, a guy I trust, but maybe he's thinking of his future and settling down. "You know you can stay with me as long as you want."

"I know, but now that the market is opening up, it might be a good time to get my own place. Like Taylor said, someday you'll need the extra rooms."

I nod, understanding everyone needs their own space. "I can hook you up with my realtor if you want to check it out," I say.

"Well," Sahara begins. "I'm not currently looking for a roommate, Taylor, but it sounds like Elias might be." As soon as the words leave her mouth, her eyes go big and her gaze flies to Taylor, like she might have said something she shouldn't have. She's right. No way would Taylor want to move in with Elias, and Sahara must realize she shouldn't have suggested it. Obviously it was just her trying to help her friend and she looks sorry that she put voice to the thought. No doubt Taylor is sick of the two of us telling her what to do, and wants away from all the fatherly advice she gets from us both.

"I'm pretty sure Taylor wants out from under Elias's thumb too," I point out with a laugh as I stab a meatball.

"Yeah, I do not want to be under Elias's thumb," she agrees with a smirk that seems out of place and when she casts Sahara a look I don't understand, I'm about to ask what's going on but Elias pipes in.

"What do you think of your Halloween costume, Sahara?"

16

SAHARA

I glance at Elias. "Oh, I actually haven't seen it yet. Have you?"

Before he can answer, Kalen gestures with a nod toward the hall. "It's upstairs. I can show you later when you're done helping Taylor. We should make sure it fits."

I grin at him, because I suspect there's a lot of things upstairs that he'd like to show me later, and of course there are things I'd like to show him too.

"Why don't you just tell me what it is," I say. Again, I can only imagine it's some tiny thing that barely fits. "Do you know what it is?" I ask Taylor.

"Nope." She finishes her last bite of pasta. "But we should probably get to work."

"You're right. Let's get at it. I have some bedtime reading to do." A noise crawls out of Kalen's throat and when everyone glances at him, he tries to cover it with a cough. "Book club,"

I explain. "It's on Thursday night and I'm only halfway through."

Taylor sighs and rubs her tired eyes. "I can't wait until summer so I can join. I just don't have the time right now." I don't have a lot of time either, but it's nice to get out and meet new people. "You're going to love all the WAGs," Taylor tells me.

"I've only met Gina, and she was so nice. Wait, does the 's' in WAGs stand for sisters? You know with you being a player's sister and all," I joke. Not that it's a great joke.

Taylor gives me a big smile. "It does now." Tuning her attention to Kalen, she bats her eyelashes. "Would you mind doing the dishes tonight, big brother? I know it's my turn but I'm swamped."

Kalen shakes his head. "Go. You'll owe me two clean up nights."

I stand and pick up my plate, ready to take it to the dishwasher but Kalen takes it from me. "Thanks for dinner. It was delicious." I wipe my mouth with a napkin. "You'll have to let me cook for you sometime. I don't have any family recipes but I can get by." I don't dare tell him we had staff doing the cooking.

He grins. "Sounds like a plan."

I note the way Taylor is watching with a grin on her face. She loops her arm in mine and leads me to the big living room where she has her books spread out.

The first thing I tell her is, "Taylor, I'm sorry, that...about moving in with Elias...ugh, it just slipped out. I would never want to do or say anything to cause tension between you and your brother, or your brother and Elias. Sometimes my mouth engages before my brain."

"It's okay. No harm done," she assures me and I relax a bit. A wry smile cures her lips. "Now speaking of my brother. I want to know what's going on between the two of you. He hasn't been coming home at night."

"Oh, he's my knight in shining armor." I wave my hand, trying for light and casual. "You know what he's like. Overprotective. He just wants to make sure my place is safe for me. I'm your friend, and that's the reason why. He'd do it for any of your friends, I'm sure." I can't tell her I'm hooking up with her brother. Everything about that is wrong. "We're friends," I add, wishing I could just shut the hell up. She who protests too much... Taylor snorts out a laugh that tells me loud and clear she's not buying any of my crap. "What?" I ask.

"More like friends with benefits, you mean."

I glance down, my stomach cramping. God, I don't want this to be awkward, or mess up our friendship. "Taylor..."

"Sahara." She touches my arm, and I look back up at her. "I like you two together. I knew you two would hit it off. You're just his type."

Am I though? How can I be when I don't even know what type I am?

"You're not upset?"

"No. my brother could use a woman like you in his life."

A woman like me...

He doesn't even know who I am.

God, could this be any more messed up? I guess it's a good thing this relationship comes with an expiry date, because I'm not sure how long I can keep hiding things from him. It was pure luck that he didn't catch me behind the desk at the library.

"A woman like me? What exactly does that mean." My mind races back to some of the things he said about not getting married, as well as the things he said—or rather didn't say— about his father. He sure puts it out there that he doesn't want more. But then I see how he is around married friends, and it seems like he wants what they have.

"It's just, you two are good together."

I point an accusatory finger. "I know what you're up to, Taylor. You're trying to keep your brother busy with me so you can make your move on Elias."

Her eyes go wide. "Well, I mean...that might have crossed my mind a time or two. Maybe at first, but then I watched you two together. Pure magic."

"The other night, when you gave Elias a ride and I was going home, I agreed to go for a drink to give you alone time with Elias."

"You rock."

"I know," I laugh. "I even kept him at my place all night." I look upward. "The things I do for you, my friend."

"It was a hardship, huh?"

"Yeah, it was hard." I cover my mouth. "Ohmigod, I can't believe I'm saying these things to you."

"Here's the thing. He's my brother, yes, but you're my friend and I want you to be able to talk to me about whatever you want to talk about."

"I don't want anything that's happening..." I stop and glance at the doorway. "...with Kalen and me to come between you and me. Kalen and I are just temporary. When it's over, I don't want to lose you. He's worried about that too, but I assured him that we're adults and can handle it." I give her hand a little squeeze. "We can, right?"

She nibbles her bottom lip like she has a secret. "Of course, and I owe you for keeping him out the other night."

"Oh, do tell?"

"Nothing happened. Not really." She leans toward me. "Other than I accidently walked in on Elias coming out of the shower."

"Accidently, on purpose?"

"I mean no, not really. We share a bathroom, you know," she huffs out, playing innocent. "It can happen. He should have locked the door on my side."

"It's like he was just asking for it."

Her eyes shine with mischief as she points her finger down and then brings it up. "I think he was happy to see me."

I laugh as I think about Mr. President. "I bet he was."

"It's just." She pauses and scrunches up her nose. "Maybe he was thinking about one of his bunnies. I don't know. I'm not sure if he likes me and most times I'm so damn awkward around him." She groans. "And even if he does, he's not going to do anything about it."

I sigh. "Kalen..."

She sinks back against the sofa. "Yeah…"

I grab a pillow and lean into the corner, placing the cushion over my stomach. "When you go away for New Year's, maybe you'll have to change his mind."

"Honestly, I'm shocked that he asked me to go, or that Kalen seems to be okay with it. But it just proves how much he trusts his best friend with me. Elias isn't going to betray that trust." She groans, tosses her head from side to side against the back of the sofa, leaving her hair a static mess. "Pretend girlfriend. That's right out of a bad romantic comedy."

"They're not all bad. Look how the good ones turn out?"

She angles her head to look at me. "How?"

"Happy ever after."

"I don't think that's in my future. Not with Elias. More like crappy ever after with him having two black eyes and best friends breaking up."

"Ugh. But there's got to be something you could do."

"What?"

"You're a smart girl. You'll figure it out. Also…" I cock my head. "Isn't it kind of a double standard that he can hook up with your friend and you can't hook up with his?"

"Big double standard," she agrees. "But he's been taking care of me since Mom died, and I don't want to do anything to hurt him, ever."

I nod, and when she stretches out her legs, I give one a little squeeze, understanding her worry. I go quiet, giving her a chance to explain their childhood, but she doesn't. Instead, she says, "Elias is a lot older too. He probably thinks of me as his little sister."

There were times tonight I saw the way Elias looked at Taylor when he thought no one was watching. He's into her. Of that I'm sure. "Something tells me he doesn't."

She pushes upright and grabs a script. "Okay, let's do this. I don't want to keep you here all night. You have reading to do."

I take the script and for the next couple of hours, we go over lines and rehearse, taking breaks to talk and sip water. Every now and then I spot Kalen, or Elias walking by, always taking a glance in to see us. As the night ticks on, my eyes grow tired and I pull my glasses from my purse.

"I had surgery years ago, but reading puts a strain on them."

"They're super cute and totally completes the sexy librarian thing you've got going on." She tosses her script onto the coffee table and stretches out. "It's getting late. I should be getting to bed. Thanks so much for your help." She pushes to her feet. "You should crawl into bed in the spare room." Grinning, she wags playful eyebrows and I just shake my head. I know what's going on here: operation distraction. "No sense driving home in the dark, and I don't like you walking from the car to your place after the break in."

"Thanks, Mom."

She laughs, and movement near the doorway catches my attention. "I agree with Taylor." I lift my gaze to find Kalen standing there, his arms crossed, his legs wide, as he stares at me. My body takes that moment to quiver and deep between my legs, my sex is siding with the Coolidge siblings. "I don't like the idea of you on the street late at night," Kalen adds.

"Okay, Dad."

He pulls his keys from his pocket, and twirls them around his finger. "But if you want to head home, I'll follow you, to make sure you get in okay."

Elias walks up beside Kalen and leans against the wall. "I'm heading out."

"Where are you going?" Kalen asks.

Taylor throws her hands up. "See what we have to put up with? Big brother needs to know our every movement."

"I only asked because..."

"Because you're nosy," Taylor provides and Kalen rolls his eyes at her.

"Brady messaged." Elias adjusts a ball cap on his head. "He's over at his buddy's house. The one down the road that's for sale. He told his friend I might be interested, and they invited me over to take an early look."

"Oh, can I come?" Taylor asks and I sense she wants to leave to give Kalen and me time alone. Not to mention having a bit of alone time with Elias. "I'd love to get a look at it."

"Oh, why is that now?" Kalen asks, and Taylor stiffens a bit. Before she can respond, he answers for her, "Because you're nosy."

Taylor sticks her tongue out at him. "Takes one to know one." I just laugh at their childish antics, and a part of me wishes I had this kind of comradery with my siblings. It must have been so nice to have each other growing up, and even though Kalen is overprotective, he has a good heart.

Elias pushes off the wall. "Sure."

"Maybe I'll pick out my room," she teases, just to get under her brother's skin.

"Thought you didn't want to be under his thumb, either."

"I don't." Kalen turns to say something to Elias and Taylor leans into me and whispers, "I want to be under his body. I have other uses for his thumb."

Unable to help myself, I let loose a big laugh, and that's when Kalen goes quiet and focuses in on me. I bite my lip to quiet myself. Damn, I hope he doesn't ask what his sister whispered to me.

Taylor and Elias head down the hall, and when the front door opens and closes, Kalen gestures with a nod toward the stairs. "Come on." He winks. "I've got something to show you."

Snatching a pencil from Taylor's case, I curl a few loose tendrils of hair around my finger. Doing my best librarian stereotype, I secure them to the top of my head with the pencil before tugging my glasses down an inch, looking at the hottest man in the universe over the rims. I'm rewarded with a growl, as he crooks his finger, beckoning me to him,

My pulse jumps, excitement bubbling up inside of me. "Better make it quick," I murmur, breathless from my racing heart. "I have some bedtime reading to do." Opening my eyes wide like I just had a revelation, I tug the pencil free, nibbling on it slightly and remind her, "Oh, wait, didn't you say you were going to read to me?"

"Oh, fuck yeah…"

17

SAHARA

Kalen takes my hand, like he's anxious to get me alone. "I'm glad you came to dinner," he says.

"Me too." Honestly, I like what we do in the bedroom but I really enjoyed sitting around the kitchen table with him, his sister and his friend, chatting about things. I have a feeling Kalen liked it as much as me.

I have no doubt this man wants a family of his own, but something is holding him back. I want to pry, but I really shouldn't get too close to a man who seems hell bent on keeping this about sex. I don't want him thinking I want more, and then scare him off.

"Come on." He tugs on my hand.

"Just a second." I hurry to the front door and pick up my bag, and when I glance at Kalen, and take in his grin, I have no doubt he's wondering if I have a few sexy books with me. He takes my bag and hikes it over his shoulder, then leads me upstairs to his bedroom. Inside, he shuts the door and walks to his closet. As he closes the double doors, I get a better look around his room. The last time I was in here it was dark and we had other things on our mind.

"You know, I love that you have family pictures around. It makes this house warm and cozy for your sister." I pick up a picture and glance at Kalen over my shoulder. "You'd be a good father, Kalen. Something tells me you don't think you would be, but Taylor is a testament to how attentive and caring you are. She's pretty amazing."

A look of warmth and love comes over his face, and I know he's proud of his sister. "I can't take all the credit. She was always an amazing young girl. Strong, resilient...forgiving." As soon as he says forgiving, he glances away, a distant, look of hurt in his eyes, like he's remembering something painful from long ago. Whatever it was he just thought about, it's still raw.

"Something on your mind?" I ask, in a light tone.

He steps up to me and takes the small picture from my hands. He lightly runs his finger over the frame, a small smile touching the corners of his mouth. "You know they talk about time healing. It does and it doesn't, if that makes sense. I put these pictures around for Taylor." As he speaks, I can almost feel the guilt radiating off him. Why does he feel guilty? He angles the pic to show me. "This was Mom and Taylor at Christmas. Taylor was only two in this photo."

"They look very happy."

"Yeah. I was eight, and I do remember being happy. I guess maybe my earlier years weren't so bad."

As if he just said something he shouldn't have, something he doesn't want me to know, he sets the picture back down.

I push my glasses up and lean over to take a closer look at the photo. "Do you have one of you and your mother?" I glance around but don't see one.

Sadness moves over him. "No."

Sensing I touched a sensitive spot, I ask, "Where were you and your dad in this picture?"

"Dad was probably making breakfast, and I was probably blowing something up."

I laugh at that. "I doubt that. I can just picture little Kalen babyproofing everything after opening all the presents to make sure nothing hurt your baby sister."

He gives me a sheepish look. "Yeah, probably."

"Always so responsible, taking care of everyone else." I give him a shove. "Who's taking care of you, Kalen?"

"I can take care of myself."

"Maybe I'd like to take care of you tonight." I push him again, and he backs up.

"Babe."

He's about to protest, so I go up on my toes and press my lips to his. As I swallow his response, I pop the button on his pants and slide my hand in.

"Fuck," he murmurs into my mouth. "You don't have to..." I stroke him from crown to tip and he moans. "Okay, if you want to."

I chuckle at that and drop to my knees, tugging his pants down. I honestly love pleasuring this man and making him happy, because if anyone deserves it, it's him. He lightly runs his fingers through my hair as I take him deep into my throat, and his soft moans curl around me. I suck him deep, and run my tongue along the long length of him, and he rocks into my mouth. This time, though, I want to be on top of him again. It's less about me, and more about him laying back and relaxing while someone else takes care of him.

His cock falls from my lips as I go back on my heels. I tap his leg and when he realizes what I want, he kicks off his pants in record time. "Done protesting?" I tease.

His voice is surprisingly low, enchantingly tender, when he cups my face and whispers, "Done protesting, babe."

I swallow as my heart expands, and I push to my feet. I tug on his shirt and he peels it over his head. Once he's naked, I nudge him and he falls back onto the bed. He pushes back until he's flat on his pillow. I grab my phone from my bag and turn on music. I can hardly believe I'm doing a strip tease for this man, yet here I am doing it. I'm not even sure what I'm doing but judging from the heat and lust brewing in his eyes, I'm not disappointing him.

"You're so beautiful, Sahara."

My throat constricts at the deep tenderness in his tone. His gaze drops as I remove my button-down blouse and my pencil skirt. I reach for the clip in my hair and meet his gaze, gauging his reaction.

There's vulnerability in his blue eyes as they almost fall shut. "I...I really want you."

I nod, feeling extremely emotional at this strange, almost dazed, yet widely open and honest state he's in. In a quick move, I remove my glasses, set them on the nightstand, and crawl over him. His big hands land on my hips and that's when I realize just how much I've missed his touch.

"I want you, babe," he whispers, and there's a hitch in his voice, one that makes me think—maybe even hope—that he's talking about more.

"You've got me," I answer, as he lifts my hips ready to pull me down onto his cock.

Condom.

As my inner voice screams at me, I put my hands over his to still him. "Protection."

He shakes his head, like he's mentally scolding himself. "Nightstand."

I turn and glance at the drawer, and while I should be moving, I'm not. What is going on with me? "Maybe...." I begin, and his eyes soften even more as he puts his palm on the side of my face. "Maybe I don't want to use one. Maybe I want to feel you come inside me." I don't tell him I've never done that before, but I get the sense that he knows.

"Aw, babe. I want that too, and I'm clean. I promise."

My entire being tells me this man would never do anything to hurt me. "I'm clean too, and on the pill."

"I know. I trust that you are," he says and it's like someone just punched me right in the solar plexus, because he shouldn't trust me. "You okay?"

I gulp. "Why do you trust me?" I ask, sensing trust doesn't come easy to him, and I'm playing with fire here.

Something comes over him. His eyes narrow, a storm brewing in the depths, as he goes quiet. Too quiet. For too long. When he finally breaks it, the turbulence in his eyes settles. "Because you've never given me a reason not to, and I'm...I'm tired of being a chicken shit."

I nod, even though I have no idea what he's talking about, although I suspect it's something from his childhood. I touch his hair, all twisted up inside. Even though it's true, I haven't given him a reason not to trust me, I am keeping things from him. Mainly that I know who he is, and I'm not who he thinks I am. Dammit. Dammit. Dammit. My throat tightens to the point of pain, and while I'm a good actress, I'm not a great one, and hiding this eruptive volcano going on inside of me can't be done.

"Babe, hey, are you okay? If you're tired—"

"I want this. I want you." I slowly lower myself, and his cock slides into my body, filling me so beautifully it brings tears to my eyes.

He lifts up, filling me even more, and his unapologetic grunt curls around me and squeezes tight.

"It's good," I tell him. "So good, Kalen."

"Yeah, it's good, babe."

Everything about this, while it was supposed to be sexual, feels different. As I move my body, wanting to take care of him, this joining has turned tender and emotional, and my insides are a hot mess of overflowing lava. Perhaps it's the skin-on-skin contact that is messing with me, pushing me past an invisible line I shouldn't be crossing.

His grip on my hips tightens, and I put my hands on his chest, our gazes holding and locking as we move as one. We push and pull, each giving and taking, and I can't help but wonder if he too thinks that what we're doing here is more than just sex.

It could be all in my head, but if it's not, well...if we're both delving into something deeper, that's not good. Nope not good at all considering he just said he trusted me and I haven't been completely honest.

I'm going to need to end this sooner, rather than later.

He removes a hand from my hips and circles his finger around my sopping wet clit. My eyes begin to close, but I force them to stay open, wanting to bask in this magical moment, because there won't be—can't be—another.

But for now, I'm just going to push all my worries aside and give my body over to his touch.

My orgasm crashes over me like a tsunami, dragging me under until breathing is nearly impossible, and I don't care. Right now I'm sure that breathing is overrated. Kalen groans as liquid heat pours from my body and sears his cock. Sex without a condom is unlike anything I've ever felt, physically and emotionally.

"Sahara. Jesus. You are incredible." The warmth and appreciation in his eyes, swirls through me and settles deep in my chest. There is absolutely nothing repressed about this man between the sheets. He's open and honest and...deserves better than me.

"You...this...incredible..." I manage to murmur as he reduces me to one-word sentences and for some reason that has a bubble of laughter climbing out of my throat. I think I might be losing it.

As I spill, he clenches down on his jaw, and puts both hands on my hips, holding me as I lift up and down, grinding, wringing every last pulse from my body. He looks like he's in awe as I completely let go and a part of me knows...knows this isn't just the actress from the stage...this is me. A part of who I am. A part of Darien Lewis. I have Kalen to thank for helping me discover this about myself. I'm not sure I could be so free with any other man.

"You want my cum?" he asks. "You want it inside you?"

"Yes," I practically scream, dying for him to spurt inside me, for his sperm to fill my body, anything to keep a part of him with me, even if only for a short while. He pulls me down to him, his lips meeting mine and I gasp into his mouth as his seed spurts inside me. Warmth spreads through my body and I close my eyes, enjoying the delicious sensations. Damn, I know I said I have to end this, but how can I possibly do that when this feels so incredible.

He runs gentle hands along my back, his fingers hot against my skin as he touches my sides and lightly massages my shoulders. Once he stops spasming, his hands still and we hold each other until our breathing regulates.

"Babe," he murmurs. "Are your legs okay?"

My heart clenches. Why does he have to be so thoughtful? I sit up and put a smile on my face, hoping it hides the bevy of emotions erupting inside me. "They are."

His smile is sincere, genuine, as he begins to lift me. "Let's get you in a more comfortable position." He moves me around like I'm a rag doll, and once I'm lying beside him, he drops a soft kiss on my mouth. As emotions hit me again, I turn my head and put my hand over my mouth.

"You're tired."

"I'm okay, it was a long day."

He lightly brushes my hair back. "I should have just tucked you in."

"I like what we did better."

He grins. "Good. I'll be right back."

This time when he leaves the bed and disappears, I know he's coming back with a cloth to wash me. I'm not entirely sure I can handle much more of his sweetness tonight. Later, when he shows me the sexy costume he picked out for me, it should help remind me what this is and what it isn't.

I stretch, feeling languid and spent, while the ensuite water runs. Suddenly the outer door downstairs opens and closes and I scramble to grab the sheets to pull them up as the sound of Taylor and Elias' voices get louder as they climb the stairs. Shoot, I hope she doesn't poke her head in here, or check the spare room to see that it's empty. I listen for a long time and let out a breath, my shoulders relaxing as I hear doors across the hall close.

"Did I hear them come back?" Kalen asks, walking back to me and climbing onto the bed. He taps my legs like washing me up is just so natural and I can't believe how at ease I've become with the process. Then again, I did masturbate in front of the man, and dammit, that was so much fun.

"Yeah, I think they went to sleep."

He cleans me up and sets the cloth aside. His gaze moves over my face and he narrows his eyes. "You should get some sleep."

"I want to see my costume, and..." I sigh and glance at my bookbag. "I really have to finish my book." I rub my tired eyes. "Book club is coming up."

"Right." He stands and walks to his closet. He crinkles up his nose as he looks back at me. I sit up and arch a brow. "I hope you don't think it's stupid."

"I'm sure I won't."

He chuckles, but it holds no humor. "The last time I went to a dress-up party was just before I left for college. It was a masquerade party and I guess you can say we had couples' costumes."

He goes quiet for a brief second like he's remembering something and my blood drains to my toes. Is he putting it together? After seeing me in my glasses, is he making the connection between me and the girl in the library? I look nothing like her anymore, and that was the point when I moved here, but there's still a chance.

"Hey, are you okay?" he turns to me, the costumes in his hands, but my vision is currently so fuzzy, I can't focus in on what he's holding.

"Just tired." It's not a lie. I am tired.

He glances at the costumes in his hands. "We can wait until tomorrow."

"No, show me."

He grins. "Okay, so you're salsa and I'm chips." He holds them up and I sit there, my jaw agape, my eyes bugging out of my head as I look them over. He can't be serious. He frowns. "You hate them. I just...I know women like to dress sexy..." He pauses and gives me a sheepish look. "I didn't want any of the guys looking at your body." He shakes his head like he's being stupid, but he's being anything but.

My heart stalls, and I crook my finger. He walks over, and I go up on my knees, put my arms around his neck and kiss him. He drops the costumes and pulls me to him. By the time we finish, we're both breathless.

He angles his head, his brows furrowed. "What was that for?"

"For the costumes you picked out. I love them." I love how thoughtful and protective he is of me. I know Taylor hates it, but deep down, their bond is strong and she appreciates him. Honestly, he only wants what's best for her. My parents say the same about me. I have a hard time believing it, though. In their eyes, my success, or lack thereof, is a reflection on them.

I'm sure the only way they'd ever come to a local community theater to see me act is if they were hog tied and forced. Honestly, I've been in Boston for months now and they aren't even talking about visiting, or seeing my place. Not that I want them to. They'd be mortified that I'm living in a place that had been broken into.

"Damn, I would have shown you them earlier if I knew you were going to react like that." His voice brings me back and as I focus on him, he wets his bottom lip, like he's still tasting me and I rub my tired eyes.

"Okay, in bed now," he commands in a soft voice. I slide between the sheets. "Where do I find your e-reader?"

I gesture toward my bag, putting all thoughts of my family behind me. I don't want anything to ruin this night with Kalen. "In there."

He circles the bed, and opens my bag, pulling out the erotic books. He grins. "This is for another night." He reaches for my e-reader. "Tonight. I'm going to read your book club romance to you until you fall asleep. That way you can't blame me for not finishing it, because I've been keeping you busy at night."

He grins and as I laugh at that, he tugs the covers up.

"Do you enjoy reading?" I ask.

"I used to read a lot in high school. Every chance I could and I always read to Taylor when she was young. I wish I had more time now."

"I didn't know that about you."

"How could you? You didn't know me in high school."

I swallow the lump in my throat and settle into my pillow as he reaches into his drawer and puts on a pair of glasses.

"I didn't know you wore glasses," I say. He's full of surprises tonight.

"I do for reading." He winks and adds, "Tell no one."

"You look hot."

He grins. "You're tired. I think you're confusing hot and nerdy."

"What's wrong with nerdy?" I ask quietly.

"Nothing. If you want to know the truth, I'm really a nerd at heart."

"Hardly." He shrugs and I study him. If he doesn't think there's anything wrong with nerds, and if he thinks he really is one, maybe he would have liked that side of me.

Ah, but it was the woman on stage he was attracted to, not the nerdy girl from high school.

He tucks the covers around me. "Now settle in."

He opens my e-reader and picks up where I left off. I lose myself in his words, and while a part of me knows I need to run away, I can't help but think I should do it after the Halloween party. He went through the trouble of finding us cute costumes, and I'm so freaking touched that he wants to protect my body, not showcase it to his friends, that I can't leave just yet. He'll wonder why, and he can never know the reason. No, I'll play this out until after the party, and then like we both agreed, we go our own ways.

Of course, none of this has to do with the fact that he wants to read erotic stories to me…

KALEN

As I step back into the bedroom, Sahara stirs in my bed. I take a long moment to watch her, to just enjoy having her here. Last night was pretty spectacular, and I'm not just talking about the sex, or how she wanted to take care of me. Fuck, no woman has ever wanted to put my needs first before, and I have to say, it fucked me over a little.

One eye opens, and I smile at her. "Good morning."

The second eye opens and as she focuses in on me, she grumbles, "How long have you been standing there like a big old creeper?"

I laugh. "Not long. I brought you coffee."

She pushes her hair from her forehead. "Okay, I forgive you for being a creeper."

"That's all it takes. A cup of coffee?"

"Yeah, apparently I'm pretty easy."

"I'll have to remember that."

She takes a fast look at the clock and sits up, pressing her back against the headboard. I hand the cup over and she cradles it with her palms and inhales. "Omg, this smells delicious."

"Hazelnut vanilla. Tanner Bang got us all hooked." She arches a curious brow. "He went to Scotia Academy in Nova Scotia. There's a fair-trade coffee roaster there, and this is their specialty. He got us addicted, so now he brings it in for all of us."

"How nice of him."

"You'll likely meet Maeve at the book club. She's the club's physiotherapist. I think you'll really like her."

She crinkles her nose, and glances down, like she's trying to pull something from the recesses of her brain. "I heard about her. She had a stalker, right?"

"Yeah. Jesus, it was awful. Turns out it was her best friend from childhood." I briefly close my eyes and shake my head, still shocked by it all. "It's crazy to think her former best friend was behind it. You think you know someone and then..." I pause and snap my fingers. "Just like that they turn out to be something or someone you never saw coming." She looks almost pale as she takes a fast sip of her coffee. "Hey, did you get enough sleep?" She nods, and holds the coffee close as she glances at the clock again. "Somewhere to be?"

"Yeah." Before I can ask what her plans are for the day she continues, "Now I have to slip into last night's clothes and do the walk of shame to my car."

I laugh at that, and walk to my closet. "I have sweats, or you could borrow something from Taylor."

"I'll take your sweats, actually." I pull out a pair of sweats that tie at the waist and a sweatshirt and hand them to her. "Thank you."

"Hungry?"

She shakes her head. "No, I'm good. I have to get a move on it."

"Does that mean we won't be going for a jog this morning?"

Her shoulders drop like she's completely disappointed. "Well, darn. Can I get a rain check?"

I ruffle her hair playfully. "Sure." I lean into her and press my lips to hers. "Last night," I begin. "I want a repeat."

"Of course, you do. I did all the work." She huffs out an indignant laugh. "All you had to do was lay back and enjoy." She rubs her thighs and winks. "Kind of a great thigh workout, though. Probably a better work out than you'll get on your run this morning."

I laugh at her antics, enjoying the fuck out of this woman's smart mouth that I'm so desperate to devour again. "Fine, tonight I'll do all the work."

She arches a brow. "Don't you need your stamina for your game?"

"Yeah, are you coming?"

With a cock of her head she asks, "Are you inviting me?"

"Of course, I am. You have an open invitation for the season if you want it."

"Well, aren't you nice." She turns her head from side to side, stretching it out.

"Keep that to yourself," I tease.

"You still want me to come to the games after our arrangement ends?"

"Yeah, sure. If you want." Not wanting to sound too possessive I add, "I mean, I know Taylor would love to have you there. So...you can make it?" Dammit, I shouldn't be pressing. I just really fucking loved having her there the other night.

She taps her chin playfully. "I'll think about it."

I shrug. "I understand if you're busy."

She grins and whacks me. "I'm coming. Taylor and I already talked about it." She leans toward me. "Besides, we only have a little time left in this...arrangement. So, let's make the best of it."

"Right," I say, and bite back what I really want to say: Can we make it longer? "My place or yours?"

"How about my place?" she asks. "That way we're close to the Nook for a delicious breakfast."

"I don't care where we go, just as long as I can get you naked."

She goes quiet, thoughtful for a moment, her smile falling as she stares into her coffee cup, and I fix the blankets over her legs, running my hands up and down her thighs on top of the sheets.

"Kalen."

"Yeah, babe?"

Her head lifts, something turbulent in her eyes. "Were you always responsible growing up? I know you don't talk to your dad, and you've watch out for Taylor since she was small, and I was just wondering if you had to take on a parental role?"

My stomach tightens at the seriousness in her tone and I turn to glance out the window. "I don't really like to talk about it."

"Oh, okay. We can talk about something else."

I swallow. Would it be so bad to tell her? She opened up and told me about her family, how they don't respect her choices and how she feels left out.

"Taylor talked to Dad. He wants us to visit for Thanksgiving," I blurt out, wanting to give her something but it's fucking hard thinking back to his betrayal.

"Are you going?"

She takes a sip of coffee, and eyes me over the rim. "She really wants to and I don't ever want to disappoint her."

"Why does she want to go?"

I exhale, and run my fingers through my mess of hair. Lowering my voice, I whisper, "Dad and his partner bought a new house. They want to make new memories."

"Partner? Do you not like his partner?"

"No, not really." I suck in a breath. "It's fucking complicated."

She sets her coffee down and takes my hand. Everything in the supportive way she gives it a squeeze unlocks things deep inside me. "I don't know his partner, Miles, but no, I don't like him."

"Miles," she says quietly. "I see."

"No, you don't see." My voice comes out much harsher than I intended and she pulls her hand back, and reaches for the blankets like she should go. "I'm sorry," I reply quickly. "I didn't mean to say it like that. It's just complicated..."

"Is it because your father's partner is a man?"

I snort out a laugh. "Actually, no. I don't care about his sexuality. Love is love, but loving someone while your wife is dying and having sex with him in the spare room right next to the room you share with your sick wife...that's the shit that gets to me."

She gasps and takes my hands again. "Oh, Kalen. I'm so sorry."

The pain in her eyes, pain for me and the hurt I'm still carrying, whooshes through me, confusing all my emotions.

"That must have been devastating for you."

I nod, and choke back a sob. "I didn't know until the other day that Taylor knew about it." Thinking about that steals the air from my lungs, and I force in a breath as I take her hand in mine. "I thought I had sheltered her from it, but she knew. Jesus."

"She still talks to your father?"

"Yeah, she still has a relationship with him." I nod.

Lines form in her forehead as she stares at me, trying to wrap her brain around all this. "She was young when it happened. Maybe that makes a difference."

I puff out a humorless laugh. "No, it's just that she's far more forgiving than me." A long beat of silence, and she gazes at me. It's easy to tell she wants to say something, but isn't sure she should. "Go ahead," I tell her.

She pinches her lips tight and then begins, "It's hard holding onto that pain for all these years, Kalen." I angle my head and her eyes open wide. "I'm not saying you should let it go." Her gaze drops to our linked fingers. "Forgiveness is hard. Especially something of this magnitude, but it's just a lot to hold onto and I don't like seeing you suffer." She blinks a few times and adds, "Have you ever talked to him about it?"

"He tried, but I didn't want to. I was angry." I swallow the lump punching into my throat. "I guess I still am." I bite the inside of my cheek to stop the sob trying to rise up in my throat. "Mom didn't deserve that."

"No, she didn't, and neither did you or Taylor."

As her words bounce around inside my head, I stiffen. "You know, I never really thought about it like that. I just always thought about how it affected Mom, and I wasn't so worried about Taylor because I had no idea she knew. I wish I could have shielded her better. I hate that she knows. I hate that I couldn't protect Mom, too," I murmur around the lump in my throat.

Her gaze moves over my face and I can almost feel her looking into my soul, understanding why I don't have any framed pictures of Mom and me. I carry so much guilt that I'm not sure I deserve to be in the same frame as her.

"Babe, you weren't the adult. Parents protect kids. It's not the other way around, and you're Taylor's brother, not her parent, and you were young. There's only so much you can do, so much responsibility you can take on, Kalen. Don't beat yourself up about that." A long moment of silence and then she explains, "Kids should have their parents to turn to when they're going through something like that, and your dad failed you." We fall quiet and I stare out my window. She finally breaks the quiet. "I wonder if he didn't know how to help you guys."

"I mean, when Mom was sick, he still took us to our sports

and things like that," I tell her, remembering my conversation with Taylor.

"That's good. Maybe that's the only way he knew how to show you he was there for you when everyone was hurting."

"Yeah," is all I answer but then I snort as a wave of anger hits like a bucket of cold water. "He wasn't hurting, he was fucking his lover."

She winces and I get it, that was harsh. "Sometimes men hold things in emotionally. Is it possible he needed help and emotional support and...love, and that's why he and Miles started a relationship?"

"I don't know. Taylor said something similar to me."

She glances at the picture on my dresser. "There were good times though, right?"

"There were."

Lips pursed she says, "I'm surprised your father let you guys move to Darien."

I roll one shoulder, not at all surprised he let us go. "I guess he wanted us gone so he could be with his new partner after Mom died. You know, to start a new life."

She cocks her head to the side, a new kind of seriousness about her. "Have you asked him that?"

Her question takes me by surprise. "No, we don't talk." She nods, and I ask, "What?"

"I don't know, Kalen. I don't know why he let you guys go, but if times weren't all that bad growing up, maybe it was really hard for him to let you go, and maybe he did it, because it was what you needed at the time."

I let that sink in for a moment. As my anger begins to subside, I consider asking him. "You know Brady's wife Melanie is the therapist in the group, right?"

"I know that now," she jokes.

I give her a playful wink. "Now, apparently there are two therapists in our circle, always analyzing everything." I roll my eyes jokingly. "That's fun."

"I'm far from a therapist, but I do love self-help psychology books and I read a lot."

"My wicked smaht girlfriend."

She smiles at me, and I stare back, knowing she has more on her mind. I arch a brow and she begins, "I know you're trying to change the subject—"

I laugh. "Like I said, wicked smaht."

She crinkles up her nose. "I was just wondering if I could ask one more thing."

"Sure."

"With everything that happened with your dad, do you think that's why you have a hard time trusting people?"

My head rears back. "What makes you think I don't trust people?"

She taps her head. "Wicked smaht, remember?" Her smile falls. "Actually, it's pretty obvious that you have a hard time letting people in...here," she adds, patting her chest, slightly to the left.

She's so fucking right about that, and I damn well know it. I also know I'm so goddamn tired of being a chicken shit.

Footsteps sound in the hall, and I stand. "Looks like everyone is up. You'd better get dressed."

She nods and tugs on my big sweatshirt, then stands to pull on the sweats, and I shake my head as she begins to fold up the sleeves.

"What?" she asks.

"I kind of like you in my clothes. I mean I'd like you better out of them..." I step up to her, grab the drawstring on the pants and tie it tight for her. "But this is fucking sexy."

I push against her, and she laughs and shoves me away. Pointing down, she says, "You'd better get that under control before going for your run or you're going to hurt yourself."

"I'm already hurting, babe," I tell her, and she just shakes her head at me. But the truth is I am hurting in many ways, and if I continue to hold onto anger and fear, then I'm never going to have what I really want in life. Fuck, if I wasn't so scared, maybe there could be more between Sahara and me. Maybe this relationship wouldn't have to be just about sex. Then again, she keeps reminding me that it is.

Maybe I should convince her that we could be more.

But you'd have to stop being a chicken shit first, dude.

Yeah, there is that...

19

SAHARA

Jaw agape, I glance around the room full of women here for book club, all of them wives or girlfriends of the players and shake my head in disbelief. "You're kidding me?"

"Nope, not kidding," Brighton tells me and taps the book in her hand. "Brandon Cannon wrote this."

"Brandon Cannon, from the Seattle Shooters? Six-foot, two hundred pounds of muscle, and can plow down every man on the ice?"

"Don't let Ash hear you say that," Gina jokes. "But yeah, that's exactly who wrote this."

I close my e-reader, and Brighton hands me the print book to examine the cover, which is your typical man chest and quite yummy. Would Kalen have read this to me had he seen this cover? Yeah, he probably would have and that's quite adorable. I glance at the name again, incredulous. I clearly wouldn't have ever put it together, considering he uses a pen name, and I'm not sure I blame him. But then again, Kalen told me Tanner Bang's nickname is Mitts because he knits, having learned it when he went to college in Nova Scotia. It's incredibly funny to me how all these guys have secrets, and how everyone on the team, all these big, tough-as-nails hockey players accept everyone as they are, no judgement.

Damn, my parents and siblings could learn a thing or two about acceptance from the Boston Bucks and I know Kalen and I have a timeline but after Gina showed me some of the things Tanner knitted for the players and the WAG's I kind of want something for Christmas.

"Does Kalen know?" I ask and take my last sip of wine. I only opted for a small glass, as I'm driving back home tonight. Last night after his game, we stayed up way too late at my place and I think the man needs his rest tonight. As much as I want to crawl into his bed, my play starts up again this weekend and our schedule is pretty hectic. We both need a good night's sleep. Unfortunately, that means after Sunday night's Halloween party, he leaves for a few games, and our time together comes to an end.

"They all know," Maeve tells me.

I smile at her and have to say, I was nervous about walking into a room of women that I didn't really know. I had wished Taylor could have come—a wing woman is always nice, but she had school. Gina was the only one I sort of knew, and now, after tonight, I feel like I'm a part of this book club, like I actually belong. It's true I'm a book nerd, but tonight was more than books. It was about reading, yes, but about friendship, comradery, and...sex. Not in a strange way either, but these women, some who have kids, and some who are pregnant, are open and honest about their bodies and experiences with sex before children, during pregnancy and after children, something that had come up in the book and gave us talking points.

I love that about romance books. People think it's just about sex, and while I do appreciate the racy scenes, and some which I'd love to try out with Kalen, it's also about so much more and being able to get together with other women and be open and honest in our discussion is a true gift.

Ah, but have you been open and honest with these women?

I mean, yes, sure, to a certain extent. What they know about me is true, and do they really need to know what happened in the library all those years ago, or that I'm not really who I say I am? Well, I am who I say I am, I'm just keeping some things from the past in the past.

"Wait," Gina grabs my leg. "I didn't tell you." She circles her finger around the room. "We all have tickets for an upcoming. I'll send out a group message."

"Ohmigod, you're kidding me."

"Nope, we're all going," Josie tells me. "We can't wait."

"I probably could have gotten more tickets."

"Forget about that. We want to support you and Taylor."

A strange wave of emotions come over me, and tears prick my eyes. I must be about to start my period. I can't remember the last time I was this emotional.

"Now, I'm nervous."

Gina waves her hand. "Don't be. Kalen told Ash you were phenomenal."

Heat moves into my face. I don't know why I get such a thrill knowing that Kalen talks about me when I'm not around. It's ridiculous, but again, I love thinking and talking about him too. "I'm not certain I'd say phenomenal."

Gina gives me a wink. "Well, he would and we trust his judgement. It's so funny you guys met through Taylor."

"Yeah, funny," I agree, my stomach tightening, because while that is true that *Sahara* met him through Taylor, he knew *Darien* from a long time ago.

"You've only been in Boston a couple of months?" Maeve asks.

I nod. "Yes." Leaning forward, I grab a carrot, dip it into the dressing and toss it into my mouth, hoping, now that I'm chewing, they'll talk about something else.

"I suppose I should be getting home," Maeve says and her phone pings. She grins. Tanner's mom is visiting, hanging out, and it looks like she and the baby have gone to bed. She laughs. "I love the woman, but finding quiet time has been a bit hard."

"Something's hard," Amelia whispers, and we all laugh.

"Which is why I'm out of here," Maeve says.

"Do you need a lift?" I ask.

She offers me a grateful smile, and then warmth moves over her face when she tells me, "Thanks, but Tanner is coming to get me."

I can feel her love for her husband, it's all over her face and I'd be lying if I said I wasn't a teensy bit—or a lot—jealous. "If anyone needs a lift." I glance around the room and try to slay that little green monster inside me when they all decline.

We chat about what to read for next month, and I resist the urge to ask if I'm invited, but I can't come right out and say that I won't be with Kalen. They don't know this is just a hook-up with an expiry date and I'd rather they didn't.

After choosing a romance based on true events that happened in the Halifax Harbor, by a Nova Scotia author, we all help with cleanup, and Brighton's walks us to the door. Ash is the first there to pick up Gina. Apparently, his dad had taken Maria's boys, Lucas and Josh, to the shop to work on vehicles. From what I understand, Maria, who works for Gina and lives in the apartment above the Nook, have some sort of history back in California.

A cool breeze rushes in and Gina rushes out. The temperatures are still above freezing so I'm not worried about driving on slippery roads. I make my way to my car as everyone piles in with their boyfriends and husbands and a noise from behind me, footsteps to be precise, grabs my attention and I spin around. My hand goes to my chest when I see a shadow emerging from the darkness, and while I thought I was over the fright of the break-in, perhaps that's not entirely true.

"Hey, Sahara. It's me." Kalen comes from the shadows and I suck in a fast breath. "I'm sorry, babe." He pulls me to him and I practically melt into him.

"You scared me," I admit.

"Babe, I didn't mean to. I texted to let you know I was going catching a ride with Noah so I could ride home with you. He took Camry and Tate to a movie."

"I didn't check my phone."

He rubs my arms up and down, creating heat from friction. "That must mean you had a great time."

"I really did," I gush. "What a bunch of amazing women. So inclusive."

He laughs. "We're not in high school anymore." Something comes over him, something dark and sad.

"What...what do you mean by that?" I ask, not sure I want to hear the answer. Is he thinking about that nerd no one really talked to?

"I just mean high school kids are not always the nicest."

"You...you didn't have a hard time in high school." Shoot, I should have posed that as a question, not a statement. He arches a brow and I hurry on with, "I just mean, look at you." He chuckles.

"What's that supposed to mean?"

"I guess I always thought athletes had it easy, you know. Popular, given breaks by teachers, loved by all."

"Moving during high school is never easy, Sahara." He looks down the road, something haunting him as a car drives by and honks. He waves and continues with, "I think it might have been easier for me because I had hockey, and it's mostly true what you said about athletes. I'm sure it wasn't easy for others."

"No, you're right." I glance down at the pavement, as I revisit old hurts.

"Hey, are you okay?" He tips my chin up. "Did you have a hard time in high school?"

"No, I'm just tired." Half-truth, half-lie. Ugh.

"Okay, let's get you home."

I pull the keys from my bag and he takes them from me. I plant one hand on my hip. "What do you think you're doing?"

"Driving you home." He pauses, a wave of panic overcoming him before he winces. "Shit, I'm sorry. I just...ugh." He tugs on his hair. "Sometimes I can be a little overprotective. I shouldn't have just showed up. I should have asked. I know you're a grown woman who can take care of herself and—"

"Kalen," I say and put my hands on his cheeks. "I'd love for you to drive me home."

He blows out a breath and relaxes. "Okay, good."

I look up and down the dark road near the resort. "As long as I'm not keeping you from anything."

"The longer we stand here and debate this, the longer you're keeping me from stripping you off, tucking you in, and holding you next to me."

I laugh and he hits the fob, walking me to the passenger side. Once I'm in, he shuts the door and I can't seem to tear my gaze away as he circles the front of the car and climbs in.

As he buckles in, I mention, "That book we read, did you know that Brandon Cannon from the Shooters wrote that?"

"No freaking way. I mean I knew he wrote romance, I just didn't know he wrote the one you were reading." He glances at me. "You seem intrigued. Have you ever thought about writing a book or maybe a play?"

"I have." I nod, and stare straight ahead. "It's played out in the back of my mind and maybe someday when I find the time..." I turn in my seat and smile. "Do you have any secrets that I should know about? You're not a secret, spicy romance writer are you?"

"Secrets yes, but nothing as clandestine as that," he teases.

"So, you do have secrets, huh?" I joke.

He grins. "Nothing big. Nothing like being a writer." Under his breath he adds, "Or having a secret life and affair like my dad." He casts me a quick glance and there's a seriousness about him.

Punch. To. Gut.

But I was the one who opened the door to this conversation.

"Okay, fine," he admits, almost jokingly. "I might have some bigger secrets." I arch a brow waiting for him to elaborate, but he starts the car, stares straight ahead and says, "Someday I might tell you."

"Same," I whisper, knowing I can never ever tell him any of my secrets, as I wonder what his might be. Heck, he shared very personal, very painful things with me. I'm sad to think he has other things that hurt just as deeply. Unless, of course, he has happy secrets. That almost makes me snort because who the heck has happy secrets.

Right now, however, as his hand snakes across the seat and lands on my thigh, I let my worries fade. I just want to bask in his presence, and how he showed up for me.

"Kalen," I murmur.

"Yeah, babe?"

"That was really sweet of you to meet me and drive me home." A bevy of emotions well up inside me and I'm thankful for the dark car.

"Tell no one. You'd ruin my grumpy reputation."

I laugh. "No one thinks you're grumpy. At least, I don't think they do."

Just then my phone pings and I pull it from my bag and read a message from Taylor. I grin, but it's hidden in the dark, which is a good thing, because Kalen is watching me and I do not want to tell him that his sister just asked me to keep him occupied.

God, I really hope she knows what she's doing, because I sure as hell don't...

20

KALEN

"**Y**ou, my sweetness," I begin as I pull Sahara against me. "...look adorable, and when I get you home, I'm going to dip my chip into your salsa."

"Um, I know there's a sexual innuendo in there somewhere, but just no..." She laughs and tosses her head back, and dammit, I love putting a smile on this woman's beautiful face.

Leaning in and not giving a shit about any public displays of affection, I drop a soft kiss onto her red lips. Something about them tonight, perhaps it's the color, reminds me of the girl in the secret library closet. It's crazy that after all these years I still think about that girl. Sahara inches back and with the tip of her finger, wipes her lipstick from my lips. "Doesn't go with your big nacho chip."

She opens her arms and glances around at our friends, who are all dressed up as well. "I've dressed as a lot of things over the years, but never a jar of salsa."

"You're sexy as hell."

"No, I look like I'm in a potato sack. You're...you're..." Her gaze rakes up and down the length of me.

"I'm pulling off a nacho like a boss. Is that what you're trying to say?" I smooth my hand over the very uncomfortable triangle nacho I could barely fit into.

She chuckles. "Something like that."

"I guess the true test is when I hit the little boys' room." I give her another kiss. "Be right back."

"Good luck."

I head down the hall, and walk past some witch decoration that cackles and scares the shit out of me. I jump, hoping no one saw that and turn back to see Sahara making her way over to Taylor who's chatting with Brighton. I can't help but smile like a fool, because...well, because I'm happy and I haven't been happy in a long time. Even the thought of visiting my father and Miles for Thanksgiving doesn't quite sting so much.

What does sting is the thought that after tonight, my agreement with Sahara is over. But that's not what I want, and dammit, I'm going to talk to her about that. I can give her another expiry date if she wants one, if that's what she needs, but I hope to convince her that maybe we could give this a try for real.

Look at you, not *being a chicken shit.*

In the bathroom, I struggle to get my pants down and when I finally do, I figure I won't have to hit the gym tomorrow because getting my dick out was a real fucking workout. Once I finish, I wash up and make my way back to the living room, where the party is in full swing. This time, however, I'm ready for the cackling witch.

I give her a wide berth and search the room. I spot Theo dressed as superman, and being obnoxious, as usual. He's headed toward Gunther, who is dressed as Wonder Woman, which is hilarious and should win best prize. Gunther is quietly chatting with his childhood best friends Paisley—who is dressed as a witch. She's visited him in Boston numerous times, and while he claims there is nothing between them, from the intense conversation they seem to be having, I think there's a story there he's not telling. Not my business, though.

I search for Sahara. The second I see Roman standing close to her, too fucking close, and she's laughing at something he's saying, my body tightens. He adjusts the firefighter's helmet on his head, and I can't deny that he's pulling off that costume like firefighting was his calling—and he knows it. Fuck me.

I stalk across the room, and put my arm around Sahara in a real fucking possessive way and pull her to me. Roman grins at me, presenting those dimples that drive the women crazy. Yeah, he's a handsome mother fucker and I don't like that Sahara thinks so too. Jesus, I need to make this arrangement a little more permanent because after tonight, our deal is over and she's free to go out with any guy she wants.

"What's funny?" I ask, my voice coming out rough and deep.

Sahara's eyes narrow. "Are you okay?"

Roman laughs. "If you ask me, I think he's jealous." He points to his dimples. "It's these, Sahara. It's a curse."

"Well, while I think your dimples are cute, I like my men cheesy," she jokes, and runs her hands over the big triangle nacho chip covering my body.

Roman laughs and puts his hand over his heart. "Girl, that cut deep."

Sahara laughs at his antics and the blood running through my veins slows, calming me as she puts her hands on my cheeks, the warm look in her eyes doing crazy things to my heart.

"Look around, Roman. I'm sure there are plenty of women here who you can charm."

He smiles and glances around. "Where's Taylor?"

My jaw drops and I shake my head as he tortures me. "What the fuck, dude? Why do you get such joy in pissing me off?"

He holds his hands up and laughs. "You make it too easy, dude. Don't worry, I'm kidding. I know all your women are all off limits."

"Will you please stop fucking with me," I grumble.

"That's my job," Sahara whispers, her voice light and full of suggestion, and it pulls a big laugh from Roman.

"Whoa, I really like this one, Kalen. Don't fuck it up." He leans into me and adds, "I was just keeping her company while you were off in the little boys' room playing with your nacho."

"I wasn't playing with my...Jesus."

Roman leans back. "Dude, it looks like you need the jaws of life to get out of that thing. What were you thinking?"

"Roman, go somewhere else," I mutter and just shake my head. He laughs and saunters off. "He's not wrong about the jaws of life," I tell Sahara.

She doesn't laugh. Instead, she leans into me and says, "You were jealous."

Between gritted teeth I answer with, "So what if I was."

"Now I get it." There's a softness in her eyes, warmth mingling with amusement as her gaze moves over my face.

"What is it you get?" I ask, and put my hand around her back, needing her close, needing to show possession. I can't seem to help myself.

"You didn't introduce me at the Nook that day." She pokes my chest. "You were worried."

"I never know what's going to come out of that guy's mouth and I didn't want him saying something to upset or offend you."

"I appreciate that."

"...and yes, I was worried. Women flock to that guy. Have you seen those dimples?"

She burst out laughing. "Dimples are overrated." Brady comes into the room, and starts up a conversation with Tuck, who is dressed as a pharaoh, and I can't help but notice how Maria keeps glancing at Tuck. Sahara goes up on her toes and gives me a kiss, and I growl, wanting to deepen it, but now is not the time or place. "We should mingle," she whispers.

I take her hand before she can move away. Okay, here goes nothing, and everything. "First..."

"First what?"

"Listen, I know we said we'd have fun these last couple of weeks, but what if I said I'd like to extend it. You and me, exclusive, until..."

"Until we're not," she finishes, and a worried look moves over her face as she tugs on her bottom lip with her top teeth.

Fuck, she doesn't want that.

Heart thumping, I try to keep my voice even, like I'm okay with whatever she wants. "Maybe that was a dumb—"

"I like being with you too, Kalen. I'm just not...not looking for anything serious. I'm new in town, and work, and...and..."

"I never said anything about being serious, sweetness," I counter, a lightness to my tone that I don't feel. "I just thought we could hang out a little longer, maybe until Thanksgiving, but if you don't—"

"I do. A little while longer sounds about right."

I bite back a smile. "Come on. You've met all the women, now it's time to meet the guys. You already know Ash."

"And Roman," she teases.

"And Roman," I grunt out.

When we reach Tuck and Brady, I introduce Sahara and she holds her hand out. "Nice to meet you both in person." She falls into easy conversation with them when they turn the conversation to her and ask about her play. Elias joins in and tells the guys how great she was. Worry moves into her face, when Ash tells her how excited Gina and the other WAGs are to see her upcoming play. Is she nervous that they're all going to watch her?

I lean in and encourage her. "You're going to be great." She gives me an odd look. Did I read her wrong? Was that nervousness not about her upcoming performance? What else could it be?

She turns back to the guys, and focuses on Brady. "Brady you made a great save in the third period the other night."

"I couldn't do it without my team," he says and I grin, because I know he's been through some shit, carrying all the team's losses on his shoulders when our games are a team effort. Melanie really helped him see that. Maybe Sahara was right about a few things when it comes to my past hurts. Had my father been hurting as much as we were at the time and just reached out for love? It was a mistake, sure, but is it worth forgiving? And did he let us go to Darien because it was what was best for us, and not because he wanted to get rid of his kids to start a new life?

I stand back, my heart beating a little harder as past hurts don't sting quite as much as they used to. Sahara laughs at something Tanner says when he walks over and I stand back and smile, loving the way she so easily fits in with my friends.

Taylor comes over, dressed in her Wednesday costume. She spins in a circle so we can all admire her, and I'm just glad Roman isn't next to me, ogling her, just to piss me off. The guy is a real shit disturber, and maybe one of these days Elias and I might have to take him outside to teach him a lesson about fucking with me.

Actually, Elias is dressed as a sheriff, so maybe we could take him out and hog tie him. I chuckle at that thought as Elias swings his handcuffs around his fingers, his gaze moving to Taylor as she laughs, which is completely out of character for Wednesday.

"Okay, time for more drinks," Gina announces, and brings in a tray. "We have bloody Marys and witch's brew." I lift my beer. "I think I'll stick with this."

Next Maeve comes in with a tray. "We also have graveyard cupcakes, brain-shaped Jell-O molds, and mummy-wrapped hot dogs."

I snatch up a small hot dog and toss it into my mouth. "Delicious," I compliment when she waits for a response.

"Who wants eyeballs?" Melanie asks. I glance at the grapes on the end of the stick, which are decorated to look like veins popping out of eyeballs.

"Sure, why not." I snatch one up and toss it into my mouth. "Not bad."

Sahara grabs a bloody Mary, and the door chimes. "Oh, good she's here," Gina calls out an excited look on her face as she hands her tray to Ash, and heads to the door. I turn as she opens it and invites in a woman dressed in a fortune telling outfit. Is she one of the girlfriends? I don't recognize her.

Gina leads her into the living room. "This is Tamara, a real-life fortune teller. She's the best in the business."

"Yeah, it's a business," Roman yells.

"She's the real deal," Gina assures him.

He makes a fist and mumbles, "*fraud*," as he coughs into his hand.

Tamara grabs his hand, runs her thumb over his palm, and says, "You don't need to believe in me, dimples." Her smile widens when he gives her a charming grin. "But believe in this. You won't be the one to run, but she will."

He scratches his head, some of the humor leaving his face. "What's that supposed to mean?"

"Time will tell."

"Wait, are you saying a woman is going to run out on me?" He snorts out a laugh and so do the rest of us because we know he's always the first to leave.

"You'll see," she answers, leaving him hanging.

As Roman frowns, Gina leads Tamara to a big wing back chair. "Who's ready to find out what their futures hold?" she asks and while the men grumble and grouch that they don't believe in it, the women are chatting excitedly, anxious to find out. Well, every woman except Sahara, who's standing back, nibbling at her lip.

I step up to Sahara and put my hand on the small of her back. "You don't want to give it a try?"

"No, I don't really believe in fortune tellers, or psychics," she tells me.

"All the more fun to do it then."

"Are you doing it?"

I shrug. "Sure, why not. It could be fun."

Taylor is picked first, and she sits in the chair facing Tamara and holds out her hand like Tamara asks. Tamara runs her fingers along the lines of Taylor's hand and many different expressions move over her face, everything from worry to joy.

"Do you have any questions?" she asks Taylor.

"Well," she murmurs quietly.

Before she can answer, Tamara says, "Yes, he likes you too, but it's...complicated."

Who likes her too?

Taylor's eyes go big. "That was my question, how did you know?"

Who cares how she knows, what I want to know is who likes her too. "Do you know who the guy is?" I ask Sahara.

"Ah, I...she has a crush," she answers and my brows punch together. Sahara touches my arm gently. "She's a beautiful girl, and you need to stop being so overprotective," she tells me.

I grumble some more, and I know she's right. "As long as it's not Roman," I grunt out.

"Deep down, you know there's nothing wrong with Roman. He just hasn't found the right woman to settle down with, but when he does, it'll change him. Right now, he's having fun, and there's nothing wrong with that."

"You," Tamara announces, and everyone moves to the side as she points her finger at Sahara.

"What?" Sahara asks, her lashes fluttering rapidly. Tamara crooks her finger.

"You," she announces again.

Sahara takes a step back, but Taylor comes running over, loops her arm around Sahara's and tugs. "Come on. It's fun."

"I...I..."

Taylor doesn't give her a chance to back out. She drags her along and sits her in the chair. Tamara angles her head, her gaze carefully assessing Sahara, and then Tamara's gaze lifts and locks on me for a second. I almost stumble backwards, her gaze hitting like a gust of wind. I don't believe in any of this, but I have a strange feeling curling around me at the moment.

She turns her attention back to Sahara and takes her hand. She studies it deeply, and leans in, and says something to Sahara, her words for her and her alone.

She lets go of Sahara's hands and Sahara is pale as she turns.

"What did she say?" Taylor asks. Sahara's gaze cuts to mine, her eyes holding a measure of worry.

"She is a woman with many faces," Tamara answers with a smile. Oh, I get it, she knows Sahara is an actress, a great one at that. But why did that seem to upset her so much? Maybe she's worried about her new friends watching her. Or maybe it upsets her that her own family doesn't respect what she does.

If only they saw her, they'd see how incredible she was, and that her talent should be respected. Maybe there's something I can do about that...

It's been two weeks since the Halloween party. Two weeks since the fortune teller whispered in my ear that I was a woman of many faces. She whispered it at first, because she wanted me to understand exactly what she was telling me and believe me, her message was delivered, received and understood. Loud and clear.

How did she know?

How the ever-loving heck could Tamara know that I wasn't who I said I was, simply from looking at my palm? At that moment, all the blood in my face had drained straight to my toes and when I turned and saw the confused look on Kalen's face, I quickly suspected my time with him was going to be short-lived, even though he'd just asked me to extend our hook-up relationship. But then when Tamara yelled it out, and everyone naturally thought it was because I was an actress.

I wanted to run that night and never look back, but we'd just agreed on Thanksgiving, and the truth is, I want to be with him for more than just a couple of weeks, but I seriously blew that when I wasn't honest with him from the start. I never felt I could be honest, though. He never liked me back in high school.

I roll over in my bed, my heart heavy. My phone pings and I reach for it, half expecting it to be Kalen. He's headed home after three days away with the team, and even though we video messaged every night, I still miss him and that scares the hell out of me because I'm falling for a man I can never be with. I'm also falling for his friends. I love the players, and the WAGs. They've all taken me under their wings and they had so much fun the night they all came to see our performance. Afterward, we went out for drinks and laughed the night away.

What the heck have I gotten myself into?

I grab my phone and see a message from my brother Charlie; he's here for a lecture at Harvard and wants to meet for lunch. I message him back and tell him to meet me at the library. I don't want him at my apartment. He'd likely run home and tell Mom and Dad I don't live in the best part of Boston and they'll either insist I go home or move somewhere else. Sure, they'll be happy to foot the bill for a place, but I want to be out from under their thumb. If I took money, they'd feel like they could rule my life.

I am happy that he reached out to me, though, and there's a café not too far from the library, where we can grab lunch. I set my phone down and head to the shower. Once I wash the fog from my brain, I check my phone to see a message from Kalen, letting me know he'll be home later this morning and that he can't wait to see me. While I'm excited to see him too, I also have a huge knot in my gut. How much longer can we go on like this? Until Thanksgiving, apparently. Even then I don't want things to be over, and I'm getting the sense that Kalen would like to keep seeing me. Dammit. Dammit. Dammit.

I message back that I'm busy for the day and we agree to a quiet night in and some take-out food at my place. I've given him a key so he can come and go as needed, just like he's given me a key, which makes this relationship feel much more real, and meaningful.

But nothing is real, is it, Sahara...especially you.

I grab a slice of toast and head outside. The November wind is cool as I make my way to my car and drive to work. The morning flies by in a rush of activity, and when lunch rolls around, I step outside to find my brother coming my way.

"Hey, Charlie." I hold my arms out and he gives me a big hug. I snuggle into him, really happy that he's here. Even though we're not close, the truth is, I miss my siblings. I wish we were involved in each other's lives the way Taylor and Kalen are in each other's.

"Hey, Darien. How are you?"

I put my hands on my hips. "I told you. I go by Sahara now."

He rolls his eyes, which really bugs me. "Fine, Sahara." He glances around. "I'm starved, where do you want to eat?"

"There's a little café across the street."

"I passed by a place called The Nook. One of the students at the university recommended it." He checks his watch. "Do you have time?"

I bite my lip. I'd rather not go there. Running into one of the players is too risky and I'm trying to keep my private life private.

"We should just go across the street. I actually don't have a lot of time."

He angles his head. "You okay, sis?"

God, I hate that he can read me so well. "Yeah, just busy."

"Okay, we can go across the street."

My shoulders relax as we walk to the corner and cross, and I turn the conversation to him, and ask about his work, which he loves to talk about. The café is busy, but we manage to snag a seat by the window. After we order sandwiches and sodas, he leans back in his seat.

His gaze rakes over my face, and I shift, uncomfortable under his scrutiny. "You look so different."

I run my hand through my hair. "New hair, no glasses. Older." Definitely not wiser.

"No, it's not that. You just seem..." He crinkles up his nose like he can't quite put his finger on it. "... different."

Oh, that's probably because I'm having sex on a regular basis and while I'm terrified the bubble I'm living in is about to burst, this is the happiest I've been in a long time.

"I'm happy here in Boston," I tell him.

He arches a brow, satisfied with my answer. "You're coming home for Thanksgiving?"

"Mom asked me to."

"Victoria decided we'd host it this year."

They'd just bought a big new house with the twins coming. I have no doubt my brother and his wife Victoria want to show the place off, and I don't blame him. "Is Victoria up to hosting it?"

"It was her idea, and we'll all be there to help."

"Yeah, I'm coming home." While I know Mom will be trying to set me up, it's better than being here alone for the holidays...or maybe not.

Just then someone stops outside the window, blocking the lunchtime sun and when I lift my head and see Kalen standing there, I nearly swallow my tongue.

"Friend of yours?" Charlie asks.

"Ah, yeah, something like that." The server comes with our sandwiches, as Kalen moves from the window. Heat floods me, worry winging its way through my body. The front door opens and Kalen walks straight over to us, his eyes narrowed in on my brother, in a very possessive way. I shiver at the possessiveness, because I like when he's jealous. God, could I be any more messed up?

"Hey," he greets, and glances at me as he taps the table, like he's looking for something to do with his fingers other than dragging my brother out of his seat.

"Kalen—"

Before I can finish Charlie muses, "You look familiar. Did you go to—"

"He's a hockey player," I cut in quickly. "He plays for the Bucks."

"That's it." My brother snaps his fingers. "Kalen Coolidge. Nice to meet you, man." Charlie holds his hand out and Kalen shakes it. "I didn't know you when you lived—"

"Kalen, this is my brother, Charlie. He's a professor at Yale, and is here for a conference," I tell him quickly, and work not to sound as shaky as I feel. Omg, why are my worlds colliding? I didn't go to The Nook for this reason, and yet here we are.

"What are you doing here?" I ask.

He gestures with a nod to the street. "Just out with Elias. He was running errands, getting some Boston gifts to take home to family and friends for Thanksgiving. I tagged along, and then I just saw you in the window."

"Join us," my brother offers.

"Oh, I'm sure he's busy," I blurt out quickly and two sets of eyes narrow in on me.

Looking almost wounded, Kalen nods. "Yeah, I should get going. You two probably have a lot to catch up on."

My brother bites into his sandwich, but I've lost my appetite. He follows it with a drink and before Kalen can leave, he asks, "How do you know, Dar..." he clears his throat, when my eyes go big. "Sahara?" he finishes.

"She's in a play with my sister. She's the star. So much talent. I wouldn't be surprised if Hollywood came knocking." Heat flushes my cheeks as he winks at me.

"Right," Charlie says, the twist of his lips a good indication that he's humoring us both. Why the hell can't they respect what I want to do with my life? I bet my mother would love that I'm dating a hockey player. Okay, so we're not really dating, we're hooking up. But man, if we were dating, Mom would love it. She'd think I finally had some value.

My brother's gaze shoots back and forth between the two of us. "Wait, are you two…"

"Yeah, sort of," Kalen answer, and as my heart leaps—why would he say that—my brother's eyes light up.

"Wow, Dar…" he begins and once again stops himself. "Wow, Sahara, why didn't you tell me?"

I shrug. "I don't know. It's new." I steal a fast glance at Kalen.

Charlie grabs a napkin. "We were just talking about Thanksgiving. Why don't you join us this year, Kalen? My wife and I are hosting. I'm sure everyone would love to meet you."

"He's having Thanksgiving with his sister," I quickly point out.

Charlie wipes his mouth with a napkin and shrugs. "Bring her too. She's a friend of yours isn't she, *Sahara.*" He emphasizes my name, and I resist the urge to kick him under the table.

"Yeah, but—"

Kalen is astute enough to know I'm hedging, so he pipes in with. "My sister and I are actually headed to my father's place. Maybe another time."

"Oh, that's too bad. If you change your mind, this is my address." My brother pulls a card from his pocket and hands it over.

Kalen tucks it into his pocket. "Thanks."

Charlie pushes to his feet. "If you'll excuse me." He glances around for the washroom.

"Just down the hall to the left," I tell him.

He leaves and Kalen leans in. "I didn't know your brother was going to be in town."

"It was so last minute. I only knew this morning. Lecture at Harvard."

He arches a brow. "Impressive."

"I'm sure Mom and Dad think so too." God, could I sound more venomous, which isn't fair to my brother. I love him and he worked hard to get where he is today.

"What's with him anyway? Why was he saying your name like that and what was he talking about he didn't know me when I lived...Why would he know me when I lived in Darien or New York?"

My heart jumps into my throat. "He's a strange one," is all I can explain, and not wanting him to think I don't want to invite him to Thanksgiving, I add, "I only said you were busy with Taylor because I didn't think you would want to come to my very dysfunctional family's Thanksgiving." Knowing he can't make it because of his plans, I feel confident state, "I mean, I would have loved it if you and Taylor could both come." It's not a lie. I would have loved it, if I weren't pretending to be someone else.

"I always wanted a big Thanksgiving dinner." That look of longing once again crosses his face.

"It's not all it's cracked up to be, Kalen. Board games with bickering. Austin and Charlie are so competitive, and when it comes to politics, London and Aspen have strong opinions." I stop to shiver. Okay, maybe it's not all bad and maybe they wouldn't be so loud and competitive if I did bring a professional hockey player home. But I don't want them to respect me because of Kalen, I want them to respect me, because I have value too.

"Got it."

"Four of you are named after places," he simply points out.

"Charlie is short for Charleston." I snort out a laugh. "Mom and Dad liked to travel."

"That's funny. I once knew a girl named Darien, from Darien. Why would any parent do that?"

Wait, what? He *knew* me. He never knew me. That's not true.

But he just said he did?

What the heck?

He taps the tabletop again. "I'm going to go. Give you some time with your brother." He leans in and gives me a quick kiss. "Looking forward to seeing you tonight."

"Same," I respond and watch him walk away, my heart in my throat because this was a close call...too close. I can't have my worlds colliding like this. My brother comes back, and we finish eating. He walks me back to my building and after a hug goodbye, and a promise to be home for Thanksgiving, I head inside and go to the circulation desk to help with the growing checkout line.

I work quickly, with a smile on my face and when the next person steps up, a little girl beside her, my legs nearly go out from underneath me.

"Gina," I murmur, barely able to get her name out. I swallow. "What...what..."

"You work here?" she asks, a confused look on her face as she glances at the name plate on the counter. Sahara Lewis. "How come you never mentioned it? Come to think of it, neither did Kalen." There's simply curiosity in her eyes as she gazes at my name plate, but this is going to go south fast.

I turn to Jenny. "Can you cover me for a second?"

She nods and I step out from behind the desk. I say hello to Zoe, and not knowing where to begin, I drag them off to the children's section. "Can we talk?"

"Zoe, go play for a second."

Zoe nods and heads to the Lego table.

"What's going on?" Gina asks. "Are you okay? You look pale."

Oh God. I take a couple of deep breaths, as my world implodes. "Gina," I begin. "I...I'm..." She puts her hand on my arm, and gives it a supportive squeeze, and my heart races, my body and brain giving up the fight. I can't keep going on like this. "Kalen doesn't know I work here," I blurt out.

Her head rears back. "I don't understand." She glances around. "This is a secret?"

"It's not...okay, it is. I didn't tell him. It's...ugh. It's so complicated."

Her gaze narrows in on me, confusion brimming in her eyes. "Why would he care if you worked at a library?"

"It's long and complex."

"I'm not in a hurry." She turns to check on Zoe who is now searching for books.

"I...I know Kalen from high school."

Her jaw drops. "Omigod, I didn't know you two went way back."

My throat squeezes tight. "He doesn't know. He didn't know me back then." Okay, so he said he knew a girl named Darien Lewis, but that doesn't mean he knew *me*.

Gina shakes her head, and pulls her purse up higher on her shoulder. "I don't understand."

"I never told him I knew him. I thought it was just a quick hook-up, you know, but then I fell in love with him."

My God, I'm in love with Kalen Coolidge.

Her eyes soften. "I'm pretty sure he's in love with you too, Sahara. I'm so happy for you guys," she murmurs. But then worry comes over her. "Wait. Why would he care that you knew him back in high school? Why is that, and this job a secret?"

"Because if he knew, it'd be the end of us..." She bites her lip, her eyes widening with concern, because I think she's putting it all together. I know we're friends, but right now, her loyalties are with Kalen, a guy she's known and has cared about for a long time. "Are you going to tell him?"

She shakes her head, and glances down. "No, but I think you have to..."

22

KALEN

After our early afternoon practice, Elias and I head to my car and once again I notice he's quiet. I've been quiet myself lately too. It's strange. Ever since I ran into Sahara and her brother at that café, she's been going out of her way to avoid me. Not entirely. We still hang out when we can, but I can't help but feel something is off. That she's pulling away.

We need to talk. I'd damn well drive to her house today and do just that if she hadn't gone to her brother's place for Thanksgiving a few days early. But maybe I'm imagining it, because I also get the sense that Gina has been avoiding me, and that's just weird. Maybe everyone is just really busy.

"You okay, man?" Elias asks me.

"Yeah, just thinking about my drive to my father's place. It's been a while. I'm not sure how it's going to go over, you know?"

He nods and scrubs his face, like he's dealing with his own demons. "It's not easy going home."

"Nope." I start the car and back out of my spot. Traffic is heavy with everyone preparing for the holiday. "You need a lift to the airport?"

"No, I'll just Uber."

We drive in silence, both lost in our own thoughts and when we get home, we grab our bags and head inside. I plan to drop my bag and grab the one I'd already packed for our road trip to New York. A part of me can't believe I'm actually going, yet another part knows it's time.

Inside, Elias drops his bag and heads to the kitchen. I lift my head to find Taylor coming down the stairs in her yoga clothes, no luggage in her hand, and none at the doorway. She doesn't look like she's ready to hit the road anytime soon. "What's going on?"

She frowns, and my gut tightens. "Miles is sick. Dad doesn't think it's a good idea for us to come. He asked if we could reschedule for Christmas."

"Shit," I murmur, and while I'm not sure about that, the hope on Taylor's face has me nodding. "Yeah, sure. Is Miles okay?"

"Dad said he has the flu, and he doesn't want us to get sick."

"Okay."

Elias comes back into the hallway. "You're not going?" he asks.

"Doesn't look that way."

"Why don't you go to Sahara's for Thanksgiving?" Taylor suggests, taking a seat on the stairs. I'm about to protest, and she holds her hand up. "She told me her brother invited us both, but I think you should go alone. I don't want to be a third wheel." With her hands still up, she continues with, "I'm a big girl, brother. I can take care of myself."

"Actually..." We both turn to Elias. He steps closer to my sister and grips the handrail. "Now that you're not going to New York, maybe you could come with me to California. Be my pretend date so I can shut down my parents' attempts at marrying me off. It'll be a quick turnaround since we have a weekend game."

"Ah," Taylor begins, a twinkle in her eye. "Get the game going early." She grins, clearly liking the idea.

"That, and I don't want you alone during the holidays, T," he explains quietly and my heart pinches. I love how much he cares about Taylor and if she doesn't want to go with me, then I'm glad she'll be with my best friend.

Taylor turns to me. "What do you say, big brother? You go see Sahara, and I'll go practice my acting skills with Elias."

Would Sahara even want me there? She was quick to point out that I was having Thanksgiving with my family—she wants to see me mend things with my dad—but she did say she would have loved it if I went with her.

"I say yes," I finally tell her, and she jumps up.

"Okay, let me get packed." A worried look comes over her face. "Wait. Tomorrow is Thanksgiving. Is it too late to get a flight?"

"Go get ready," Elias says. "I'll make all the arrangements."

She hurries up the stairs, leaving Elias and I alone. "Thanks for this," I tell him.

He nods, and averts his gaze and I get it. He's worried about the charade. But knowing my sister, she'll pull this off.

"I guess I'm going to...shit, where am I going?" I laugh. I didn't even look at the card Charlie had given me. I have no idea where he lives. I assume it's near Yale, since that's where he works.

Elias laughs. "Safe travels, wherever it is you're going, buddy."

I hurry upstairs and open my nightstand. I threw the card in there a while ago. I pull it out and for a brief moment, I consider calling Sahara, but then decide against it, partly because I want to surprise her and partly because there's a chance she might balk at the idea, and I really fucking want to see her and meet her family.

I read the name: Charlie Lewis, and find his address. Maybe I'll drive by grandma's old house. But grandma's old house and the fact that Charlie's last name is Lewis has me thinking of Darien Lewis again. Why does she always pop into my mind? I guess maybe it's because I feel like we have some unfinished business.

With the card now tucked in my back pocket, I give my sister a hug, and thank Elias again before heading outside. Back in my car, I punch in the directions, and go through the drive thru to get a coffee and banana bread for the road.

Traffic is crazy and what should have been a three-hour drive turns into four, and it's already getting dark by the time I pull up outside Charlie's house. It's big and impressive and as I stare at it, taking in the expensive vehicles in the driveway, my heart hurts for Sahara. Why can't her family see just how talented and special she is? If only they saw her in action. Maybe I can convince them over Thanksgiving dinner.

I park my car, and leaving my bag in the back seat, I walk up to the house, glancing around the elite neighborhood. It's far different from where Sahara lives. At the door, I hear laughter and voices, and I ring the bell. A few minutes later, a pretty woman with long blonde hair, blue eyes, and a very pregnant belly stands before me. She stares at me for a second, like she's trying to figure out who I am, and I hold my hand out for a shake.

"Hi, I'm Kalen Coolidge. A friend of Sahara's. Charlie invited me to dinner when I met him in Boston."

Her eyes brighten. "Right, the hockey player." Her cheeks turn a bit pink. "Sorry I didn't recognize you. I don't follow the game."

"No worries."

Her brow's bunch. "I thought you couldn't make it."

"Change of plans."

"Come in. You're just in time for dinner, actually." She steps back and I walk into the warm house.

"I'm not interrupting anything, am I? Charlie invited me, but I don't want to put more work on anyone's shoulders."

She waves her hand as she closes the door behind me. "No problem at all. Any friend of Sahara's is a friend of ours."

I smile, really liking this woman.

"Oh, I'm sorry." She puts her hand on her chest. "I'm Victoria. Charlie's wife. Charlie is going to be thrilled that you came." A smile spreads across her face. "Sahara too, I'm sure." She angles her head, a look I don't quite understand, moving across her face. "Actually, everyone will be thrilled."

She guides me into the living room, and I take in the numerous heads lifting to see me. I scan the room until I find Sahara, who is looking at me like I might have a hockey stick growing out of my head. Shit, maybe I should have called, or maybe I shouldn't have come at all.

"Kalen..." She jumps to her feet, her jaw agape as she almost stumbles toward me. "What are you doing here?"

"Your brother invited me, remember?"

"Kalen, my man." Charlie steps up to me and puts his hand on my shoulder. "I'm so glad you could make it." He turns. "Everyone this is Kalen Coolidge, Sahara's...friend."

Oohs and awes come from the family as they check me out.

"Friend?" An elderly woman who looks very much like the matriarch of this family asks.

"Mom, Kalen and I are friends," Sahara explains quickly. "I thought you were going to see your father."

"Miles was sick, so we didn't go. Taylor went with Elias and I came here." I stare at her for a second, and my heart jumps into my throat. "Maybe I should go."

"No, it's just..." Her words fall off, as she grabs me and ushers me into the kitchen. "You surprised me is all."

I cock my head. "I take it, it's not a pleasant surprise." Jesus, she looks like she's going to be ill. "I thought...I guess I thought wrong." My stomach cramps as I look over my shoulder. I need to get the fuck out of here. What the hell was I thinking? She doesn't want more and me showing up here like this, has her acting like a skittish cat.

She bites her lip, worry radiating off her. "I'm sorry." I take a step back.

"It's not..." she begins and stops. "I...I need...we need to talk."

With my heart in my stomach, because I'm sure this talk is going to be the big turkey dump, I say, "Okay, let's talk." I glance at the kitchen table, and walk toward it, to pull a chair out. "Is here okay?"

"Darling, why didn't you tell me you were dating an NHL player?" her mother asks, stepping into the kitchen. Her gaze rakes the length of me, clearly sizing me up to see if I'm good enough for her daughter. Judging by the shine in her eyes, I'd say I was. "I'd invited Jeremiah to dinner."

"Mom, I've asked you a million times not to set me up. I can find my own date."

"Yes, I see that you can. Should I call Jeremiah?"

She nods. "Can we please have a minute."

"Darien, whatever it is you need to say to Kalen, can it not wait? We'd all like an introduction." She wags a finger. "And you have some explaining to do."

Darien?

I turn back to Sahara, and her face is ghostly white. She grips the island, holding onto it like it's her lifeline, like if she lets go, she'll fall to the floor.

"Mom," she whispers, her voice low and strained, as her eyes begin to water. "We need a minute."

"Always with the theatrics, Darien." Her mother flips her hair over her shoulder. "Make it quick, please." Pleasure glints in her eyes, and I fucking hate being worthy because I'm a professional hockey player. I'm a guy who comes from a dysfunctional, broken family. I bet if that's all I was, she'd be showing me the door. "We have so much to learn about your new friend."

She leaves the room and my pulse hammers in my throat as I watch Sahara bite her lip so hard, I'm sure it's going to bleed.

"She called you Darien?" She nods, and in that instant understanding hits like a hockey puck to the face. I eye her, my gaze zeroing in on her face as the pieces all fall into place. My stomach lurches and I stumble backward.

"Darien Lewis?"

I can't be right. This isn't happening.

Oh, but it is happening, dude.

"I...Kalen..."

"What the fuck?" I croak out, sinking into the chair. "You're fucking Darien Lewis. The girl I hooked up with in the library, years ago."

She gulps so loud that I can hear it across the room. "Kalen... you...you knew it was me?"

"Yes. I ran after you." She averts her gaze which makes me ask, "Did you know it was me?" I always assumed she did, but could never be sure.

"Yes," she squeaks out, putting that question to rest.

I swallow. "When you met me at the theater, you knew it was me, Kalen Coolidge, from the closet?"

A tear falls down her face as she begins to sob. "Yes."

"What the fuck, Sahara." I snort out a humorless laugh. "Or rather, Darien." I grip my hair and tug. "Jesus, that's what was going on at the café. Your brother was about to call you Darien a couple of times, and he...he must have known I was from Darien." More tears fall down her face as anger courses through my veins. "What was this all about?" I wave my hand back and forth between us. "Were you fucking with me? Was it revenge or something?" I rub my damp hands on my pants. "Jesus, your brother was in on it too, calling you Sahara."

"Sahara is my middle name," she murmurs. "I didn't want to be Darien from Darien. You said it yourself how crazy that was, and then...then...when I moved to Boston. I didn't want to be Darien the librarian."

"Holy fuck. You're a librarian? You're a fucking librarian." As more pieces fall into place, my mind races with questions. "That day...shit, that day I ran into you."

She nods. "Yes, I was working. I'm sorry, Kalen. I'm sorry I didn't tell you."

What the ever-loving fuck is going on here? "Why didn't you?"

"I just thought it was going to be a quick hook-up, and..." She grabs a tissue and wipes her eyes. "I was trying to discover who I was. I'd just gotten out from beneath my parents' thumb and I...you seemed to like the girl from the stage."

"All this time you were pretending to be something you weren't." My father's deceit flashes in my brain. Jesus, talk about history repeating itself.

"No...yes, I mean not really. I was trying to find myself." She lifts her head and her gaze meets mine. "You never liked that girl from high school. So, I became someone I thought you'd like."

"You never gave me a chance to get to know that girl from high school." My voice jumps an octave when I repeat, "You didn't give me a fucking chance." What the hell. How little does she think of me?

She stares at the floor. "Everyone has secrets, Kalen."

"This is a big fucking secret don't you think?"

Half lidded eyes lift and meet mine. "You said you had a big secret."

I scoff, and shake my head. "My big secret was that I'd fallen in love with you, that I wanted more for us."

She whimpers. "Kalen…"

"For the record, Sahara. After that night in the closet, I went to your house. I talked to one of your brothers and he told me you'd left for college."

Her eyes grow big. "You came looking for me?"

"Yeah, I did. I liked what we did in that closet. I liked the way you reacted to my touch and I liked being touched by you. I wanted to explore that. I wanted to get to know that girl, and figure out why that night felt pretty fucking magical." I take a step back. "All this time it was you. Keeping truths from me. Not trusting me enough, not having enough faith in me to believe I could like the quiet shy girl from high school. You think that little of me?"

"No…Kalen." She sniffs. "I was going to tell you. I wanted to. I…after talking to Gina—"

"Gina knows?" I burst out, my head spinning so fast I'm dizzy. "What the hell, Sahara." I groan. "I guess now I know why she's been avoiding me." How horrible for Gina that she was put into this position, holding this in. I can't imagine how awful this has been for her.

"She's been avoiding you?"

"I can't believe a friend has been dragged into your lies." I shake my head. "You're the one thing I hate in this life. A fraud. Pretending to be something you're not."

Her tears fall harder, and each drop rips my heart open a little bit more.

"I'm sorry," she sniffles.

"Yeah, me too. Happy fucking Thanksgiving, Darien." With that I walk out the door, get in my car, and get the fuck out of Dodge.

23

SAHARA

As I watch him walk out the door, I put my hand on my stomach, but nothing can stop it from churning. I shouldn't have waited to tell him. Finding out from someone else was the ultimate slap in the face. Heck, I should have been honest from the start. He's right about one thing. I showed him little respect, had no faith in him, simply assumed he wouldn't like me, when honestly, he never really knew me—and I never gave him that chance.

Back in high school, we ran in different circles, but when it comes right down to it, I didn't run in any circles. I kept to myself, never opening up to anyone, including Kalen. It's no wonder he never spared me a glance, and now, I don't blame him. I'm not a very good person.

As my family calls out to me after Kalen slams the front door, I hurry to the bathroom. I close the door and turn on the tap, hoping the sound will drown out my tears. Even if it does, there's nothing I can do to hide my red, puffy eyes. I have loss and hurt written all over my face.

I step from the bathroom to find Charlie waiting for me. His eyes hold a measure of worry, and it's awful to say, but I like that he's showing concern. I never really felt a part of this family.

"Hey, are you okay?"

"No," I cry out, and he pulls me into his arms.

"I'm sorry, little sis. I take it I shouldn't have invited him."

I mumbled that he shouldn't have against his shirt, getting it soaked with my tears. "I'm sorry," he murmurs. "Do you want me to go talk to him? Try to fix this?"

"No, it's over."

He smooths his hand down my hair, and I hear more footsteps coming into the hall. God, this is so damn embarrassing. Why did this have to happen here? My whole family watching my collapse wasn't on my bingo ticket today. I'm sure I'm going to hear: You never should have moved to Boston, or I told you so, or something to belittle my choices in life and that I should have followed the path they wanted for me.

"Honey, what happened?" Mom asks. I don't lift my face. I keep it buried in my brother's shirt.

"I think she needs a minute," he answers her says quietly, and I really appreciate his support.

A beat of silence and then, "Should I call Jeremiah back?"

Oh, my dear God!

I push back from my brother, and square my shoulders. "No, you should not call Jeremiah." I take a deep fueling breath.

"Mom," I begin, and Dad puts his arms around her as my brothers and sisters stand still, all eyes on me. "I know I've been the black sheep in the family." Mom opens her mouth, but I hold my hand up to stop her. "I know I've never been the daughter you wanted, never followed the path you had laid out for me, and I'm sorry for that. But I needed to find my own way in life. Heck, I needed to find out who I was."

"Come sit," Dad insists and I shake my head, needing to get this all out.

"I love what I do in Boston. I love my job as a librarian, and I love being on stage in the local theater. I never thought I could put myself out there like that but I did. I'm proud of myself for that." A deep breath and then, "I know you'll never be proud of that, but it wasn't easy for me to perform in front of an audience. I pushed myself, gave it my all, acting helped me discover another part of myself. I'll never be Meryl Streep, but I think I'm pretty good."

Mom and Dad nod and I glance around at my brothers and sisters, as I spill my heart out.

"Kalen is a good man. A great man." Tears start again. "I messed up, made mistakes. But they're my mistakes. I can't grow, can't discover who I am or what I want if I don't make mistakes." My words shake when I add, "I love him, and he had every right to walk out that door because I haven't been honest with him."

"Darian..." Mom whispers, a look of sadness overcoming her. "I'm so sorry."

I snort. "Are you? You were ready to call Jeremiah."

She glances down, a sheepish look coming over her. "Right. I shouldn't have said that."

"You shouldn't have invited him in the first place. You know I asked you not to set me up." She nods in agreement. "I realize I'm not what you want me to be. I just wish you could love and respect me for who I am."

"Who are you, Sahara?" Charlie asks and I smile at him, happy that he asked the question.

My mind walks me back to the night I encountered Kalen in the closet, and all the fun we had right up until he walked out the door tonight. My God, the things I did with that man. Not just in the bedroom but out of it too. I am a woman of many faces, but all of those faces belong to me. They are a part of me. Parts that came to life, because of Kalen. Darien is a part of me. Sahara is a part of me.

"I've finally figured it out," I respond.

"Darien...uh, I mean Sahara," Mom begins and I nearly collapse. She's refused to call me Sahara. This is the very first time, and it actually steals the breath from my lungs, because it means the beginning of something new, a new supportive path forward. One without Kalen, and that hurts my heart, but I think my family might just have my back. She takes my hands in hers. "I'm so sorry. I've only ever wanted what was best for you."

I believe that. Image is important to her, but deep down, I believe she cares about me, and wants me happy. "Thank you."

"I know I pushed you in a different direction." She frowns, and pats my hand. "Maybe mother doesn't always know best."

"Maybe not."

She pulls me into her arms. "I'm sorry, Sahara."

A small chuckle rumbles in my throat. "You can call me Darien."

She inches back, tears in her eyes. "I'll call you what you want me to call you."

I nod, my heart filling with warmth. "Thank you." Everyone shuffles, and the next thing I know we're having a big family hug, and everything about this fills some of the broken spaces in my heart.

"Why don't we all sit for dinner?" Mom suggests.

We part, and even though I don't have an appetite, I follow everyone into the kitchen. We all help get the dishes on the table, and even though everyone keeps glancing at me with real concern, the conversation soon turns to the arrival of the twins, and while my heart is crushed, I'm happy that they can talk about good things on the horizon.

Once dinner is over, we all clean up, and instead of playing games, I head to my bedroom. No one protests, knowing I need alone time to sort things through. In my room, I open my phone and find a bunch of messages from Gina.

Gina: Can you call me?

Gina: Are you okay?

Gina: Kalen called me.

· · ·

Gina: He's pretty messed up, Sahara.

I understand that. Everything I did messed him up and I'll never forgive myself because he's a good man who deserves better than me. I run my fingers over the phone and stare at the words through blurry eyes. What do I even say? That's when I realize I didn't just lose Kalen, I lost everyone, including Taylor. She's going to hate me, too. I finally text back.

Me: I'm sorry Gina. I messed up, and Kalen is better off without me in his life.

With that, I throw my phone on my bed, roll over and cry myself to sleep. I wake late, and smell the turkey cooking downstairs. It actually turns my stomach, and I half consider just driving back to Boston. I pick my phone up to see a text from Taylor, telling me she's with Elias in California, and things are going well. I guess she doesn't know what I did to her brother. If he's protecting her, then I'm going to protect her too.

Is Kalen alone?

Oh God, the thoughts of that gut me. All he ever wanted was a big Thanksgiving dinner. I've destroyed the man in more ways than one. I push the covers off and walk to the window. Wind blows leaves down the street as voices rise up from downstairs. My foot hits my still packed suitcase as I turn and I bend down to unzip it.

The second I see my running clothes, they fill me with joy and sadness. I brought the clothes thinking I might get a run in, to get in better shape for running with Kalen, but now that's not going to happen and of course that fills me with sadness.

As my heart sits heavy, I swipe at the tears that are falling again and pull out my clothes. Maybe a good hard run will help me figure out how I'm going to manage my life back in Boston—without Kalen and my new friends who've become my family.

I strip out of my pajamas and tug on my sweats and sweatshirt. It's chilly out, but once I start running, I'll warm up. Though, I'm not sure anything will ever warm this new cold inside my bones.

Downstairs, I walk into the kitchen, and a hush falls over Mom, Dad, Aspen and Victoria as they turn to me. Clearly, I'm the morning's topic of conversation. They glance at my clothes, and it actually puts a small smile on my face. I guess they too are learning this new version of me.

"I'm going for a run." Their eyes go big. "I run now," I explain.

Mom nods. "Coffee first?"

I nod, grateful for a cup. "Always."

She pours me a cup and I stand at the counter and sip it as they sit around the table. Mom keeps casting me quick glances, and her worry wraps around my heart and hugs tight. I finish the coffee and put the cup in the dishwasher.

"I'll be about an hour." They all nod, worry brimming in their eyes as I head outside. On the sidewalk, I begin a slow jog. I fill my lungs with cool air, and work to clear my head so I can figure out what's next. I turn a few corners, and when I spot a coffee shop up ahead, I slow, my heart aching as I remember my run with Kalen and meeting Gina at the Nook.

I slow in front of the coffee shop and pull the door open. I'm greeted with delicious scents and walk up to the counter and order banana bread. Banana bread. Everything that reminds me what I had and lost. Honestly, I'm just torturing myself, and maybe I deserve it.

"Hey," I hear from behind and spin to find Jeremiah standing there.

God, this isn't awkward at all.

"Jeremiah," I begin. "How are you?"

He smooths his hand over his hair, and I step to the side to pick up my order. "I'm good." He puts in his order and moves to the side with me.

"Ah, about dinner."

He laughs. "It's okay, Darien. Your mom has been trying to set us up for as long as I can remember."

Of course, he still calls me Darien. My mom still does and he knows me from high school, which makes me wonder...

"You wanted to come?"

"I like you, Darien. I've always liked you." My heart jumps. "I also understand, you like me as a friend. But hey, a guy could hope, right? Until I found out you had a boyfriend."

I nod. Had, being the key word here. "Jeremiah," I say, as my order comes up. I snatch it from the counter and stand waiting until his arrives. "You said you liked me." He nods. "What is it you like? What is it you know about me that you like?"

He furrows his brow, clearly thrown by my question, but as I wait, he shrugs and starts with, "Well, for one, you're super smart."

Kalen said I was *smaht*.

I raise my brow, waiting for more. He nods and continues with, "You're a booklover, and we have that in common."

Kalen knew I loved books. He loves books too. Heck, he even read to me.

Jeremiah grins as he takes in my attire. "You're a runner now."

Kalen and I ran together. "Yeah, I'm a runner now." I fall quiet, lost in thoughts and he speaks again.

"You're supportive." I lift my gaze to meet his. "You helped me with my algebra in high school."

I also helped Taylor run lines when she needed it and supported her when she talked about Elias.

His coffee order is called and he reaches for it. He points to a table and I follow him to it. We sit and he continues, "You also give great advice. Remember when Rachel dumped me, and you talked with me, helped me through it?"

I gave Kalen advice on his father, and I think it helped.

As I listen to Jeremiah, I have an epiphany, and I shoot up from my seat. I might not have told Kalen that I was that girl from the closet, but he did, in fact, see all my different faces —even the ones from high school. He did know that girl, and he liked all those parts of me. God, I need to fix this. I can't face a life in Boston without him in it.

So, what are you going to do about it, Sahara?

Honestly, I'm not that shy meek girl anymore. I fought to get out from under my parents' thumb, fought to find my own path in this world, fought to take library science at college, and fought to discover who I really am inside. I've always lived by the philosophy that anything worth having is worth fighting for. The truth is, I'm still me, but I've grown in so many ways, learned so much of myself since moving to Boston, since meeting Kalen. I've discovered who I am and what I want. What I want is Kalen.

The man is absolutely worth fighting for, but am I fighting a losing battle? As Jeremiah watches me, I grab my phone and text Gina.

Me: Is Kalen home?

Gina: Ash invited him over last night but he said no.

My heart squeezes tight. Kalen alone during the holidays is the last thing I want.

Gina: He said he wasn't going to be alone.

My heart races. What does that mean? Is he going to spend

the night with some bunny? Taylor and Elias are away. Oh God, that would definitely be the end of us.

Gina: Don't read too much into that.

Great, now she can read my mind.

Gina: I think you two need to talk.

Me: Do you even think he'll talk to me?

Gina: There's only one way to find out.

She's right, there is only one way to find out...

I thank Jeremiah, who is completely confused, and run all the way back home, a new kind of urgency about me. The second I walk in the door and see my mother, understanding falls over her face. "Go," she orders. "Go do what you need to do."

I kiss her cheek. "Thanks, Mom." I shower quickly, dress, and toss my bag over my shoulder. Downstairs, Mom has a big Thanksgiving dinner packed for two, and her support means the world to me. After a quick goodbye to my family, I hurry out the door and drive straight to Kalen's house. When I get there, I see his car is in the driveway.

I hurry to the door, and knock. For a second, I consider using my key but if he's in there hating me—and he's not alone—

I'm not about to enter, unwanted. All hope of making this right begin to fade as his door remains shut.

Not giving up, I bang again, and hit the doorbell a dozen times. I wait and wait and when no response comes, I think about texting him, but no, he's inside and is making it quite clear that he doesn't want to talk to me. My heart sinks into the pit of my stomach.

Oh God, if he won't talk to me, maybe there isn't any way to fix this...

24

KALEN

It was a long-ass drive back from Connecticut, my mind swirling with all the lies, fed to me by the finest actress I know. Jesus, how did I not see it coming? Oh, probably because she didn't give me any reason to think she was messing with me. But seriously, talk about past lessons learned doing nothing to give me a head's up. Honestly though, I've always had lessons learned in the back of my brain. It's why I haven't been able to commit. After my talk with Taylor, who reminded me I needed to let the past go before I could move forward, I began to do that, not completely, but little by little, which is why I grew closer to Sahara.

She was different, sweet, kind and so caring.

I bark out a laugh, because yeah that was all an act. Hollywood is definitely going to come calling.

Sahara Monroe is Darien Lewis, from the closet.

I shake my head, still unable to wrap my brain around that as I pull into my driveway and stare at my big, empty house. I don't actually want to go inside. I'll see Sahara everywhere, laughing with me, helping my sister with her lines, eating at the kitchen table…making love in my bed.

Correction: having sex in my bed.

None of this was real, and that's the hardest part to accept.

I tap my fingers on my steering wheel, as my phone rings. I reach for it and slide my finger across the screen. "Hey," I greet my buddy, Ash. Fuck, I can't believe Gina knew about this. Why didn't she tell me? I'm not mad at her, but it's not fair that she had to keep a secret.

"How's it going?"

Did Sahara call Gina? How much does my buddy know?

"I'm home," I exhale, exhaustion getting the better of me.

"Yeah, I just saw you drive by my place," he says quietly, and that one word says it all. He knows who Sahara is, and he knows that I know. "Why don't you come over?"

"It's late."

"It's not that late. Come have a beer and crash here."

I stare at the big oak tree on my lawn, the branches moving in the breeze. "I loved her, man."

Ash takes a big breath, and in a low voice whispers, "I know. I'm sorry, Kalen. You shouldn't be alone right now. I'm going to come get you, okay?"

As I stare at the house, big and empty, and consider his offer. But then another idea hits, and I know in a heartbeat what I have to do. "No, it's okay."

"At least come for dinner."

"I'm good. Don't worry, I'm not going to be alone."

"You sure, buddy?"

"Never more sure about anything."

"Okay, we're here for you if you need anything."

"I know." With that we end the call, and I hop from my car. With exhaustion pulling at me, and not wanting to fight traffic or parking, I call an Uber. Forty-five minutes later, thanks to favorable traffic, I make my way through airport security. Thank God, I forgot to cancel our flights.

A few hours later, I step off the plane in New York, and since I only have one carry-on bag with me, I head straight outside and call for a car. I give him the address and an hour later, nighttime blanketing the city, I stand on the stoop and knock on the door.

I glance around. Maybe they're asleep. Shit, I should have gotten a hotel for the night, and come back in the morning. It is getting late.

I'm about to call an Uber, only to turn back to the door when it inches open. "Who is it?"

His voice falls over me, and in that instant, I honest to God don't know whether the sound of it adds to the hurt or begins the healing process. All I know is a bevy of emotions race through me and throw me off balance.

"Dad, it's me."

The door swings open and my father's jaw is practically on the ground as he flicks on the porch light and gazes at me like he might be dreaming, or I'm some kind of unexplained apparition.

"Kalen..."

"Can I come in?"

"Yes, of course. What are you doing here? Miles is sick and I didn't want you or Taylor to catch anything. I thought we'd rescheduled. Not that I'm not happy to see you. I am."

I step inside his place, and the lights are dim. I hear an old hockey game playing in the background. "Is this a bad time?"

He gives a fast shake of his head. "No, I was..." An almost embarrassed look comes over his face "I was just rewatching an old game."

As I listen to the play, it becomes evident it's one of our old games against Chicago. I scored a hat trick in that one.

"You watch my games?" Equal measures of sadness and warmth swirl around my stomach, yet I still hold onto anger. Anger that is weighing me down and that's why I'm here. I have plenty of friends to talk to, but I think I'm here because what I need can only come from my father.

"I do," he answers quietly. "Come in." He guides me into the living room and turns the TV down. "Have a seat. Can I get you a drink?"

"No, I'm okay."

He sits across from me, and while he seems genuinely happy to see me, he's confused as well. Why wouldn't he be? I haven't talked to him in years.

"Kalen, why are you really here? Are you okay?"

I lean forward, plant my elbows on my knees and press my fists against my eyes. "I don't think I am."

"What can I do?" he asks, his tone worried, cautious.

Is he afraid I'm here to hurt him, to yell at him for what happened all those years ago...for needing someone during the most difficult time of his life...

"Why did you let us go live with Grandma?" It was a question I always thought I knew the answer to, until Sahara.

Sahara....

Goddammit, I reacted, walked out on her because I'm still holding onto anger, unable to completely forgive.

You need to let the past go before you can move forward.

Maybe if I had done that, moved past the pain of my father's infidelity and lies, I would have reacted differently with the woman I love, instead of saying some pretty shitty things to her.

Fuck me.

There's a long beat of silence, and when I lift my head to look at him, he begins in a shaky voice, "Because I love you and Taylor, you both mean the world to me and I wanted to do what was best for you both." As I continue to stare, he nods and expands with, "I thought you needed distance from me, to find yourselves and reach your goals. You couldn't do that with all the anger you were holding. Anger I put there. I understand that." He rubs his hands on his pants, much like I do when I'm stressed, and glances down like he can no longer look at me. "I'm so sorry, Kalen. I'm so sorry for everything."

The sadness radiating from every pore in his body pierces my heart, and my eyes grow wet as I take in the dark circles beneath. He's been hurting. My heart squeezes tight, and I pinch the bridge of my nose to fight back a sob. Fuck, we've all been hurting—we've all lost loved ones because of the hurt —and goddammit, it's gone on long enough.

Forgiveness is hard.

Yeah, it's hard, but I can do hard.

"Hurting you and your sister, I'll never forgive myself. It was the last thing I ever wanted to do. I only ever wanted what was best for you both. I knew you couldn't stand to look at me. I couldn't stand to look at myself. I was afraid and what I did was wrong, son. I know that, and I own that mistake and regret it every day." He chokes on his words as a sob catches in his throat. "I loved your mother. I wish I could have taken her cancer away. I wish it was me, and not her, and—"

"Dad," I begin to stop him, his fear and hurt and sadness pushing back the last of the pain inside me, making room for love and...forgiveness. "You looked out for us. You did. You tried to do your best in a difficult time, but what I didn't understand for a very long time was how much you were hurting too, how you had no one helping you." My heart pounds fast in my chest, as I make a fist and hold it to my chest. "No one was taking care of you, Dad. I didn't understand that then."

Who's taking care of you, Kalen?

As Sahara's words bounce around inside my brain, my stomach clenches. Jesus, she was the one taking care of me, and look how I treated her.

Dad is about to speak, to no doubt keep blaming himself, but I speak first. "You needed Miles," I decide. "You were broken, too."

His shoulders sag, and his head falls forward. "I was broken, son. That's no excuse. I shouldn't have...not during..."

"I know, I get it, but I no longer think it was a matter of shouldn't. You had three people to take care of. I think it was a matter of need, the only way you could physically and mentally get yourself through a horrible time."

"Son..." He gives me a shaky smile as the mood in the room shifts, the darkness lifting.

I shift forward. "I'm sorry I didn't know how to take care of you."

He gives a hard shake of his head. "That's not the way it's supposed to be."

"I know, but it's who I am."

He nods and lets me own it. "I guess we all have to take care of each other, son."

Silence falls over us for a long time, and we let it as we sort through our thoughts. I finally break the quiet. "There's a girl..." I lift my head to see worried eyes. "The whole time we were together, she was pretending to be something she wasn't." He nods, understanding the question, even though I didn't pose it as one.

"Sometimes we hide who we are, Kalen. It's true. I did it. But we do it, not to be mean or spiteful, but to protect ourselves and the ones we love, for fear they won't like who we really are inside. We present a different version of ourselves."

"She said I never paid the quiet, shy book nerd any attention in high school."

"Is that true?"

"It is. We ran in different circles. It's not that I didn't like that version—I didn't know that version—it was because I was busy with hockey, and had a girlfriend, and then there was a closet incident..." I steal a glance at Dad, but there's no judgement on his face, just quiet understanding. "I thought she was my girlfriend when I went into the closet, and when my real girlfriend found us, Sahara ran away. It was only recently she found out that I knew it was her."

"Ah, I see."

"I went looking for her back then."

He angles his head and states, "You liked what happened in the closet."

"Yeah, I did. She's a friend of Taylor's and we met one night at a play. She thought I liked the character she was playing, so she pretended to be her."

"Because you wouldn't like that girl from the closet?"

"Right."

He rocks back in his chair and it squeaks. "All this time you were with her, is that the only version she showed you?"

I consider it a moment. "I...I don't know. I mean, she was fun, exciting, bold, like her character, but there were times she was deep, caring and understanding. She was the one who encouraged me to talk to you, and talked about forgiveness."

"Sounds like she really cares about you."

"She cares about Taylor too. She's been a good friend to her." A beat and then, "When she moved to Boston, she said she wanted to find herself. She said she didn't know who she truly was."

"Sounds like she had some work to do on herself."

"I just...don't think she had to hide it from me."

Dad leans forward. "Son, she was protecting herself, and in a way protecting you, by trying to hide the girl you didn't like, or rather the girl she thought you didn't like." He gives a humorless laugh. "Trust me, I know what I'm talking about."

"Yeah…"

Wise eyes latch on mine. "If you ask me, everything she presented to you might have been a part of who she really was."

"Yeah…" I murmur as I consider all the time we spent together, and apart.

"Do you think she's found herself, Kalen?"

I can't deny that I watched a woman blossom before my eyes. She might have done things that were out of character or out of her comfort zone, but in my heart, I know there was truth and honesty in everything that transpired between us. "I do."

"And what about you? What did you find?"

My pulse jumps in my throat and with zero hesitation I answer with, "I found a multifaceted woman that I'm in love with."

His lips thin as he nods. "If she found herself, maybe you should go find her too."

I swallow hard. "I said some things…"

"Forgiveness is hard, but it's in all of us. Look at us. Forgiving each other, and ourselves."

I jump to my feet, grab my phone and call my sister. She's breathless when she answers on the third ring, and normally I'd ask what she was up to, but the panic inside me has me blurting out, "I need your help."

25

SAHARA

I spent the better part of the week moping and hating myself. I checked my phone numerous times, waiting for something, anything from Kalen, but no. He's angry and he has every right to be. I made a grave mistake in not being forthright with him, but I never ever meant to hurt him. I didn't think this hook-up would last...didn't think we'd fall in love.

A sob catches in my throat and I choke it back. I'm at work and the last thing I need is to break down in tears, especially when I have to go on stage tonight. How I'm going to pull off a performance is beyond me. All I want to do is curl up in a corner and cry.

My phone pings and I snatch it from the desk drawer, my heart in my throat. I calm a bit when I see that it's from Taylor. I haven't seen her since she went off with Elias for Thanksgiving, and I really hope things went well for her. She hasn't stopped messaging me, which means our friendship is intact, for the time being.

I can only assume that Kalen kept all this deceit from her, wanting to protect her that way he always does. His biggest concern was that a relationship between the two of us might negatively affect my relationship with his sister. It will now, and I'm heartbroken over that.

I haven't heard from Gina or any of the other girls. Book club is next week and there's no way I'm just going to show up. I've been ousted from that group, I'm sure. They're tight and acting like a herd of elephants that surrounds one of their wounded members. Kalen is so lucky to have them all. Does he even realize he's always had a big family of his own?

I guess the one good thing that came from all this was me telling my family how I really felt, opening up to them and sharing my hurts. Everyone comforted and supported me, and while they spoke the words, their actions haven't changed. They're still busy living their own lives, taking very little interest in what I'm doing here in Boston. Did I really expect one heart-to-heart would change everything? At least Mom is going to stop trying to set me up. Come Christmas, there won't be an eligible bachelor around the table and for that I'm grateful.

Missing Kalen, and missing my family—maybe I should move out of Boston—I swipe at a wayward tear when a customer comes to the counter. Tucking my phone away, I'll message Taylor later even though I'm not sure what to say, I check out the man's books and busy myself in my work. Soon enough, it's quitting time and I have only one hour to make it home, grab something to eat and head to the theater.

My heart is heavy as I head outside, to jump in my car. As I drive, I notice that the nights are growing longer and longer, and by the time I pull into my driveway, I can't keep the tears from falling. Everything about my little place reminds me of

Kalen, of what we had and I'd lost. I don't even like sleeping in my bed anymore. Would it be cowardly of me to pack up and move home, or would it just be self-preservation? I fought so hard to leave Darien, to pave my own way in life with what little money I saved and currently make. Would it be like going backward with my tail between my legs?

I might have been a quiet book nerd growing up, but I fought hard to get where I am now. I fought for Kalen too. Heck, I pulled up my big girl panties after he said some horrible things and went straight to his house—only for him not to answer the door.

But did you fight hard enough, Sahara?

That thought takes the breath from my lungs. My God, did I fight hard enough? Was one trip to Kalen's house to convince him to forgive me, to maybe see things through my eyes, and run off into the future with me, enough? Maybe not, considering how long he's been angry with his father. But forgiveness is hard. I do understand that.

Gathering myself up, I head inside, take a fast shower, and gulp down some leftovers. Nothing as delicious as Kalen's spaghetti, but I'm not tasting much these days anyway. Once my belly is full, I get back in my car and drive to the theater. Maybe tonight, getting into a different character, will help me forget about who I really am, and how I messed everything up.

The warmth of the small dressing room hits, but does little to warm the chill in me as I step inside, and see the cast all chatting and running lines. Taylor hurries over to me and throws her arms around me.

I put on a big smile. "I hope you're this happy because of Thanksgiving," I say.

She bites her lip and glances around. "Elias' parents are something else, but I think we pulled it off."

"Did you pull anything else off?" I tease.

Her eyes go wide, a playful look on her face. "Sahara. What exactly are you asking me?"

I laugh. "It's not my business, but I love seeing you happy."

She cringes. "It's so complicated, though. Nothing can come of us." She blows out a breath. "Big brother."

"I get it."

"Yeah, I know. You've seen how protective he is of those he loves. I think it's killing him that Elias is going to move out. He wants to keep us all in bubble wrap."

Not me, though. He's having no trouble poking each individual bubble and popping the wrap he once had around me.

"Anyway," she continues. "Full house out there tonight."

"Oh, really?" Why would they all be here so early? I make a move toward the door leading to the stage to peek, but she grabs my arm to stop me.

"Oh, no one is there yet. I just mean I heard it's a sold-out show. Can you help me with this zipper? It keeps getting stuck." She turns around and lifts her hair to give me access.

"No problem." I grab the zipper and easily pull it up. "It doesn't seem to be stuck at all."

"Oh, jeez, maybe I'm just not as flexible as I used to be." I'm about to say something, but she averts my gaze and points to a man I've never seen before. "Did you see the new prop guy? Gary's wife had her baby and he's the replacement. Not bad to look at, huh?"

Okay, that is strange. If she thinks I'm with her brother, why would she be pointing out other men. Oh, God. My pulse jumps. She must know. She must know what happened and is trying to keep things between us normal, which of course is never going to happen, judging by the cagey way she's acting, and maybe wanting me to hook up with someone else to get me out of her life.

My heart tumbles as the gravity of this situation hits harder than Kalen's parting words. Our relationship isn't going to make it. A fresh wave of tears is about to fall, but I pinch them back when the director comes into the room and claps her hands.

We all stop what we're doing and get instructions from the director. Then a flurry of activity begins as we all get our makeup done, get into our costumes, and go over last-minute things. Soon enough, voices and shuffles can be heard on the other side of the curtain, and I force all my concentration into the play and the happily ever after that happens before the curtain falls.

Do not cry, girl.

I suck in a tight breath, and note the way Taylor is watching me. Yeah, I get it. She knows everything and is just trying to make the best of this play like I am. Moving off to a corner to be alone, I focus in on my script, pretending to rehearse even though I know every word by heart. I push the real world away, and fall into make believe, needing, somehow, to believe there really is happily ever after out there somewhere.

Once again, the director claps her hands and we all gather. Noah, the man who plays the professor I fall for, and I, take to the stage, and the second the curtain opens, I fall into character. For the next couple of hours, we all give a mesmerizing performance and before I know it, we're all back on stage, holding hands and taking a bow to the thunderous applause.

I stare into the audience, not seeing anyone or anything at all, really. How could I? The stage lights are blinding. It doesn't matter anyway. There is no one out there for me.

The curtain closes again and we all turn to each other, hugging before we make our way off the stage. Backstage, I go straight for my things, wanting to go home and go straight to bed, even though it's going to be cold and empty.

I go to the change room and get into my street clothes. The others are making plans for a drink, and I'll be invited. I'll just make an excuse. I wipe off my makeup and by the time I'm done, everyone is headed out the door. Not one person asked me to go, or bothered to look back. Okay, great. Did Taylor tell them what I'd done to her brother and now everyone hates me? God, no, she'd never do something like that.

I'm about to head out myself, when my name is called. I spin to see Taylor standing there, also in her street clothes. "What's up?" I ask, and I don't think I've ever seen her so antsy before, even though I sense she's trying to showcase casual. She's a great actress, but tonight, she's not pulling off calm, because what I did has really affected her.

She jerks her thumb over her shoulder. "Can you come back on stage with me? I messed up one of my lines and if you wouldn't mind, I'd like to be in my exact position on stage and run it again, with your help."

"Uh, sure." I wrack my brain. I don't remember her flubbing any line. But I'm happy that she's asking me for my help. Is it possible that I read her all wrong and we *can* have a relationship? Still, why would everyone leave without even asking me to join them?

Certain that the guests would have left the theater by now, and the curtain would still be closed I agree, "Sure." We head to the stage and she turns to face me. As she wrings her hands together, an uneasy feeling races through my blood. "Taylor?"

"My brother," she begins, in a low voice and my blood drains to my feet.

"Taylor—"

She holds her hands up to stop me. "I love him, but he can be dense at times."

"What?"

What is she talking about?

"He had some things to work through, but I think you know that already."

I nod. "I wasn't completely honest, Taylor. With him or you."

She shrugs, her eyes full of understanding. "We all make mistakes. I think you two should talk."

I swallow, remembering that Kalen told me she had a lot of forgiveness in her. "I tried. I went to your house. He wouldn't talk to me."

Her eyes go wide like that bit of information surprises her. "I actually think he's worried you won't talk to him."

"Why...would he be worried about that?"

She winces. "He said some things..."

"Yeah, he did." My heart sits heavy as I stare at the floor. "He was upset and had every right to be. I wasn't who I said I was."

"Yes, you were. You were always who you said you were. Your only mistake was not telling him you were Darien. But like I said, Sahara, we all make mistakes, and my brother needed to put some things in place to show you what forgiveness looks like." She gives me a wink. "Actions...far more convincing than words..."

I frown, having no idea what she's talking about. "What are you..."

My words fall off as the curtain opens and now, with the lights on in the theater, and not blaring on the stage, I can see everyone in their seats. I gasp and clasp my chest as tears fill my eyes.

"What...what?" I glance at Taylor as she inches away. I look back out over the audience, identifying them all.

My family.

The hockey players.

The WAGs.

Two men I don't recognize, but one who looks an awful lot like Kalen.

I catch movement near the side emergency exit door and turn to see Taylor opening it. I nearly fall to my knees when a very familiar figure walks through it. Tears fall as a sob catches in my throat.

"Kalen..." is all I can manage to get out.

He rubs his eyes, which are dark and puffy, full of worry and pain. "Sahara." He holds his hand out to me, like he's terrified I won't take it, but I do.

I look at the audience again. "What is happening? Why...why? How?"

His chuckle is soft, yet full of nervousness. "The how part was tricky, especially with everyone's schedules. The why part is easy. We are all here because you're important to us. I wanted to show you that. We're all proud of you and your accomplishments. Tonight's performance was off the charts, and your family is brimming with pride out there. Just look at them."

I turn to see them all smiling at me, and for the first time in my life, I actually feel 'seen' by them. Valued. Respected.

My God, he really did all this for me? My heart wobbles, the love I feel for this man exploding inside me.

"Sometimes people make mistakes, they do things because they think it's what's best for you. Sometimes it's to protect you." He turns and makes eye contact with his father. "I understand that and asked for all these people to come here tonight so they could see what I see."

"What...what do you see?" I ask, almost afraid of the answer after the way he walked out on me.

His smile is warm, and soft. "I see a woman who is talented, kind, and giving. I see a woman with strength, who always fought for what she wanted. I see a woman who is indepen-dent, and adventurous. I see a woman with many faces, and I love every single one of them." Before I say anything, not that I think I can get any words out past the lump in my throat, he takes my other hand. "I didn't know until tonight that you came to my place, to fight for me." I swallow and tears spill. The warm tender look he gives me, wraps around my heart and pieces it back together. "No more secrets, okay?"

I nod. "I'm sorry, Kalen."

"I'm the one who's sorry. I shouldn't have reacted—"

I touch his lips to stop him. "I understand why you did, and I forgive you."

He smiles. "I don't deserve you, but it's not going to stop me from doing this." He drops to his knees and pulls out a box. I gasp and catch Taylor hugging herself in the corner, a big smile on her face.

"Darien Lewis Sahara Monroe, will you make me the happiest man in the world and be my wife."

The audience falls quiet. "I can't..." I begin and Taylor gasps. Kalen falters on his knees, a gurgling sound in his throat. "I can't be Darien Lewis Sahara Monroe," I say quickly, and he briefly closes his eyes.

"Jesus, girl," he whispers.

"If it's okay with you, I'd simply like to be Sahara Coolidge."

A big smile spreads across his face and wraps around my heart. "It's all I've ever wanted," he says and takes my hand, to put the ring on my finger. He rises to his full height, pulls me into his arms and the audience gives us a standing ovation as he kisses me and spins me around. "I love you, Sahara. No matter what name you want to go by."

"I love you too, but how about tonight, you call me Monroe," I playfully tease. He arches a brow, and I run my finger down his shirt. "And I'll call you Mr. President."

EPILOGUE

Kalen

As I drive across town, I glance at Sahara, my stomach in turmoil in the best possible way. I haven't asked her to move in with me, even though it's everything I've ever wanted, because I needed to do some renovations first. I hate her living where she is, but when I explained that carpenters were coming and going because I was making a small dance studio/theater for Taylor, she totally understood. I've mostly been sleeping at her place, but tonight, with the construction finally completed, I'm going to ask her to move in.

It's Christmas Eve and tomorrow our families will be coming for a big Christmas dinner, something I want to do annually. When I say families, I mean everyone: her parents, all her brothers and sisters, my dad and Miles, and of course my sister. Even though Elias is in the process of moving into his own place, a slow progression with us in the middle of our NHL season, I'm happy my hockey brother will be having dinner with us tomorrow.

Honestly, he never talked much about what happened at Thanksgiving, other than having Taylor on his arm really helped keep his meddling mother off his back. Taylor didn't say too much either, which is odd for her, but she's had her head down studying and I'm proud of her.

It's funny really because Sahara's family had been trying to marry her off to a man of their choice. Elias' family is doing the same, but Sahara and I found each other, and now she's my fiancée. Hopefully my buddy, my brother in every way but blood, will find his own fiancée too, without family interference.

Fiancée.

Will I ever get used to that? I hope not, because as soon as the season is over, we're getting married. I want to call this incredible woman my wife. Tonight, Taylor is helping Elias with a few things—she's been mostly staying there with the construction going on, which means Sahara and I have the place to ourselves.

I reach across and take her gloved hand in mine. She gives me a smile so full of happiness and joy it fills my heart with all the love I have for her.

"Looking forward to tomorrow?" I ask.

She laughs. "Did you forget what I said about big family dinners, Kalen? Chaos. Total and utter chaos." I laugh, and I don't care. I can't wait. Although the last time I visited her brother's house for a big dinner, surprising her, that didn't turn out so well. This time, however, no surprises, other than the one I have waiting for her, and I'm pretty sure this is a good one.

"I'm making a special dish," I tell her, and she arches a brow.

"Oh? Do tell?"

I whistle innocently and she whacks me. "Tell me."

I laugh. "Let's just say it has something to do with noodles and cheese."

"You're making mac and cheese." I grin, giving her a minute to catch up and her eyes go wide. "You're kidding?"

"Not kidding. I had a truck load of Beecher's cheese delivered."

"Kalen no way."

"Merry Christmas babe."

"That's the best gift ever."

We reach my driveway, which is a bit slick, and I ease the car in. "Let me come get you."

She laughs. "Kalen, my knight in shining armor."

I hold my hand up. "No armor, but I do have gloves." I carefully walk around the front of the vehicle and open her door. I take her hand and help her out.

"My bag," she reminds me, and I open the back door and pull it out. Soon enough she won't need to pack an overnight bag, and I really hope she's open to the idea of moving in. I know her independence is important to her, and our wedding isn't until next summer, but I want her in my house and in my bed.

I hike her bags over my shoulder. "What's in here?"

"Clothes and presents for everyone."

"Everyone?" We all drew names because buying gifts for everyone was too much work with all the busy schedules.

"You, Taylor, Elias, and your dad."

She drew Dad, and I drew her sister London. Thankfully she helped me pick out a gift for her sister. We got her some feng shui crystal tree thing that I know nothing about. Sahara didn't ask for my help with Dad, and that doesn't surprise me. She's wicked smaht, and no doubt got him a fabulous gift.

I open the door and as soon as we step inside, I set the bag down and pull her to me. I press my lips to hers and I will never ever get tired of the way she melts into me. Jesus, I love this woman.

I inch back and her eyes go wide as she glances around. She was here at the beginning of construction and the place was a mess, and there were numerous carpenters coming and going. "Is Taylor's room finished?" she asks. "It's so quiet."

"Finally done."

Excitement moves over her face. "Has she seen it?"

"No, it's been blocked off. Too much dust and danger."

She nods. "I can't wait to see her face when she sees it for the first time."

I cock my head and arch a brow. "Do you think you might want a peek?"

Her eyes widen. "Really?" Her curiosity instantly fades and she makes a sound, like she's unsure. "I don't know. Maybe I shouldn't be the first. It's her surprise, and that somehow feels wrong."

Dammit, I really wanted her to say yes. Playing it off, I shrug my shoulders. "Okay, if you don't want to."

She chuckles. "I actually do."

"Okay, come on then. I know Taylor won't mind. I'm sure she'll be delighted."

She eyes me, like she's not so sure about that. I pick her bag back up and carry it upstairs. We stop at my bedroom and I put it on my bed.

"I can't believe you built her a dance studio. It's going to be amazing to have her own place to dance, and to rehearse." She grins at me. "Do you think she'll let me use it?" A quick shake of her head. "No, it's her space. I can't ask that."

"Would you like your own space too, Sahara?"

"Someday, sure. My apartment seems to grow smaller every day."

"Probably because I'm practically living there with you." We stop outside the newly built room, and I put my hand on the knob. "But now that this is done and men aren't coming and going and there's no dust to make you sick, I'd love it if you moved in here with me."

Her smile is soft and warm and curls around my heart and tugs tight.

"I would love that, Kalen. But are you sure you want me moving in before we get married?"

"No one in my family is old fashioned," I tell her.

She laughs. "My mom is, but she's so happy I 'snagged' an NHL player." She does air quotes around the word snagged. "She'll want us shacking up, because it takes us one step closer to the altar."

"She has nothing to worry about. You're not getting away from me."

"Ooh, possessive. I never knew."

I laugh. "Right." I twist the knob. "Ready to see this?"

She nods as I push open the door, and wave for her to step inside. The minute she does, a gasp escapes her throat.

"Kalen..." She spins around, taking in the floor to ceiling bookshelves, the sliding ladder, and the comfy chairs and tables. "Kalen," she whispers again. "This...this isn't a dance studio, it's...it's..."

"Your brand-new library. Just for you, my sweet fiancée." She spins to see me, tears spilling down her cheeks.

"It's...mine?"

"Merry Christmas, babe."

She gulps and stands there, shock and happiness and disbelief all moving over her face at once. "Babe," I begin. "It's yours. I fibbed about it being Taylor's, because I wanted to surprise you. You're not mad that I fibbed, are you? I know we said no more secrets." My heart races because she's not speaking. She's just standing there looking at me like I might be some kind of monster. I take a step toward her, put my hand on her arm.

"I can't believe you built me a library."

"Do you like it?"

"I...I love it. I love you. I mean, I thought the cheese was amazing, but this...this is the nicest thing anyone has ever done for me."

"It has its own nook with a comfy chair for reading, and Gina helped me fill it with books we thought you'd like."

She sniffs. "I'm the luckiest person in the world."

"Nah, I think I am."

She backs up. "I got something for you." She crinkles her nose. "I'm not sure..."

Reading the worry in her eyes, I assure her, "Sahara, all I want for Christmas is you." Jesus, I sound like a song. "Now show me what you got me?" I joke and touch her blouse. "Is it under here?"

That lightens her mood. "No. Wait here." She disappears and I walk around the library, admiring the dark wood, and the cozy nook in the corner, her private spot for reading. There isn't even a chair in here for me, because I want it to be her private space, for her and her alone.

Well, almost...

She comes back with a bag in her hand. "I...I...didn't have time to wrap it. I can do it now."

"I don't need it wrapped, babe." Worried eyes meet mine. "Show me."

She reaches into the bag and pulls out a picture frame. The second I look at the picture, my heart is in my throat. "Sahara," I murmur, my eyes lifting.

"It was the one thing missing from this house." Her smile is wobbly. "Besides this library, of course."

I look back at the picture of Mom and me. I'm about six years old, sitting on her lap, a book in my hands. Memories of that happy day come rushing back in a whoosh and my heart overflows with love. "This is the best gift anyone has ever given me," I say, and bend down and press my lips to hers. "I love it, Sahara."

"You have so many of Taylor and your mom, and none of you, and I thought—"

"You're right. I did need this. I wasn't ready for this until you."

"Your dad sent me some old photo albums. I kept them hidden at my place. I was terrified you were going to find them." She reaches back into the bag and pulls out another picture. "This is what I got for your dad."

Tears well up in my eyes, when I see a framed picture of Dad and me. His hand on my shoulder after a game. I was about thirteen in the picture, and it was when Mom was sick. The pride in Dad's eyes as he looks at me reminds me of happy times, of love and forgiveness.

She worries her bottom lip. "Do you think he'll like it?"

I nod, and tears fall down my face. "He will love it."

I put my arms around her and hug her tightly. "One more thing," I manage to push out past the lump in my throat.

"No, Kalen. You can't give me anything else. This library is everything."

"It's just something small."

She folds her arms and gives me a warning look. "It had better be small."

I lead her to a section of the bookshelf. "Pull the book on Kama Sutra."

She gives me an odd look. "Is something going to jump out at me?"

I wink. "Possibly later."

She grips the book, tugs and a little clicking sound fills the room. "No," she practically shrieks when a panel opens to reveal a secret room. A laugh bubbles out of her. "You didn't?"

"Oh, but I did. You see, after we fill this house with kids, we're going to need our own, private hiding spot to do, you know...things."

"Things?" Her grin is playful and mischievous.

I pull her to me. "You know, things that are in that book."

Laughing, she rubs against me and my cock thickens. "Hey, I thought you said it was just something small."

"Another fib," I laugh and push Mr. President against her. "I wasn't lying about something jumping out at you, though."

She shakes her head and frowns. "You're not my knight in shining armor at all." Before I can ask what she means, she grabs my shirt and tugs me into the secret room. "You're my beast."

I laugh. "And you're my beauty."

I close the door behind us, draping us in darkness, and pull her against me. "Now why don't we finish what we started all those years ago."

"Ah, but we're not finishing anything," she says, going up on her toes to kiss me. "This is just the beginning of our own fairy tale."

"Yeah babe...it's just the beginning..."

ALSO BY CATHRYN FOX

Boston Bucks

Stick Move

Sticking Around

Sticking Out

Hook 'em Hard (Written in the Boston Bucks World)

Scotia Storms

Away Game (Rebels)

Warm Up (Rebels)

Crash Course (Rebels)

Home Advantage (Rebels)

Shut Out (Rebels)

Moving Target (Rivals)

Face Off (Rivals)

Scoring Fast (Rivals)

Opposing Teams (Rivals)

Fake Out (Rivals)

Deal Breaker (Rebels)

Hard Burn (Rivals)

End Zone

Fair Play

Enemy Down

Keeping Score

Trading Up

All In

Blue Bay Crew
Demolished
Leveled
Hammered

Single Dad
Single Dad Next Door
Single Dad on Tap
Single Dad Burning Up

Players on Ice
The Playmaker
The Stick Handler
The Body Checker
The Hard Hitter
The Risk Taker
The Wing Man
The Puck Charmer
The Troublemaker
The Rule Breaker
The Rookie
The Sweet Talker
The Heart Breaker

In the Line of Duty
His Obsession Next Door
His Strings to Pull
His Trouble in Talulah

His Taste of Temptation

His Moment to Steal

His Best Friend's Girl

His Reason to Stay

Confessions

Confessions of a Bad Boy Professor

Confessions of a Bad Boy Officer

Confessions of a Bad Boy Fighter

Confessions of a Bad Boy Doctor

Confessions of a Bad Boy Gamer

Confessions of a Bad Boy Millionaire

Confessions of a Bad Boy Santa

Confessions of a Bad Boy CEO

Hands On

Hands On

Body Contact

Full Exposure

Dossier

Private Reserve

House Rules

Under Pressure

Big Catch

Brazilian Fantasy

Improper Proposal

Boys of Beachville

Good at Being Bad

Igniting the Bad Boy

Bad Girl Therapy

Stone Cliff Series:

Crashing Down

Wasted Summer

Love Lessons

Wrapped Up

Eternal Pleasure Series

Instinctive

Impulsive

Indulgent

Sun Stroked Series

Seaside Seduction

Deep Desire

Private Pleasure

Captured and Claimed Series:

Yours to Take

Yours to Teach

Yours to Keep

Firefighter Heat Series

Fever

Siren

Flash Fire

Playing For Keeps Series

Slow Ride

Wild Ride

Sweet Ride

Breaking the Rules:

Hold Me Down Hard

Pin Me Up Proper

Tie Me Down Tight

Stand Alone Title:

Hands on with the CEO

Torn Between Two Brothers

Holiday Spirit

Unleashed

Knocking on Demon's Door

Web of Desire

ABOUT CATHRYN

New York Times and *USA today* Bestselling author, Cathryn is a wife, mom, sister, daughter, and friend. She loves dogs, sunny weather, anything chocolate (she never says no to a brownie) pizza and red wine. She has two teenagers who keep her busy with their never ending activities, and a husband who is convinced he can turn her into a mixed martial arts fan. Cathryn can never find balance in her life, is always trying to find time to go to the gym, can never keep up with emails, Facebook or Twitter and tries to write page-turning books that her readers will love.

Connect with Cathryn:
Newsletter https://app.mailerlite.com/webforms/landing/c1f8n1
Twitter: https://twitter.com/writercatfox
Facebook: https://www.facebook.com/AuthorCathrynFox?ref=hl
Blog: http://cathrynfox.com/blog/
Goodreads: https://www.goodreads.com/author/show/91799.Cathryn_Fox

Pinterest http://www.pinterest.com/catkalen/